# LINKED
# FOR LIFE

# LINKED FOR LIFE

## HOW SIBLINGS AFFECT OUR LIVES

MARVIN D. TODD, PH.D.

CITADEL PRESS
Kensington Publishing Corp.
www.kensingtonbooks.com

CITADEL PRESS books are published by

Kensington Publishing Corp.
850 Third Avenue
New York, NY 10022

All Kensington titles, imprints, and distributed lines are available at special quantity discounts for bulk purchases for sales promotions, premiums, fund-raising, educational, or institutional use. Special book excerpts or customized printings can also be created to fit specific needs. For details, write or phone the office of the Kensington special sales manager: Kensington Publishing Corp., 850 Third Avenue, New York, NY 10022, attn: Special Sales Department, phone 1-800-221-2647.

First Citadel printing: November 2001

10  9  8  7  6  5  4  3  2  1

Printed in the United States of America

Designed by Leonard Telesca

ISBN 0-8065-2235-6

Library of Congress Control Number: 2001092761

# Dedications

My wife
*Mary Carol*

My children
*David Matolo*
*Molly*

My parents
*Hazel Violet Moody Todd*
*Vernon Dennis Todd*

My sister
*Marilyn*

My brothers
*Harold*
*James*
*Charles*
*Stan*

*To the Creator, who is the parent to all
the sisters and brothers on the planet*

# Contents

# Foreword

When Marvin and I first discussed the possible title for his new book, *My Brother Ran over Me With a Tractor,* I laughed (a sign that he must be on the right track). What a perfect title for that mixed bag that we call family. I'm reminded of Dickens's words: "It was the best of times; it was the worst of times." I'm also reminded of the mixed messages that we are all presented with as we grow up:

"If you have time to kill, work it to death," but, "All work and no play makes John a dull boy."

"Blood is thicker than water," but Cain killed Abel.

"Fools rush in where angels fear to tread," but, "He who hesitates is lost."

"Only the good die young."

"No good deed goes unpunished."

"The more things change, the more they stay the same."

Life is not simple. Families mirror life. One minute you're as close as brothers. The next minute the tractor is running over you, and your brother is driving it. How could this be? Who can explain it? Well, if anyone can, it would be my friend Marvin Todd.

During our biweekly get-togethers, road-trip adventures, and retreats at Esalen, I have listened to Marvin's struggle with the pain, paradoxes, and puzzles presented by families and siblings. Through it all, I think we have both decided that, despite the fact that families and siblings can often drive us crazy, they are also a gift to be appreciated and enjoyed.

Can we reconcile the pleasure/pain polarity that many of us experience with our families? I think Marvin's book does an excellent job of telling us how. As Marvin explains, sometimes we get run over by the tractor; but if it doesn't kill us, maybe we get to enjoy the kind of closeness and support that only families and siblings can provide.

John Kohls, Ph.D.

# *Preface*

You are at the start of a journey—a journey from birth until death. This journey is about the time in between these two events and the players who accompany you on your journey. These special people are your sisters and brothers. Some of you have only one sister or brother and some of you have many more. I have four brothers and one sister who have been and continue to be with me on my journey.

Brothers and sisters are peers. Parents are the generation that comes before, and your children's generation comes after yours. Sisters and brothers, most likely, will be your longest relationship. This special relationship may have elements of being positive or negative; however, this relationship will always be strong.

While reading this book, you will reexperience memories from childhood, you will experience feelings that, at times, are difficult, and you will experience feelings that are fun, satisfying, and exciting. These feelings, while based on something in the past, are here-and-now experiences.

You also will reexperience memories and current activities of your adult years with your siblings. Whether you love them or hate them, they are your sisters and brothers. Love and hate are on the same continuum. When you love them you are connected. When you hate them you are connected. You are not indifferent about your sisters and brothers, and they are not indifferent about you.

You will learn how birth order, age differences, and blended families create a difference in an individual's personality, and the role each plays in a brother or sister relationship.

Brothers and sisters, or course, have frequent spats and disagreements, but they generally work them out within the guidelines provided by parents. This teaches siblings how to negotiate conflict and arrive at compromises. These skills become important later in life.

Finally, this book explains why brothers' and sisters' relationships are often an untapped source of support. During the past fifteen years I have devoted a part of my practice to working with adult siblings. This work focuses both on adult brothers and sisters who work in the same business, as well as on siblings as unique historians in each other's life journeys. You will understand how you can tap this resource for inner strength and it will help you clear the air, resolve problems, and reestablish a good, solid relationship between you and your sisters and brothers.

# Acknowledgments

To my secretary and receptionist, Judy Novak, who mailed each chapter to my editor while giving me encouragement to carry on with my writing. To my secretary, Patty Caldwell, for her clerical support. To Pat and Ed Vorhees, office managers, who have also offered their support and encouragement to complete this book.

To my editor, Duane Newcomb, who guided me from the beginning of this book five years ago. He has offered suggestions and editorial expertise. His chapter-by-chapter editing and his suggestion to "pull it all together" have proven invaluable in the completion of my book.

To my dear friends and colleagues Eric Olesen, M.F.C.C., and Dr. John Kohls. Eric for writing his book, *Mastering the Winds of Change,* and for being my friend. John for suggesting the title of this book while at a workshop in Esalen, California. To John and Eric for our biweekly two-hour lunches that are a source of fun and "brotherly" love for me.

To each of the more than thirty clients who have participated, with their brothers and sisters, in adult sibling sessions, for their willingness to allow me to guide these very special relationships in exploring their "then and there" of childhood and their "here and now" of adulthood, and for their willingness to be surveyed about their reactions.

I received permission from each of the first sixteen surveyed clients to share some of their reactions. I have made changes that will protect their identity. I have used the thread of a sibling idea and changed parts of their stories. Some of the examples are a compilation of my many years of working with adult brothers and sisters.

Each of the surveyed clients was grateful for the experience and offered suggestions for some changes in the format and in future sessions. I am thankful they gave me the opportunity to assist them on their brother and sister journeys.

To my clients, colleagues, and friends who have continued to ask me, "How is the book coming?" Thank you for asking and thank you for your support.

# 1

~

# *What Difference Does the Birth Order Make?*

The birth order has a lot to do with our behavior. Because of our position in the family, we learn to react to other people in certain ways that eventually become habits and part of our personalities. If you are the oldest male in the family, you expect the others to look up to you for leadership. Firstborns often grow up knowing they're bigger, stronger, and smarter than their younger siblings. They are generally jealous and status-conscious. Firstborns are also, by reputation, the list makers and control freaks. "Show me a librarian who's not a firstborn," says Kevin Leman, author of *The Birth Order Book* and *Growing Up Firstborn*. "They live by the Dewey Decimal System." Firstborns are often at home in trades such as accounting and architecture. Studies have found that firstborns are more neurotic than later-borns, more responsible, organized, and achievement-oriented. Some famous firstborns are Clint Eastwood, Marcia Clark, and Hillary Clinton.

If you are the youngest in the family, you may look up to the oldest, do what he or she tells you, and look to him or her for leadership. Later-borns, since they can't get their way by force or bluster, are usually more social and agreeable. Later-borns, in studies, are consistently deemed more agreeable and are overwhelmingly more open to experience. Since they have a lesser stake in the family order, they are more open to novelty and innovation. Some famous later-borns include Michael Jordan, David Letterman, and Madonna.

These are not genetic traits but learned ones. They, however, become so much a part of us as we grow up that they follow us into adulthood. The youngest child often finds himself or herself a follower while the oldest often becomes a leader of others. Birth order can often explain why one person launches out and builds a large company, another works on a production line his entire life and enjoys it, and another easily runs a large staff in an office.

## The Ten Birth Orders

Psychologists have discovered that there are ten birth orders that essentially predict our behavior as adults. These behaviors depend primarily on where you were born in the family and whether you are male or female. They become part of your personality because of the way you react to your brothers and sisters and, conversely, because of the way they react to you.

Today families are extremely fluid. An oldest child in one stepfamily may suddenly find himself or herself the youngest child in another stepfamily. While this does affect behavior, birth order is still useful in explaining how and why we act as we do.

Since I personally come from a large family, I got interested in the dynamics of birth order in the seventies. And the more I studied birth order, the more fascinated I became.

I no longer see people as individuals but as a reflection of the families they come from. In my practice I always spend twenty to thirty minutes of the first session taking family and marriage history. I find that these characteristics, as determined by the birth order, are pretty well established.

Even though the individual usually isn't aware of how much birth order affects him or her, these birth-order histories, combined with the birth-order histories of his or her mother and father, give me a pretty good picture of who my client is. Now let's examine these ten birth orders individually to see what characteristics each contains.

## The Oldest Brother of Brothers

You become the leader as soon as your brother is born. As you grow older you take on leadership naturally and become extremely comfortable around other men; sometimes you feel uneasy around women. In general, the oldest brothers of brothers become leaders or heads of companies, or own their own businesses. If this individual has learned about females from his mother, or has sisters, he may be comfortable around women; otherwise he often feels more at home working with men. When he does work with women they must fully understand that their role is to unconditionally support him. Bill, the oldest brother of brothers, opened a ski shop in which he hired only men. At one point he tried female sales help but felt uncomfortable working with them, and when they quit he replaced them with men.

Gerald, on the other hand, the oldest in a family of four brothers, found himself working for a wireless-communications company that expected him to run an office of five women. For the first four months he felt confused because the women resented being ordered around. His solution was to find a woman to put in charge who could lead others and still take direction from him. As a result, his office now runs smoothly.

In the space program, twenty-four out of twenty-six of the first astronauts were firstborns—people who could lead, could take orders, and were committed to completing the job.

## The Oldest Brother of Sisters

You're also a leader and know a lot about females. You are often a manager or the owner of a business that employs a lot of women and you generally expect them to respect and listen to you. This individual often supervises women and sometimes deliberately surrounds himself with them. You may find him at gatherings where he is the only male present. He understands females and is comfortable among them as long as they listen and defer to him.

When he hires a female employee, he instinctively picks a woman who will let him be the leader. If he accidentally picks someone who doesn't understand his leadership needs, there can well be conflict.

When he marries, he often takes a wife who puts his needs ahead of her own. His friends are often their friends; on vacation they go where he wants to go; and when they buy a car, he invariably makes the choice. If he marries a woman who is also a leader and they can work out the conflicts, the relationship may well be strong. If not, this marriage will probably end in disaster.

## The Oldest Sister of Sisters

You are a natural leader. You like being around your sisters and other women and often wind up taking care of and listening to other women's problems.

The older sister of sisters expects women to understand that she is in charge. She is always helping other women, but often neglects her own needs. Because her job as a child was to take care of her younger sisters, it becomes a lifestyle trait that extends into adulthood. At home she may have been expected to give up her own pleasures to baby-sit her sisters. At work she may take on additional chores to bail a "sister" out. Firstborn girls, however, are typically more confident, assertive, and verbally aggressive than their younger brothers or sisters.

I have observed that while these firstborn females often take care of other females, they often have trouble taking care of the child within themselves. They usually can't let go and just have fun. If they go on vacation they habitually stay in touch to handle office problems. If they go out for a night, they may call home four or five times to make sure the children are okay.

This older sister of sisters often works well with a male boss, but only if he respects her and allows her to stake out her own turf. For instance, if she reports to a man, she will probably be running an entire office full of women.

## The Oldest Sister of Brothers

You love working around men, and often find yourself in a work situation in which most of the other employees are men. Even though you are a female, you could very well be the senior manager, supervising dozens of men.

This woman may very well have a male boss if she respects him, but, even so, she is nearly always in a position where she heads her own department. Sometimes her position is informal rather than official. We have all seen offices where one woman, regardless of her title, really runs the business. When someone wants to know what is going on, she's the one approached. She is a good team member. While she is usually supportive of other women, she often keeps them in a junior position. This woman deals from strength and always has a problem with women who act like little girls. She not only doesn't understand them, but is impatient for them to grow up. The oldest sister of brothers is usually the leader in her marriage, and may well be behind her husband's success. She pushes her husband constantly, although he may not be aware of it.

Her husband relies on her to make most of the family decisions. When they buy a car, she picks out the color and the model. She selects the home, the neighborhood, and their friends. Often she is the leader in the neighborhood, and at work. Sometimes her house is full of the neighbors' kids, and she never knows how many children will show up at the dinner table.

## The Youngest Brother of Brothers

You tend to be artistic, creative, and intuitive. You may be an artist, a writer, a photographer, an entertainer, or an advertising copywriter, or you might have these pursuits as a hobby. You are a good team player and are very comfortable supporting other males. Sometimes you are overdependent and a bit irresponsible.

The youngest brother of brothers generally needs to work with other men and for a male boss. He doesn't like working in an office full of women and he certainly doesn't understand them.

If the youngest brother of brothers marries a strong woman who gives him direction, that marriage will usually work. He, however, never does well with a woman who needs direction herself.

## The Youngest Brother of Sisters

You get along well with and don't mind working with mostly women, or for a female boss. You also like and expect to be taken care of by women.

When the youngest brother of sisters marries, he usually marries a woman who gives him direction and who loves and takes care of him. She does all the shopping, buys his clothes, and makes sure he always gets his favorite meals. Even if she works full-time she usually comes home and cooks his dinner.

This couple generally has a very strong relationship, even though the woman works harder than the man does. If, by accident, the youngest brother of sisters picks a wife who can't lead, the marriage often becomes a disaster.

## The Youngest Sister of Sisters

You nearly always look to your sisters for leadership. You like doing things for them and often find yourself taking care of their hair or filling in for them. At work, you are most comfortable in an all-female office. You don't much like working with men, and stay out of situations where the majority of employees are male.

This woman often goes into a profession like nursing or teaching, where she works primarily with women. Children don't bother her, but male bosses and male coworkers do, since she doesn't understand them. She tends to be feminine and spends time taking care of her appearance. She often wears frilly dresses and never puts on a pair of blue jeans. When she marries she chooses a strong man who dotes on and takes care of her. If her husband has a younger sister, he usually understands his wife and gets along well with her.

## The Youngest Sister of Brothers

You like and understand men. You don't mind taking orders from men and work well with a male boss. You get along well with male coworkers and often strike up platonic relationships with them.

In an office, this youngest sister of brothers doesn't mind handling menial chores. She cheerfully takes care of details and actually enjoys bringing coffee to the men. She is not comfortable as a leader and seldom rises above a junior level unless a man takes a special interest in her. Most of this woman's coworkers, however, really like and support her.

The youngest sister of brothers usually marries a man who dominates and leads her.

## Twins, Triplets, Quads

You have an extremely strong bond and a unique relationship with your sibling or siblings. Usually you have a special language between you that no one else seems to understand. Often you can glance at your brother or sister and know exactly what he or she is thinking.

This is the pattern of multiple births with no other brothers or sisters. However, there can be many variations on this behavior:

### Twins with Younger Siblings

Firstborn twins often overshadow the young children in the family, especially if there is a real age difference. Rachel and Ruth, for instance, fraternal twins, formed a strong bond before their sister, June, was born seven years later. This bond completely excluded June, who was never allowed to enter their world. Rachel and Ruth, now both successful attorneys, are still close. June, however, seldom sees her sisters and has moved several hundred miles away to avoid contact with them.

### Twins Who Are Middle Children

These twins often have a fairly close relationship with all the siblings in the family, but no special twin bond. I have twin clients who are the middle children in a family of five, with about four years between the oldest and youngest. At thirty-five they don't consider their relationship any closer than the one they have between their other brothers and sisters.

### Twins Who Are the Youngest Siblings

The bonding between the twins depends on the spacing. If the spread is between three to five years, they act as the youngest children of brothers or sisters. If the spacing is greater than five years, they generally have a strong twin bond that excludes the other children.

*Multiple Twins*

The personality characteristics here are again determined by the age spread. For example, in one family, the oldest two are twins, the middle child is a girl, and the youngest two are twins. In this case the oldest twins act as the older brothers of a sister, the younger two as the youngest of brothers and sisters.

*The Death of a Twin*

The impact of this situation depends on the age of the surviving twin at the death of the other, and how the parents grieve the loss. In southern California, the Mcquire twins did everything together, including playing high school football. At USC they both became stars and went on to play for the Los Angeles Rams. They had insisted on playing together for the same team. Then Jim Mcquire was killed in a Los Angeles automobile accident. The parents grieved for several years, and his surviving twin has significant difficulty in his grieving process.

Sometimes twins achieve almost identical results in the same profession. Abigail Van Buren and Ann Landers are almost equally famous. Although they have had their conflicts over the years, they take time off each year to spend their birthday together. Sometimes one twin will be the achiever the other the backup. John Lindsay (former New York City mayor) and his twin brother are an example. John was the star, his twin the career manager. When the relationship is negative, however, the association between the twins can be extremely destructive.

Today, fertility drugs have increased the possibility of multiple births of triplets and quadruplets. These siblings are bonded because the developmental milestones: walking, talking, and toilet training all occur within the same time frame.

## The Only Child

Early in life you learned to talk and think like an adult. If you had other children to play with, you probably grew up to be a positive, productive individual. Because you were an only child, however, you learned to take care of and entertain yourself. Generally you do what you want to do and pay very little attention to other people's opinions. You are extremely self-contained.

Only children are the center of their parents' universe, and they often have the undivided attention of their mother and father. They get their way much of the time and have a problem sharing with others. As adults they frequently strike out on their own.

There are a number of reasons parents have only one child. Let's take a look at some of them.

### The Only Child with Divorced Parents Who Haven't Remarried

In this case, since both parents are generally satisfied with their lives, neither parent wants another child. The parents of Angela, who is seventeen, are both busy people in their mid-thirties. Angela's mother is absorbed in her career as an attorney. Her father, the middle manager of a small company, likes his life as it is. Although Angela lives with her mother she is frequently shuttled from parent to parent, and sometimes it is painfully obvious to her that neither parent wants to spend much time with her. For instance, she often arrives at her father's house for the weekend to discover that he is headed off on a trip, leaving her alone with the housekeeper. Although she is self-sufficient and capable of being by herself, Angela often feels left out and lonely and would like a little more support from her parents.

### One Parent Doesn't Want Another Child

One parent is satisfied with an only child; the other wants the child, but can't convince his or her mate. Thomas's mother wanted another child; his father refused. Finally she gave in and accepted his wishes. At first Thomas would have liked a little brother and sister, like his friends had. But gradually he got used to being the center of attention, especially his mother's, and now his life is complete. Another child would be an intrusion.

### When the Mother's Life is Endangered

Tina's mother came close to death when Tina was born. Her doctor indicated that the mother would face great danger if she became pregnant again. When this happens, the only child often takes on some of the responsibility for causing the mother's problem and frequently assumes a great deal of the guilt. In this case, Tina, even as an adult, felt partially responsible for her mother's failing health. This greatly affected her relationship with her husband because, no matter what he wanted to do, Tina always put her mother first.

*Older Parents*

When career parents have their first child after forty, many often decide that they are too old to raise another. When Roberta was born her mother had just turned forty-six, and her father was fifty. She grew up around her parents' older friends, and even as a youngster she never felt like a child and had trouble relating to her schoolmates. They always seemed too young and childish. Even as an adult, she still has relationship problems with others in her age group.

*To Heal a Shaky Marriage*

At least one of the parents believes that a child will help hold a failing marriage together. Brenda's mother decided the solution to her problem was to have a child. Without telling her husband, she simply stopped taking her birth control pills. When she became pregnant she convinced her husband that they needed another family member. After Brenda arrived, the marriage didn't get any better. As Brenda got older, she begin to feel that it was her responsibility to keep the family together. She also found herself becoming the mediator. Her father talked to Brenda about her mother. Her mother kept complaining about Brenda's father. Neither mother or father talked much to each other. Brenda needed to realize that she was an innocent bystander. The war between her mother and her father existed long before she came along. The only solution for her was to give up being the buffer for her two parents. Usually these people break free when they want to connect with another person. When the parents center their lives around their child, however, it becomes extremely difficult for him or her to get away.

## The Only Child As an Accident

Lennie was a complete surprise to her parents, since her father had had a vasectomy. Her mother was extremely resentful but carried the child to term. When this happens, it frequently turns the parents around and they thoroughly enjoy the child. If they continue to talk about the child as an accident it usually affects that child. When the child realizes he is an accident, he often plays it out. I had one client, for instance, who convinced herself she was accident-prone and had six or seven accidents within four years. The person subconsciously thinks, "I am an accident, I am supposed to keep creating accidents."

Surprisingly, those individuals with only-children personalities don't have to be the only child in the family. They simply have to be far enough apart from the other siblings that they are not influenced by them. If an individual remains an only child until about the age of eight, his character is already set, and even if his parents have another youngster, he will probably act like an only child the rest of his life.

## The Only Child with Younger Siblings

The only child actually is a state of mind influenced by the attention the parents focus on him or her. Children with eight years or more between them and the next brother or sister act like only children. Alan Alda, the actor, has a brother twenty years younger (same father, different mother). He essentially, however, considers himself an only child, and acts like it. He is independent, self-centered, and extremely opinionated. President Clinton has a brother, Roger, who is ten years younger. Roger has said that they grew up knowing very little about each other and that he doesn't consider himself close to his brother.

## The Only Child with Older Siblings

Again, when there are eight years or more between this younger child and the older brothers or sisters, this individual functions like an only child, and his parents treat him like one. The young child, however, is often fearful and frequently hides these fears. I had a client whose brothers and sisters were ten years older. When she started kindergarten, her brother was a high school freshman. He played freshman football and was the center of attention in his group. As a result he had very little time for a five-year-old who wanted help coloring within the lines. Typically my client grew up fearful of reaching out and doing things on her own.

## Middle Children—Mixed

This is not an additional category, but a mixture of the original ten. A second-born middle son in a family of five male children, for instance, will take on many of the characteristics of the oldest brother of brothers. The fourth-born daughter in a family of five girls will take on most of the characteristics of the last-born sister of sisters. You will find numerous groupings here. In a three-sibling family, there can be an authentic middle child only if a middle child is born within five years of the other children.

I have a client who has three children: Kevin, twelve, John, ten, and a three-year-old daughter, Marie. John functions not as a middle child but as the youngest brother of brothers. There are many other combinations of this: three older siblings with a much younger fourth child, a four-sibling family with two older children, a six-child family with the last child born five years after the first five.

The character of middle children depends on the number of children in the family, their position, and their gender. My younger brother is fifth in a family of six and has the personality traits of a last-born. He married a loving, nurturing, firstborn female who controls the marriage and provides the direction he needs.

My father, on the other hand, had two younger brothers until he was ten years old; then his parents had a daughter, To this day he acts like the firstborn brother of brothers and has very little understanding of and interaction with females.

In my family I am the third of six children, with two older brothers, a younger sister, and two younger brothers. We were divided into the three big boys and the three little kids. I functioned as the youngest brother of brothers. My sister functioned within the three little kids as the oldest sister of brothers. There came a time, however, when my older brothers pulled back and I became the leader of the younger group. Variations of this behavior frequently happen in a growing dynamic family. As children get older, the birth order characteristics may change.

## Stepfamilies

In our present culture we often talk of "your kids," "my kids," and "our kids." When children go from one family to another the birth order characteristics change.

My wife has a son from an earlier marriage, and together we have a daughter. Her son spends part of his time with us, and part of his time with his father. In our family he is the older brother of a sister. In his father's family he is an only child.

If this blending takes place at an early age it is easier on the children. After about the age of ten, their character is formed for life. At that point, forcing them to shift birth order from family to family often results in conflict.

## The Parents' Influence

Parents can influence a child to take a lesser position, one other than that dictated by his or her birth order. The parents of one of my clients always interfered with the relationship between their son and daughter. They insisted that the boy give his sister preferential treatment at all times. As a result, the son grew up taking an inferior position to his sister, and his characteristics as an adult more closely resembled those of the younger brother of sisters than the older brother of sisters.

When the parents have problems such as a rocky marriage, or the mother or father is an alcoholic who abuses the children, the child may become excessively compliant or tremendously rebellious. Oprah Winfrey is a good example of a firstborn from a disruptive family who broke away from her parents' influence and went on to chart her own course.

Birth order has a lot to do with our behavior as children, as adolescents, and as adults. By determining your birth order and then observing your behavior, you can learn a lot about yourself. The remainder of this book will help you see yourself in many types of sibling relationships and offer tips for improving what will probably be the longest of all the relationships you will ever have.

# 2

*You and Your Brothers
and Sisters*

John and Paul, ten and thirteen, respectively, constantly take advantage of the naivete of their younger brother, Mark, who is seven. When he gets a treat they demand a little-brother tax. Sometimes they tie him up in a closet. Mark, who wants his brothers' approval, accepts this treatment cheerfully. John, who hasn't discovered girls, continually teases Paul, who has. Cindy, on the other hand, the sister in the family, whines and complains that the boys are picking on her.

There are many combinations of brothers and sisters in a modern family—all boys, all girls, or a combination of both. It is possible to have many ages in the same family, from three grouped around the same age, or an older group followed by a younger group. These children can have the same mother and father, or one biological parent, and a stepparent. Clint Eastwood has older adult children followed by a much younger daughter. Hugh Hefner has older adult children and two younger children. Clint and Hugh, however, accomplished this with much younger wives. William Jefferson Clinton was ten years old and in the fourth grade when brother Roger arrived. Older children with much younger brothers and sisters, like former President Clinton, may have the same biological mother and different fathers. They are a sibling group that is more akin to only children.

Sisters and brothers respond to each other with rivalry, hate, love, envy, jealousy, resentment and more. How they react often depends on the sex of the individual, and age and position in the family.

This is complicated by the fact that even today, after about age nine, boys don't express feelings well. Brothers have a brothers' club that they don't share with girls, and girls often have a sisters' club not shared with the boys. It's still okay for girls to be afraid and cry, but not be angry, and it is okay for boys to be angry, but not be afraid or cry.

This chapter takes a close look at brother-sister relationships (from youngster to adult) and explains typical reactions. The readers should find themselves in many of the examples and come to understand why they reacted the way they did to their brothers and sisters. If they are still having trouble as adults, the chapter offers tips for improving the relationship.

## The Early Scenes—Birth through Seventeen

I was five years old; my brother Stan was eight. I was furious at him for taking my scooter without asking. Being the angry, self-righteous, wronged younger brother, I located a large metal file and, when he came near me, I threw it at him. Luckily, the file hit him on the flat side across his face. I don't recall now what happened next. In our adult years Stan told me that the reason he took my scooter was that I left his bicycle out in the street. As a kid, I forgot that part!

What are your early scenes? A scene can be viewed from as many perspectives as you have brothers and sisters. The child bond begins with the birth of the second child and in some families with the entrance into the family of a stepbrother or -sister. Early childhood bonding is determined in large part by the ages at which the children join in each others' lives. New stepsiblings, Belinda, three, and Tony, two, have a better possibility for a strong sister-brother bond than new stepbrother and -sister Barbara, twenty-three, and Richard, seventeen. Barbara and Richard do not share early scenes. Barbara's mother married Richard's father after both parents divorced their first spouses.

The sibling bond is significant inasmuch as that relationship in childhood within the *family of origin* is a unique one. Family of origin is a catchy phrase that gives a name to the individuals who live under one roof. "Under one roof" may include parents, stepparents, children, stepchildren, grandparents, and anyone else who may spend significant time living with the family. The early scenes in the family have a division between the child generation and the adult generation. Privileges and responsibilities reside within each generation.

## What Happens When Biological Brothers and Sisters Reside under Different Roofs?

Jonathon was given up for adoption soon after his birth. His mother was a teenager who would later marry and have three more children with a different man. The four children are siblings who have significantly different early childhood scenes. My grandnephews, Tyler, six, and Aaron, five, and their older half brother Joshua, ten, lost their mother in a car accident four years ago. Tyler and Aaron live with my sister, their fraternal grandmother, and Joshua lives with his maternal grandmother. These three brothers are connected while residing under different roofs.

Oprah Winfrey, Maury Povich, Sally Jessy Raphael, and others air on their shows numerous stories on the "reconnection" of adult children later in life. A future television show may indicate whether the adult siblings remained in contact with each other.

The early bonding under the same roof determines the power of this unique relative bond. These early years, prior to schooling, are most likely a time when young children share the most time together. The onset of schooling causes children's relationships to change, because the child is now acquiring new friendships on a regular basis. Few other relationships that a person has in his or her childhood will match the longevity, intensity, and opportunity that siblings have with each other.

Who were the family members who resided under your roof? Under my roof was my father, my mother, my four brothers, my sister, and me. When I was eight years old my father moved out. Who were your brothers and sisters? Were your childhood relationships changed by a death, or a divorce or other separation? Jason, eight, and Elizabeth, six, lost their younger brother, Brian, to cancer. Their younger brother Billy was born after the death of Brian. Brian's death left a traumatic opening that will never be filled. The loss of Brian can be grieved. Younger brother Billy will have a history with Brian only through the stories related by his parents, brother, and sister.

Roger and Don are biological brothers. Ten years separate their births. Their parents divorced when Roger was four and Don was fourteen and Don soon moved out of the home when their mother remarried.

Henry was the middle-born child into a family of three children, and he was removed from his family when he was seven to live in foster care after repeated physical abuse by his father. Henry's mother was overwhelmed as a single parent and she agreed to have Henry adopted by her sister. From age seven Henry grew up as an only child. Most likely Henry continued to function more like a middle child because of his early childhood experience.

Susan Scarf Merrell, in her book *The Accidental Bond*, addresses the power of the brother and sister relationship, "the least appreciated of all family and emotional connections." Unlike other choices in life, these early same-generation companions are, for better or for worse, a result of the choices made by parents.

## Siblings' Views of the Parents

During the past twelve years I have conducted thirty adult brother-and-sister sessions, each five hours in length. These were sister-and-brother combinations that ranged from two to six per session. These brothers and sisters were *family of origin historians* who offered their unique view of the early childhood years.

The following accounts are in response to a survey the author conducted after the sessions.

Brenda learned from her sister and brother what a negative, somewhat violent relationship her sister had with her parents, compared to the relatively benign relationship she had with them.

Carol learned that "My mother isolated me from my three brothers and one sister."

Diane learned, "We all had different views, and yet some things were confirmed."

Marilyn learned, ". . . that my sister had developed a much better system of being with my parents and maintaining her individuality than I had."

Robert learned, "That it was just as crazy for them as I had experienced."

Charles learned, "That I was treated the worst."

James learned, ". . . what form of abuse our father's alcoholism took; . . . the cause of estrangement of my brother from our aunt and uncle."

Gordon learned, "My father was proud of my accomplishments."

Claudia learned, My mother told my sisters that I sustained brain damage at birth and that something was wrong with me and to leave me alone."

Elaine learned, "That my older brother was always afraid I'd hurt my younger brother."

As the leader in the above adult sister-and-brother sessions, I was not involved with these unique relationships. I was the guide that facilitated a deeper look for each of these brothers and sisters as they looked into the significance of their unique relationship. For me the experience was an honor, a pleasure, and an education into the power of these relationships.

Firstborn siblings are the pioneers in training parents. Later-borns reap benefits and burdens from the firstborns' pioneer efforts. My mother's repeated words to us five later-borns were, "I am not going to make those same mistakes five more times." My oldest brother, Stan, paved the way for the rest of us. The benefit, for us younger siblings, included not having to teach the parents the lesson again. The burden included not being able to teach the parents the lesson again.

## Kids Viewing Kids

The worst day of five-year-old Jennifer's life was the day her younger brother, Oliver, was born. Jennifer had been an "only," and her new brother entered her "territory." Over time he may win her over and she may learn to enjoy him. My mother's sister had the first two grandchildren in our family, both boys. My mother then had the next two, my two older brothers. My mother and her sister wanted a girl in our family. Eighteen months later I was born, another boy, and my aunt wept. My mother would comb my blond hair and leave a curl on top of my one-year-old head, and my four-year-old brother, Stan, would flatten out the curl and remind her that I was a boy. Eighteen months later my sister was born, which relieved me of carrying the burden of my aunt's tears and my mother's comb. I admired Stan and looked to him for protection. Within three more years two more boys were born. My second-born brother, myself, my sister, and my younger brother were the middle-borns filling in the sandwich of early childhood life. My oldest brother and my youngest brother were the bread. The oldest slice had a theme of seniority and the youngest that of a junior. We middle-borns had a combination of senior and junior. My childhood fantasy involved an automobile accident in which all of my siblings were killed and I became an "only child," with all of the benefits that being an only child would give me. I am eternally grateful that my fantasy never came true.

I invite you the reader to ask yourself:

> *What is your view of your brothers and sisters? (i.e., your childhood companions)*
> *What is their view of you?*
> *Have you ever asked them?*
> *Have they ever asked you?*

The answer to the question about *your view of your childhood companions* is that you are most likely more accepting of them, more loving of them, more forgiving of them for their transgressions and feel closer to them than they realize.

The following are responses received by participants in the adult brother-and-sister sessions when they asked their same-generation relatives to attend. My comment follows their exact words.

Brenda: "Positive but a little hesitant." Her sister participated.
Jennifer: "Frightened of confrontation and no show." Her sister and brother participated.
Diane: "I worried about the logistics and expenses of getting us together physically, but was excited about doing it." Her two sisters traveled from Kentucky to attend.
David: "Scared but hopeful." His three sisters participated.
Jason: "I didn't think they would come." His two brothers and three sisters participated.

The answer to the question about *their view of you* is most likely that *you believe* that they are less accepting of you, less loving of you, less forgiving of your transgressions, and more distant than you realize. Your behavior with your siblings will be reflected by *your belief* of how they view you.

These are quotes regarding the fear of inviting siblings:

Janice: "Felt unsafe/worried about criticism from one sister." Her two sisters participated.
Liza: "They wouldn't come." Her three sisters participated.
Barbara: "The only fear I can think of is that I didn't want them to decline the invitation." They both consented.
Robert: "That my thought about what happened in our childhood would not prove valid." Three sisters confirmed childhood memories.

Participants in these adult brother-and-sister sessions were pleased and surprised that their requests were honored.

In the adult brother-and-sister sessions many of the below-listed items were addressed.

Ask yourself:

*What do you want to ask of your sibling(s)?*
*About an unresolved conflict.*

*About your parents.*
*About your family rules.*
*About your family secrets.*
*About your family losses, i.e., death, divorce, separation.*
*About your family myths (untruths believed to be a truth).*
*About your family "cutoffs."*

## About an Unresolved Conflict

The unresolved conflict in the family may be between the mother and father (who are also known as wife and husband), between you and your siblings, or between parents and children. Conflict is normal, natural, and a healthy part of family existence. Conflict means that each person in the family is an individual with his or her own wants, wishes, and desires. How the family members go about resolving the conflict will determine the strength and/or weakness in the family fabric. Abusive, neglectful, aggressive, and passive behavior undermine that fabric.

Mom wants to eat at the Mexican restaurant and Dad wants to eat at the Greek restaurant (conflict). Dad says, How important is your choice? (negotiation). She says that on a scale of one to ten, this is an eight. He says Greek is a six (compromise). They eat at Mexican this week (resolution) and enjoy each other's company.

*What are your unresolved conflicts with your parents?*
*Mom? Dad? Both?*
*What are your unresolved conflicts with your sibling(s)?*

## About Your Parents

When my daughter was five years old she said, "Dad, you were married before, weren't you?" I want to tell the truth and teach my daughter to tell the truth. I responded, "Yes, I was," and wondered what my daughter would say next. She asked, "What did you and your other wife do?" I was impressed with her question. I said, "We traveled." We had lived in Europe and traveled back on one occasion. My daughter said, "Okay," and went back to her playing. I know that she will ask more questions later in her life.

My stepson, David, is six years older than his sister, my daughter. He was excited about his new sibling. Prior to her birth, he believed that the child would look like him. David's father is from Kenya and his mother is Caucasian. David had difficulty understanding how his sister or brother could look different. They are close in their relationship, even though they are six years apart in age. He has some characteristics of being an only child and some characteristics of being an older brother of a sister. She has some characteristics of being an only child and some characteristics of being a younger sister of a brother.

My parents were both firstborn in their families. My mother was the oldest of three and my father was the oldest of six. My parents' twelve-year marriage began when he was twenty-six and she was twenty-four. Their six children arrived within a seven-and-a-half-year period. My parents separated when my youngest brother was four years old.

When I was thirty-seven I had an extended breakfast meeting with my father. It was at my invitation, and he accepted. I had been angry at my father for his leaving when I was eight, and I extended the invitation in order to tell him of my feelings.

The breakfast was an event for an adult, thirty-seven-year-old son and a sixty-eight-year-old father. I was scared. He was scared. We were in a restaurant with customers moving in and out. We ordered our food and settled into brief small talk. I realized that the conversation for us would not be between father and son, but between two grown men. I thanked him for meeting me, and we began eating. I mustered the courage to say, "I am mad at you for not being the father I wanted." My statement initiated putting both of us at ease. I told him the truth about my feelings, but didn't blame him, and he didn't back down. In the past, my father had been passive in the face of expressed feelings.

As our conversation continued, I became unaware of the others in the restaurant, and he also appeared to be fully involved. I asked him why he left, and his quick reply was, "I didn't take care of myself." I asked why he and my mother had six children, and his quick reply was, "We both wanted a large family." My father is from a family of six and his father was from a family of six. He asked me about my previous marriage and expressed how surprised he was when it ended. I was suspended in the conversation with him, and I believe he with me. We had no blame, no shame, little or no criticism, and the words flowed.

All times come to an end. This time lasted one and a half hours. The time had come and we both knew it. It was Thanksgiving morning and both of us had to return to our own towns. Outside at the car, he said, "I'd like to do this again sometime." During the next year he requested breakfast with me on two separate occasions. I attended, but we were not able to rekindle what had happened in the first meeting.

The breakfast meeting was an ending and a beginning for me. I learned to accept my father for who he was and not try to change him, and my energy was then released to freely love him without remaining angry at him. I shared this experience with each of my siblings and encouraged them to have breakfast with him. Although the six of us share the same father, the relationship with him is different for each of us. They declined my invitation and continued the relationship that was good for each of them in their unique way. My father died in January 1998 at the age of eighty-four. He was healthy and alert up to his death. I often thought of him as I wrote this book.

My mother lived for nine years at a convalescent hospital in a small town. Ironically, this small town with a population of three thousand is the town of her childhood. She had severe Alzheimer's symptoms, and though her eyes were clear and richly brown, her mind and voice were not present. Occasionally, a yes or no would be her response to a question. Her eyes reflected frustration, and when fed chocolate pudding by my brother, her eyes softened.

She was a pioneer. She went to college when many women did not. She raised six children on her own while finishing her studies for her college degree and while teaching school. She waited many years for the return of her husband.

I "interviewed" my mother when I was thirty-eight and she was sixty-seven years old. I have an ability to put people at ease, and as we talked in her apartment she relaxed. I asked about her parents, and my nurturing and loyal mother began to tell of her childhood, her parents, her younger sister, and her brother. Her parents had a cold war that they put on hold when company visited. The tension in her home was centered on the marital relationship. Both of her parents were good and supportive. My mother did not speak of the reason for the marital tension as that would require her to be disloyal to both of her parents, who were deceased for some years. She seemed to enjoy the interview, as I did, and I got a glimpse of what her life had been like while growing up. As we talked I became aware that she tired of talking about her family of origin and she moved to the subject of her *family of procreation,* her beloved children.

## Siblings in Therapy—a Hidden Resource

I am a clinician, and we clinicians pursue different avenues to assist people in therapy. The very nature of therapy is a journey of support and discovery. Resources for this journey include trust, together with the competence of the clinician. Some clinicians are explorers. I combined my deep interest in my same-generation peers and sibling relationships in general to develop a practice that would assist in brother-brother, brother-sister, and sister-sister understanding. As a family-therapist clinician, I find that family therapy encompasses two and sometimes three generations in a single family. Children and parents are a two-generation family-therapy journey. Children, parents, and grandparents are a three-generation family-therapy journey. Adult brother-and-sister sessions are a one-generation family journey. I have expanded the adult session concept into work with adult siblings outside of the therapy setting. The other settings include siblings who work together (see chapter 8) and siblings who want to mediate conflict over the care of their aged parents.

Banks and Kahn (1982) identified the sibling bond as a significant factor in people's lives. Lewis (1990) cited a literature review and her own clinical examples and ideas about how to utilize this resource in therapy. Her hypothesis is that whether negative or positive, the sibling relationship has significant influence. She used three categories to identify how siblings could assist in therapy: (a) sibling as a participant in therapy, (b) sibling as a consultant, and (c) sibling as mutual nurturer.

Translated into everyday language: The sibling relationship

may be an unremembered family relationship. We grew up together and the bond now crosses both time and distance. Adulthood is characterized by our emancipation from our parents and our siblings as we form our families of procreation, our work careers, and our wider community involvement. This is the time when we have less frequent verbal contact, less physical contact, and less emotional contact as we develop our own families. The sibling bond is a lesser priority during this time; however, the bond based on history continues to exist.

The following responses about parents are from participants in adult sister-and-brother sessions. The question each was asked was, What did you learn about your parents from your sibling(s) that you did not know?

Brenda: "What a negative, somewhat violent relationship [parents' marriage] they had had, compared to the relative benign relationship I had with them."

Carol: "Learned my mother isolated me from my siblings."

Diane: "We all had different views and yet some things were confirmed."

Irene: "I learned my parents knew each other less than six months prior to getting married."

Marilyn: "I learned that my sister had developed a much better system of being with my parents and maintaining her individuality."

Paula: "I learned that our dad has a strong hold on us even today."

Robert: "That it was just as crazy for my sister as I had experienced."

Charles: "That I was treated the worst."

Gordon: "My father was proud of me."

Have fun with these questions and keep in mind that this is not a trial.

*What do you want to learn from your sibling(s) about your parents?*

*What are you willing to learn from your sibling(s) about your parents?*

*What do you want to tell your sibling(s) about your parents?*

*What are you willing to tell your sibling(s) about your parents?*

Your sisters' and brothers' facts, feelings, and perspectives about parents may be quite different from yours and wisdom requires that you be gentle, kind, considerate, loving, and truthful without doing damage when you go on this journey. The truth can set you free, and at times the truth can be difficult.

## About Your Family Rules

Family rules are the methods by which a family functions. The form of functioning may range from extreme enmeshment (no room for separate mental, emotional, or physical movement with family members) to extreme disengagement (nobody says anything, nobody cares, everybody feels like a nobody). Most families function somewhere between these two extremes.

Rules can be clearly stated—such as be in bed by nine o'clock, Mom does the cooking, Dad does the driving.

Rules can be not stated—they evolve over time and are not questioned.

Rules can be discovered after they are violated—getting a speeding ticket when the limit is not posted.

Who makes the rules in the family? Who enforces the rules in the family? What are the consequences of violating family rules? How are the rules different for sisters? How are the rules different for brothers? How flexible are the rules? Some rules are common sense. Some rules are cockamamy.

My father's family rule was, "We have to hang together or we will hang separately." From my perspective, their hanging together by way of alcoholism was destructive to relationships.

My mother's family rule was, "Don't ask."

My siblings' family rule was, "Don't take all." This statement was primarily for food at mealtime. Nobody asked us to eat anything. If I didn't eat something, one of them would. It was both a reality and a humorous response. We never starved; we just acted that way.

My family rule about feelings was, "Don't be too emotional." Somehow feelings were perceived as a threat. If one of us was too emotional we might be viewed as being crazy. When one of us went crazy everyone else got calm until the crazy went away. At that point guilt hung around for a while.

Some of us got good at faking crazy.

Responses about family rules learned during an adult sibling therapy session:

Pat: "Families stick together even if you have little in common."

Judy: "For me it was don't get close to people, they will hurt or leave you."

Erica: "Work, don't relax too much, keep your feelings in."

Kay: "Dad had rules for us based upon his own criteria or what lay ahead for us. For example, a pretty child [girl] could rely on looks, charm, and eventually being a good mom with a husband who would provide financial support. This I already knew, but it was confirmed."

*How aware were you of your family rules?*
*Were you allowed to question your family rules?*

This is not a test! Have fun asking your childhood sidekicks about family rules.

## About Your Family Secrets

This is a big one. Families often expend more energy in keeping a family secret than in releasing the secret. We conduct secret exercises in our weekend group-therapy marathon. We give members a sheet of paper and instruct them to write a secret on the sheet. Members protest about the exercise and then are told that they can "lie" and write any secret. When they finish, they fold the sheet in half and put them all in a brown paper bag. Each member reaches into the brown paper bag and pulls out someone else's written secret. The person reads the secret to the group and then tears the paper up and throws it away. The group members then query the new secret owner about the reasons for the secret. Nobody knows who wrote the secret, and now the secret is open to the universe. The person learns about how others feel about the secret, and most of the group members report feeling relief.

One of my family secrets was that when my dad left, his leaving caused my parents' marriage to break up. I learned later in my life that all was not well in their marriage before he left. He was a passive man who didn't know how to fight fair with a woman. She was a woman who was "right." They both failed to find compromise when conflict appeared. His passive behavior led to his aggressive act of leaving.

Responses from participants in adult brother-and-sister sessions regarding what they learned about family secrets from their childhood "sidekicks":

Claudia: "My mother told my sisters that I sustained brain damage at birth and that something was wrong with me and to leave me alone."

This information enabled Claudia to understand the hostility she felt from her sisters.

Felix: "Some secrets became confirmed. Other secrets were new or had been unnoticed. I have a confirmation of what was never said."

Some secrets are known and not discussed. The benefit of secret confirmation was that Felix no longer has to carry the secret by himself. The secret can be "released" without using the energy required to keep it hidden.

Elaine: "I had a better idea of how my brothers had felt around me and how we could work together to be healthier and more in touch with each other. We agreed to always talk to the one we wanted to know about rather than filtering that knowledge through someone else. That my older brother was always afraid that I would hurt my younger brother. That both brothers had learned to talk to my dad more intimately than I could, and that it seems to have more to do with understanding 'male' things/interests better than I did. My younger brother felt 'overshadowed' by my achievements. My older brother had been suicidal for a while. My contact with my family was too heavily filtered through my mom for my dad."

Elaine's "released secrets" assisted in clearing some communication channels in her family. In the *ideal* family, each and every member of the family can speak directly with each and every member of the family. No switchboard! The sibling generation is as unique to the siblings as the parents' generation is unique to the parents. The talk is:

(1) between brothers and sisters,
(2) between the parents, and
(3) between the parent generation and the children generation.

Connie (when they discussed her dad's death of twenty years ago): ". . . it was as if he just died yesterday. We hadn't cried all of our tears. But I don't know that that was a secret. It became a revelation. I got some healing from opening my heart wide open."

Connie calls the shared experience a revelation and not a secret. When a significant topic is not discussed it is a secret. Some secrets are shielded because the subject is forbidden, and siblings are the keepers of the secret unless parents give permission to examine it.

Loyalty to the parent generation will sometimes restrict siblings from examining the secret(s). Children absolutely want to protect parents. In part because happy, pleased parents won't go away. This two-generation loyalty travels in both directions, parent to child and child to parent. When the loyalty has positve qualities, both generations benefit. When the loyalty has negative qualities, such as alcoholism, abuse, or abandonment, both generations may be harmed. Exploration of a family secret may be blocked by loyalty. Evan Imber-Black, in her excellent book *The Secret Life of Families,* provides examples of how family loyalties may keep family secrets.

When adult brothers and sisters are around each other there is an area that is okay to discuss, and there is an area that is not okay to discuss.

Ask yourself:

> *What are the areas that are okay to discuss with my sibling(s)?*
> *What are the areas that are not okay to discuss with my sibling(s)?*
> *Who is being protected? And what is the reason for the protection?*

The code I recommend when approaching a family secret with your sibling(s) is to insure that they will not be harmed when the secret is examined. That may require a disinterested third party such as a family therapist to assist on the journey.

The original reason for keeping a secret may be long gone, yet the secret remains after having gained a life of its own. Most secrets are benign and are dusty old relics. The more energy-laden secrets need to be confessed, examined, shared, and understood by you and your sisters and brothers. This can be a risky business and requires treading with compassion, care, and a loving attitude.

## About Your Family Losses: Death, Divorce, Separation

Losses are big and small. Death, divorce, separation, emotional/physical injury, miscarriage, and finances are big losses. Bobby and Eddy lost their mother in a car accident when they were toddlers. Raymond, Eric, and Samantha's parents divorced when they were teens. Jeannie and Barbara's father deserted them before they were ten. Jerry and Hank's father became disabled after an accident. Johnny and Linda would have had another child in their family if their mother had not miscarried. When their father lost his business, Frank, Joan, and April were reduced to a lower standard of living.

These are big losses. How you and your sibling(s) grieve over these losses will determine whether you move on from the loss or stay stuck with the significance of the loss.

Responses regarding losses examined during adult brother-and-sister sessions:

Francis learned from her siblings that, ". . . parents [both] lost their parents at a young age."

The early death of parents (before children become adults) is significant in that the person(s) most able to care for the child is gone. The "gone" parent leaves a gap in the child's life and in the sibling relationship.

> *Did you have an early loss of a parent?*
> *Do you and your sibling(s) talk of the loss?*

Small losses don't have the significance of a big loss. Big losses remain and get bigger if grieving is absent. Compare with your sibling(s) about the significance of losses from your shared past, your ongoing shared present, and your upcoming shared future. Losses are a part of a family and a part of life and living. Ask your sibling about the family losses and understand that the significance of the loss may vary with you and your sisters or brothers.

My brother Harold disappeared. I don't know if he is alive or dead. He disappeared in 1994. He is my youngest brother and the father of three children. This outgoing, amiable, lovable dreamer left without saying anything. He left his children, his wife, his parents, his sister and brothers, his friends, and his community. If he is alive he has created a life apart from all of us. I miss him and long for his return. My loss is incomplete and I have learned to move on in my life without his warmth and humor. My siblings and I, along with his children and the other people who love him, yearn for his return.

Things don't always get wrapped up in a nice neat package with a bow across the top. Some losses continue to be a part of life, and life goes on.

Ask yourself:

> *Do you have a sibling loss?*
> *When did the loss occur?*

Amy, Barbara, and Richard, all adults now, have a sibling loss. Their older brother, James, whom they never met and never knew, died one hour after birth. This family lived in a small Vermont village, with a small hospital that did not have the resources to prevent this child from dying. Because life in this small mining town had to move on, the father quickly arranged the funeral. Within the next five years the two younger sisters and brother were born. The unresolved grief over the loss of this first child continues to this day.

Thirty-eight-year-old Linda's older brother was always sick. He was born with a defective heart and did not live past his tenth year. At the age of five, Linda became an "only child" after the loss of her brother. Her first five years of life included her older brother, and during the last thirty-three years she has lived only with memories of him.

## Family Myths

Helen's mother was not the innocent she portrayed. She had affairs that were common and hidden. She looked wonderful, delightful, sunny, acceptable, and appropriate in the community. She seemed all of these things and more.

The myth is a belief in the family that does not have a factual basis. A fact that is counter to the myth can destroy the myth. Bernie's father was a minister who had been married to Bernie's mother for over thirty-five years, and the church community liked Bernie's father and mother. The community did not know that Bernie's parents had not lived in the same house for over twenty-five years.

No one starts a myth. Ask yourself:

*Does your family have myths?*
*Do you and your sisters and brothers know the myth(s)?*
*Will you and your brothers and sisters speak of the myth(s)?*
*What are your child and adult myths (yarns)?*

### Myth Number One: My Sisters and Brothers Will Not Be There for Me

This myth is easily sent the way of the tooth fairy when you reverse the statement and say that you *will* be there for your sibling(s). I don't always like my own siblings; however, I do continue to love them.

I attended my sibling(s) baptisms, hospitalizations, graduations, birthday parties, weddings, births of children, holidays, and pains at the end of their relationships with significant others and will continue to do so. They in turn have attended mine.

### Myth Number Two: You Can Divorce Your Brothers and Sisters

You can love your brother or hate your brother and you are still connected. The strength of the connection waxes and wanes over time and just won't go away. You can lie about it, you complain about it and deny it, but it remains.

The connection started when your sibling was born and continues to this day. Down deep inside of you it lives.

### Myth Number Three: "I Wish You Were Dead"

You did *not* mean what you said; however, you *did* feel what you were feeling. This is a throwaway line. Six-year-old Herbert told his friend Leroy while watching a scary movie on television that he wished his younger brother, Simon, would die. Herbert, sixty-two, and Simon, fifty-eight, have spent the last thirty-nine years working together in their trucking business. Herbert is grateful that his wish did not come true.

*What is one of your childhood fantasies about your sibling(s)?*

## Myth Number Four: They wish You Were Dead

They did *not* mean what they said; however, they *did* feel what they were feeling. None of my siblings ever killed me, and their feelings could not make me disappear. *What is one of your sibling(s) childhood fantasies about you?*

## Myth Number Five: All Sisters and Brothers Are Equal.

Diana is the oldest of five children. When Diana was nine years old, and shortly before her mother's early death from emphysema, Diana's mother told her that she was expected to take care of her father and her three younger brothers and her sister. Diana's mother's death gave Diana the parental role. Now in her sixties, Diana has learned that her job of parenting her brothers and sister is completed. She stayed loyal to her mother's comment.

## Myth Number Six: You Can Disown your Siblings and Your Siblings Can Disown You.

When you have ongoing unresolved conflicts, look to your parents' generation. When parents become the judge and jury in the brothers' and sisters' childhood then the children are not taught the tools for conflict resolution. Unresolved adult brother-and-sister conflict can be traced to these early childhood conflicts. Disowning is an ultimate denial of conflict and resolution of the conflict. Brothers and sisters often focus more energy on disowning than in maintaining a relationship.

Brian was a brilliant attorney who disowned his sister. His relationship with her had a long history of unresolved conflict that he attributed to his sister's unfairness in resolving disagreements with him. He disowned his clients when they displeased him by not following his counsel and then by refusing to pay their bills. He set up his clients with vague, confusing contracts. He disowned his feelings by living in his head and always being logical. Worst of all, Brian disowned the opportunity of grieving over the loss of his mother when she died when he was only eleven years old.

What you *do* is not who you *are*. What your sister *does* is not who she *is*.

Forgiveness is the delight that appears when you continue to own the relationship with your sisters and brothers. Delight appears when your family members forgive you and continue to own the relationship with you.

Hurt comes from what we do and not who we are. Track your own hurt down by asking who did the hurt.

*What do you want to do with your hurt?*

## Myth Number Seven: Sisters and Brothers Are Not Strangers

Comments from participants in adult brother-and-sister sessions when asked after the session, What, if any, subjects would you like to have been brought up in the session?

Barbara: "How to establish a relationship with these strangers."

Howard: "More about how it was when Momma was home sick. We only had one session and it seemed like we would have needed more time or more sessions."

Bob: "Loss of 'closeness' between my siblings. I did not want to control the session. I wanted my siblings to freely discuss me, based on subjects proposed by the facilitator."

Calvin: "I felt good afterwards when I realized my siblings loved me so much, but never told me."

My longtime family friend Josephine Kuhlman's belief and practice was, "I never knew a stranger." Siblings are not strangers; they are just distinct from each other, and these differences, when honored, strengthen this relationship.

In the movie *The Prince of Tides,* the mother tells her ten-year-old middle-born son that he is her favorite. Later in the movie the son shares this with his sister. Her reply is that their mother told each of her three children he or she was her favorite. This comment split the brothers from each other and from their sister. Some families do have favorite siblings, and the favorite brother or sister has both added privileges and responsibilities. In childhood, the younger siblings in my family would accuse our mother of favoring my oldest brother. She probably did, as he was her first. Unfortunately this may have had the effect of driving a wedge in the same-generation relationships.

*What are your myths and what is the truth behind your myths?*

*What safe risk will you take with your sibling(s) to find the truth behind the myth?*

## About Your Family "Cutoffs"

A "cutoff" is a decision to no longer associate with a family member.

Cutoffs revealed in adult brother-and-sister sessions:

William: "Each of my siblings experienced a cutoff [the sibling initiated it] with my mother."

Joan: "Obvious 'cutoffs' were discussed as well as 'cutoffs' that were family secrets."

Yvonne: "My aunt [mother's sister] was cut off for long periods of time. My divorced uncle was cut off for a while, as he was the first on his side to divorce."

Jennifer: "I understood them because my sister knew some history I did not."

Nancy: "I learned that my dad had cut off lots of relatives."

Siblings are historians about:

(1) the origin of the cutoff and
(2) the family members that fortify the cutoff."

My own family cutoff was of my father's cousin Royce. Someone hinted to me that Royce would not toe the family line on my father's side of "hang together or hang separately." This severely limited contact with Royce, and talk of him dripped with indignation. I never met my second cousin Royce, and as of this writing I have no idea where he is or what happened to him.

*Who is "cutoff" in your family? A sister? A brother?*
*What was the "wound underlying the cutoff?*

Now that you feel stirred up and anxious about your questions, keep in your mind and your heart that your siblings will most probably have the same questions. Most likely one of you will have the answers to each of these questions. If you are willing to risk the question you also must be willing to risk hearing the answer. So much for clearing up confusion for you. As my friend and colleague Maria Nemeth asks, Would it be okay with you if your life got easier? Karen Gail Lewis, author of *Journal of Strategic and Systemic Therapies,* views siblings as a hidden resource in therapy. Like most treasures, they are in our own backyard.

## What Do You Want Your Siblings to Ask?

I want my own siblings to ask me to participate in their lives. They have honored me with requesting participation in theirs. Saying yes to a sibling is participation. Saying no to a sibling is participation. Not responding to a sibling is nonparticipation.

The participation may take the form of a letter, a telephone call, or a face-to-face experience. The magic of the past, the present, and the future is with that moment.

Further comments in response to the adult session:

(1) How close to your brothers and/or sisters did you feel before the adult session?

Ken: "We had once been very close but became more distant as I underwent therapy."
Steve: "Moderately close."
Donna: "Closer to my younger sib than my older one."
Lavar: "Closer then, than now."
Arnie: "Felt close to my sister and neutral with my brother."

(2) During the adult session how comfortable were you with your brother and/or sister?

David: "Felt very tense, a little defensive."
Madalyn: "Good to see in them their feelings of support."
Bernice: "I was surprised at how easily we were able to reveal or talk about things."

(3) During the adult sibling therapy session, what feelings did you have about your sibling(s)?

Alice: "More uncomfortable than distant."
John: "I did feel attacked by my younger sister."
Eric: "I felt distant due to my anxiety of the situation."
Pat: "The fact that she cared enough about me to come made me feel close to her."
Judy: "I loved them for their cards and desire to help."
Phillip: "I felt close to them but I also experienced moments of feeling distant when I wanted to keep my emotions in check."
Gordon: "I felt deep love and compassion as we shared hurts and pain."
Dennis: "I felt a great deal of support."

These siblings met in a neutral setting (my office), with a facilitator (me) and a willingness to be mutual historians and mutual supporters.

## What Do You Want Your Siblings Not to Ask of You?

One of my clients said; "I do not want my brothers and sisters to ask me to do something that they can do for themselves. I believe in assisting people in my life. If my assistance helps them to flourish, they grow and I am rewarded in many ways. Saying no to a sister may be the start of growth. I may have to be hated (temporarily) when my vision is of the growth of my brother. Conversely, when my brother tells me no, does he have the vision that I do not have?"

A telephone call from Kansas City to Los Angeles came from his twenty-six-year-old younger sister. She asked for enough money to ride the bus to Los Angeles. She had earlier left her children in Los Angeles with friends and traveled with her boyfriend to Kansas City. Alcohol and drugs had become a part of her life. Her older brother initially agreed to send money for the trip back to Los Angeles, but on second thought he reasoned that he was being asked to do something he did not believe in. He believed in her, not in her behavior. He made the painful decision *not* to send her money. She returned to Los Angeles on her own initiative. Ten years later she marched into an Alcoholics Anonymous gathering in order to straighten her life out. Not helping sometimes appears to be cruel. You must determine whether or not to help your brother or sister. If your help assists growth in your siblings and you are committed to growth, then help them. If your help retards growth in your siblings and you are committed to growth, then don't help them.

The required care and feeding of elderly parents has recently become a growth industry. Your parents moved from being the caretakers to being the caretaken. They must be cared for, and you and your siblings are it. You are not required, legally, but moral law requires you to act.

The care and feeding of elderly parents can be a strong point of contention. Every sister and every brother has an opinion, whether or not she or he verbally expresses it. A withheld opinion still carries an opinion. What do you ask of your sibling(s) in the care of your parent(s)? What do your sibling(s) ask of you in the care of your parent(s)? There is no magic on this journey, and what you do or don't do can leave a sweet or bitter taste in your mouth. An assumption about elderly parents is not a question asked. As siblings you are required to ask the questions.

Comments about mother from adult brother-and-sister session participants when asked the question, "What did you learn from your sibling(s) about your mother?":

> Brenda: "I am more honest in what I recognize about my mother, and more of my own person; I respect her more."
> Jaime: "I no longer see my mother and have very little exposure to my father. As a result I am more comfortable making decisions without Mom's input."

Mary: "I am able to be her adult child instead of her little girl. I can disagree with her without anxiety, and love her as she is."

Brian: "Positive in that it was easier to express my feelings about my dad and mom as the session wore on. I think my mom felt threatened when she heard about adult sibling therapy. It is hard to say."

Rod: "We are finally gaining in this area. 'Work in progress'— I'm not crazy; so I feel okay knowing the past happened the way I perceived it. I don't need her confirmation."

Elaine: "I can talk much more freely with my mother."

Tim: "Mother is supportive."

Comments about father from adult brother-and-sister session participants when asked the question, "What did you learn from your sibling(s) about your father?":

Louise: "Father is dead but my relationship to his memory is more honest."

Billie: "I don't get to see my dad much. I miss him."

Jason: "I learned that he was not 'the heavy' I had thought and am able to talk with him more than before. I can accept him as he is and ask advice in ways I couldn't before without feeling quite so childish."

Jeanie: "I expressed some repressed feelings of sadness and loss I let come to the surface in great force. I got to express my love for my dad too."

Mike: "I feel closer to him now—I'd like to see him more."

Gary: "I could see my father for who he was."

Asking the adult children who grew up with you about your parents and being asked by these same sisters and brothers about your parents can be a delicate stroll through intention versus content, intention being the purpose and content being the substance of the stroll. These early childhood historians want to know your reason for asking and what you are doing with the information. You want to know the same from them. A little trust goes a long way on this stroll. When you tell them, will they keep the secret? Will you?

Keeping a confidence that has been shared with you by your sisters or brothers will deepen your relationship. Use this delicate family information to enhance your own life, and don't use the information to hurt other family members. They will appreciate your thoughtfulness as you will appreciate theirs.

The participants in adult brother-and-sister sessions had the joy of having answers to questions that they did not have to ask. They were in a room with people who have an intense childhood as well as an intense adulthood with one another. Each person in the room had a virtually untapped well of information. As their guide, I had to win them over, these people I had recently met, in order to uncap this well of information. I am friendly, humorous, effective, curious, and protective as a guide, and this allows me to enter their unique world. My presence in their world is an honor for me, and this unique relationship will flower when nourished with acceptance and nonjudgment. I strive to provide nourishment during the session.

Comments from participants when asked, How has the quality of your relationship with your sisters and brothers been since your adult session?

Judy: "Perhaps more honest."

David: "Maybe slight improvement."

Bobbie: "We can talk more straightforwardly about our feelings, needs, and fears."

Ann: "My sister said that she always thought of her childhood as happy. After [the session] she started talking about her anger at Dad much more than I ever heard her do before. I got to know my sister and her feelings about Dad. Intimacy developed between us."

John: "It still fluctuates. I know that in a crisis we'd be there for each other, but knowing how to keep it going under normal' times is challenging."

Pat: "I feel closer to all my siblings than any other time in my life."

Tom: "I feel more free to talk openly with my brother."

Beyond the anger, hurt, resentment, blame, fear, illusion, history, and whatever other story you have is your sibling(s). You did not choose these people to be in your life, and yet there they were in your past, here they are in your present, and they will be in your future.

## What Is Left Over from Your Past about Your Sisters and Brothers that Is Not Completed.

A "complete" carries the positive energy of love, forgiveness, and acceptance.

An "incomplete" carries the negative energy of resentment, bitterness, and hate.

## Bonds Formed through Emotions

Love and hate are extremes on the same journey. When you love your sibling(s) you are bonded. When you hate your sibling(s) you are bonded. I have yet to see sisters who are not bonded. Positive brother bonds lead to a joyous journey with the shared sweats, the shared sweets, and the shared sorrows. Negative adult brother and sister bonds lead to a journey of leftover hurt, resentment, and wasted energy. The ultimate negative sister-and-brother bond leads to murder.

The opposite of love and hate is a relationship of indifference. Can you be indifferent to your sisters and brothers? I think not. Unresolved conflict in this unique relationship, whether it occurred in the past, in the present, or is anticipated in the future, can be resolved. The skill in conflict resolution in this unique relationship is within each person. Conflict resolution leads to a sense of closeness. What is your fear of feeling close with these special people? The extent to which you are willing to risk being close to your sibling(s) is the extent to which you are willing to lose the closeness. Translated—there are no guarantees in life. The reward of risking your feelings to obtain closeness with your sibling(s) is your option. It is not about your sibling(s). It is about you.

## Anger

Remember when you were a child, and became angry with your brother or sister? Some people fib and say they didn't get angry. Anger came with us at birth. The newborn turns up that pouty lip when angry. So what did you do with that anger when you were a child? Our culture says that nice girls don't get angry. What a burden for young girls. I told my six-year-old daughter, even when I was mad at her, that I still loved her. She said I did not. One year later she came to me and said, "Dad, don't you know that when I am mad at you I still love you?" I said, "Yes." An unexpressed anger is the block to an expression of love.

Now ask yourself: In your childhood, how did your mother display her anger? How did your father display his anger? When you were a child and angry what was your father's response? When you were a child and angry what was your mother's response? When you were a child and your brother or sister was angry what was your parents' response? When you were a child and you were angry what was your brother's or sister's response? Anger is an emotion and the emotion will not harm, hurt, or kill if you can remain objective. Behavior that comes out of anger is not anger itself. When my eight-year-old older brother took my scooter without my five-year-old permission, I hurled a metal file at his head. Throwing the metal file was not a healthy expression of emotion; it was a behavior. Did your family distinguish between anger the emotion and anger the behavior?

What anger do you have left over from your childhood directed at your brother or sister? Did your parents' generation model the healthy expression of anger? Telling the truth about your anger can be a difficult behavior to relearn. If you have leftover childhood anger, what happens to your anger when you look on the face of your adult brother or sister? Can you recognize their unexpressed anger? What would occur if you risked expressing it in a healthy way? What would occur if your sibling took the risk of expressing his or her anger in a healthy fashion?

Twenty-seven-year-old Devon first told his sister Pauline that he loved her very much and that he had also been angry with her. He went on to explain that his anger came from her not inviting him to her annual block party. She accepted his feeling and she apologized.

Love flows when anger is expressed in a nonthreatening, nonblaming, and personally responsible fashion.

## Sadness

The origin of the emotion of sadness is linked to a loss. The loss can take the form of death, disability, separation, disappointment, injury, accident, a slip of the tongue, a missed opportunity, or anything that feels like a loss. Loss is a part of life. How we deal with the loss is the key to a process I call "good-bye, hello." We say good-bye to kindergarten to say hello to first grade; we say good-bye to high school to say hello to adulthood. When the good-bye is not experienced, the hello waits around the corner in our lives. An unexperienced good-bye keeps you stuck at the point of the loss.

In our culture, sisters can acceptably experience the emotion of sadness and express the emotion through tears. As the song says, "Big boys don't cry," and after the age of nine, the healthy expression of sadness disappears for brothers. As anger is not acceptable for sisters, then sadness is not acceptable for brothers. When she is angry does she substitute tears? When he is sad does he substitute anger?

When my daughter was eight years old she told me that she had never seen me cry. I want her to know that men have tears. I told her that I had cried at my grandfather's funeral, and she said she wasn't there.

Did you experience your father's expression of tears? Did you experience your mother's expression of tears? What about sibling tears? What are your unexpressed tears from childhood about your sibling(s)? What are their unexpressed tears from childhood about you?

Two adult sisters and their adult brother had lost their father through death twenty-five years ago. During their session each one of them expressed their tears as if the death had just occurred. The outpouring of emotion enabled each of them to support themselves and each other in this healthy expression over the death of their father. Tears can come in the form of a current loss or an old loss.

Their loss was an old loss expressed in the now. Tears bring relief from the pain of the loss, and the expression is never too late.

An unexpressed sadness can result in depression and despair. An expressed sadness can lead to a new happiness.

## Fear

Gavin De Becker's book *The Gift of Fear* gives us permission to know that our fears alert us to a danger or potential danger. The key is to develop a strategy for dealing with that fear. De Becker described one of his childhood scenes. He was ten years old, and his mother was poised to shoot his stepfather. He backed away from it, passing through the kitchen where the forgotten dinner was burning and into the small bedroom where his two-year-old sister slept. As he went to wake her, he heard the gunshot he was expecting. He was startled, but not surprised; however the silence afterward concerned him. He had originally planned to take his sister out of the house, but he told her to stay in bed. He knew she was too young to understand the seriousness of the situation. He was not.

Fear, real or imagined, takes a strategy to reduce. The strategy may be dramatic like De Becker's, it may come in the form of comfort, it may come in the form of reassurance that people and things will be okay, it may come in the form of counseling, it may come in the form of law enforcement, or it may come in the form of simple words and healing through physical touch.

In your childhood how did you and your family deal with fear? An unexpressed fear is a block to trust. What are your leftover sister and brother fears from childhood? How are the leftover fears in the way of a relationship with these family members now? What courage would you have to muster in order to address your fears? Fears come in two forms: (1) real fear and (2) imagined fear. When you were a child the "bogeywoman" and the "bogeyman" brought imagined fear. Your sibling hitting you brought real fear. The emotion of fear is authentic, no matter the form.

In your childhood, how did your same-generation family members react when you were afraid? How did you react when they were afraid? In my own childhood family, I kept the fear inside. I don't know how that rule got started. In retrospect, when my father was afraid, he became quiet. When my mother was afraid, she worked harder to survive.

## Conflict

Ten-year-old Dennis and nine-year-old Kevin brought their unresolved conflict to their mother. This wise mother, not wanting to be judge and jury, told the brothers that she was going to the store and that when she returned, the boys were to tell her how they solved their conflict. Thirty minutes later when she returned, each brother approached her with excitement. After meeting with each other in Dennis's bedroom, they had arrived at a fair resolution of the conflict and both felt okay with themselves and each other. They had learned to structure their conflict resolution. They traveled the path of conflict, to the path of negotiation, to the path of compromise, and to the path of resolution. Their resolution led to a bond of closeness. Twenty-four-year-old Dennis and twenty-three-year-old Kevin continue the path of resolving conflicts.

What are your unresolved childhood conflicts? What are your unresolved adult peer family member conflicts? How did you resolve brother and sister conflicts in your childhood? How are you resolving sister and brother conflicts in your adulthood? Did your parents "get out of the way" after giving you conflict resolution tools? Do you want to travel the path of conflict resolution with these special same-generation people? If not, ask yourself, How come? By the way, parents are *not* to blame. If they did not teach you, you can still learn.

## Happiness

Pleasure, delight, satisfaction, merriment, excitement, laughter, elation—take your choice to describe your happiness. Some families are happy families—not happy all the time; however, they have a theme of happiness running through their lives together. Some families are unhappy families—not unhappy all the time; however, they have a theme of unhappiness running through their lives together. My experience as a marriage and family therapist is that a happy family begins with a happy marriage. The happy marriage trickles into the sibling generation.

The trickling is only a part of the happiness in a family. Contrary to some beliefs, I believe there is no such thing as a "dysfunctional family." However, each and every family has some dysfunction. When the "dysfunction" changes into "function," then the family purpose and work continue on the path of happiness.

In childhood, what were the happy moments and times with your family members that you can recall?

In my childhood:

With my brother Stan: He carried me to my bed after I had spilled scalding water on my bare feet.

With my brother Chuck: He was the "cook" in the family, and made sure that everyone had something to eat.

With my sister, Marilyn: She moderated the brothers' masculinity with her femininity.

With my brother Jim: He was the craftsman who could create order out of chaos.

With my brother Harold: He was the companion ready and willing to have a good time.

I have many other times and moments with my sister and four brothers in childhood, and our happiness was not always present; however, we were, and are, "characters." We know how to play, laugh, have fun, joke, and continue to create more happy times together. I want them in my life, as they add happiness, and I hope I add happiness to their lives.

Happy comments from participants in adult brother-and-sister sessions:

Nancy: "This was a special experience that I will always remember as very positive."

Robert: "Marvin, I still think you're a little nuts, but love you anyway. Without your support [Adult Sibling Therapy©] and patience with me, my life would still be a considerable mess."

Daniel: "It was a very positive experience for me. It was scary to think about at first, but it brought a lot of issues together and helped to finalize some problems. I felt good afterwards when I realized my siblings loved me so much, but never told me."

*Do you know that your brothers and sisters love you?*

*Do your brothers and sisters know that you love them?*

# 3

*What Your Brothers and Sisters Taught You*

## Not All Sisters and Brothers Are Created Equal

Imagine a clone of you, not your sister or your brother but a reproduction of you—no differences and all sameness. Your clone has all of your genetic makeup; your brothers and sisters have some of your genetic makeup and some of their own. Your clone could stand in for you when you don't want to take that test in school. Try your sister or brother with a bribe. That might work. Your clone thinks like you; the others think somewhat like you. Your clone loves like you; the others love somewhat like you. Your clone is as boring as you can be; your sisters and brothers are less boring. (Just ask them.) Your clone likes the same food you like, the same movies you like, the same books you like, the same lovers you like, the same travel, and never differs. Your sibling(s), on the other hand, can both look, talk, and act somewhat like you and look, talk, and act somewhat differently from you.

One egg and one sperm is how we got here. You the egg and you the sperm came from two separate donors. We call these donors *parents*. Parents at conception can be different from the caretaking parents throughout life.

You and your brothers and sisters may have come from the same donors, but with a different egg and a different sperm.

You and your sibling(s) are unique.
*Vive la difference.*

Brother and sister differences include gender, height, weight, body shape, body size, intelligence, looks, talents, ambition, determination, goals, tastes, dislikes, and any other ingredient in the sibling salad. The salad starts with ingredients you are born with and then begins to acquire ingredients from your life experiences. The wise parent perceives the differences with each child.

In our childhood we were "the Todd kids," or "Hazel and Vernon's kids" to the outsiders (all the people who are not in the same family generation). Not much chance to be experienced as separate by outsiders. Within our same-generation world we were different. All six of us worked to break out of the pack. The pack provided familiarity and change, support and criticism, fighting and forgiving, companionship and confinement, and love and hate—very little indifference and a lot of bonding.

I want my siblings close, but not too close. I want them distant, but not too distant. This is the childhood dance of nearness and closeness. Excessive nearness is suffocating. Excessive closeness is restraining. As the philosophers say, everything in moderation and know thyself.

Distinction, variation, dissimilarity, contradiction, contrast, open conflict, and dissent are terms describing a healthy sibling relationship. Sibling conflict is a sign of contrast between siblings, and sibling resolution is a sign of strength between siblings. Paul and Edna are forty-eight and fifty-one years of age, respectively. They have the same parents and same childhood life together. Edna took the path of pioneer in their family of origin by challenging the parental generation. Paul learned from Edna's example and took a passive position on the pathways of life in their family. She became resentful and angry, and Paul became resentful and passive. Fortunately, in their adult years they addressed their family drama in an adult brother-and-sister session. We provided space for both of them to address her aggression and his passivity. Their pathways of aggression and passivity then led to their pathway of assertion. Both Edna and Paul were able to say who they are and glimpse how they are alike and how they are different.

Telling the truth about what you want and telling the truth

about what you don't want is the pathway to an uncluttered relationship. Unresolved conflict collects clutter. Paul and Edna tossed away their clutter by telling the truth to themselves of what they wanted and didn't want, and having the courage to then share their truth with each other.

## You Did Not Choose Them—They Are a Nonreturnable Item

Six-year-old Sandy says the worst day of her life was the day her brother, Theodore, was born. Sandy will come to both love and hate Theodore, and he will admire her and look to her for leadership. She will be won over by him, come to appreciate him as he learns to appreciate her. He was an intruder in her safe world, and, if she could, she would have "returned" him to his own world.

Sixteen-year-old Sandy is a high school sophomore, and ten-year-old Teddy is a fourth grader. She has a boyfriend and he has friends. He is a kid and she is a young lady. She is glad her parents did not return him.

Twenty-two-year-old Ted was at the hospital with his brother-in-law, Brian, when Sandy gave birth to her first child, Brian.

Thirty-one-year-old Sandy was a bridesmaid at Ted and Hannah's wedding.

Aunt Sandy and Uncle Ted share five nieces and nephews between them and have attended many birthday parties, holiday gatherings, graduations, sick days, and various nonlethal accidents of broken skin and bones.

Seventy-six-year-old Sandy called seventy-year-old Ted to tell him of the death of her husband, Brian. Ted was nurturing and supportive, and offered whatever assistance Sandy wanted. Their sibling relationship has outlasted, in the length of time, the relationships with their parents, their spouses, and their children.

Nine-year-old Brian and seven-year-old Kevin have a newborn brother, Arnold. Kevin is bounced out of his seven-year position of being the youngest child in this family. Brian retains his firstborn senior position and continues to be the oldest brother in the family. Now Arnold has arrived, and because he requires his ever-present needs to be met by his parents, Kevin has to adjust in order to receive recognition from his parents. As with all babies, Arnold wins the baby contest and Kevin has to redefine his safe world. He opts for being the academic in the family, and his parents begin to give him recognition for his school efforts.

Kevin was able to successfully adjust when his birth position was changed from being the youngest to being a middle-born. Twenty years later, twenty-seven-year-old Kevin graduated from Cornell University's medical school.

Feelings are not facts, and the sayings about sibling feelings are mostly throwaway lines. Sandy and Theodore love each other even when they don't like each other. Arnold, Kevin, and Brian are brothers who have established their individuality as separate members of the family.

## You Are a Nonreturnable Item

Look at this from your sibling(s) position: You did not make the decision—those two people with the egg and the sperm made it. Your sister and brother may want you or they may not want you. It depends on the world they have created, and if they have room for you in their created world. Their initial enthusiasm may dwindle as they realize that you are not a weekend guest. You are here for the long haul, and along with the tree of love they have for you, there are some branches on the tree of hate: resentment, jealousy, envy, and wishes for your psychological death.

So here you are! The deck is stacked against you and you just arrived! My brother Chuck was eighteen months old when I arrived. My brother Stan was three years old when I arrived. As brothers, our recovery time from a new arrival was often interrupted by an even newer arrival.

Human behaviorists widely debate the spacing between each new birth in the family. If the family has enough stroking recognition to go around, then close spacing may not be a problem. During my teenage years I worked in construction for Mr. Williams. In an informal lunchtime discussion with him, he told me that he has four grown children and they were all spaced four years apart, and his reason for that was that he did not want more than one child in college at a time. Mr. Williams was a practical person!

There is always a story about your arrival. Perhaps the story is clouded in secrecy because of the conception date, place, time, or biological parents. Do you know your own story? What do your siblings know about your story? What do you know about their story? The story will follow you through your life, and the story can be based in fact or fantasy or some variation of both.

In your own life at least one person knows the stories. It is sometimes a mother, sometimes a father, and sometimes someone else. Your simple curiosity may solve a long-standing question of fill in some family gap. What you do with the information and what will your other family members do with the information is your choice and theirs. Keep this simple, fun, loving, and educational, and be protective of yourself and others.

You won't be "returned" by your sibling(s) for asking the questions when they understand your motives, or for clearing up misunderstandings and helping grow your sibling relationship.

## You Don't Have to Savor Them, but It Helps If You Do

Savor means to enjoy the flavor of. Taste the flavors you gave to your sisters and brothers back then and there, and the flavors you give to them in the here and now. Notice the flavors they gave to you back then and there, and the flavors they are giving in the here and now. At times flavors change. They may be sweet, sour, or salty.

As with most things in life, we can change the sour taste of a lemon into lemonade. Your attitude about your brothers and sisters can either be one of abundance or one of scarcity. The outcome is your option.

## You Cannot Divorce Your Sisters and Brothers—Even If You Try

Divorce has six components:

1. Legal  The sibling relationship is not a legal relationship, although you may experience it as legitimate.

2. Financial  You exchanged money with your siblings. They exchanged money with you. You do not owe and they do not owe.
3. Coparenting  You coparented the pets in childhood, perhaps even coparented your parents, if your parents do not take care of themselves.
4. Community  You shared the community of your neighborhood, your family, your extended family, your schools, and any other common community activity.
5. Emotional  The bond that exists between you and your siblings is mainly emotional—remember that blood is thicker than water. The emotional bond can't be seen, it can't be touched, and it can't be heard. You can see, touch, and hear your sibling(s) but not the relationship.
6. Psychic  This encompasses the stuff inside of each of us. I am my siblings' brother—nothing will ever change that. They are my brothers and sister—nothing will ever change that.

Nothing will change the fact that they are your blood relatives from the same generation, and the fact that you are also from the same generation. Divorce is out of the question. What you do with the relationship is in question. Like all relationships, care and feeding will nourish and strengthen the sibling relationship, and disregard will starve and weaken it.

Every Thursday morning at seven A.M. for the past fifty-three years brothers Lloyd and Calvin have met at the Elks Lodge for breakfast. Both are married with children and grandchildren. Neither Lloyd's wife nor Calvin's wife has ever complained about these Thursday-morning breakfasts. Both wives know their husbands are happier when they come home from breakfast. Lloyd and Calvin take care to nurture and feed their brother relationship.

Caroline and Leonard are different. When Caroline was twenty-five, she invited Leonard to be in her wedding. He accepted, and on her wedding day he did not show up, refused to give a reason for his absence, and further refused to apologize. During the past two decades they have not spoken to or seen each other. Their lack of care and feeding of their relationship caused it to decline. Their relationship could be revived with their assistance.

## Sibling Love and Hate

### *They Hate You While Loving You*

Love and hate are on the same continuum. The pathway to hate starts at the opposite end of the pathway of love. Indifference is not on the pathway at all. Movement between love and hate can be a brief moment in time or of long standing. Children move from love to hate and hate to love in brief moments. The time is extended when someone else has a vested interest in maintaining the hate between children. Children have the wonderful capacity to forgive and forget. Big people, who have difficulty with the closeness of intimacy, have difficulty with forgiving and forgetting.

With some minor assistance from parents about fairness, a win-win attitude, and tools of conflict resolution, siblings soon learn that to get along, they must compromise.

John took his two young sons, four-year-old Danny and seven-year-old Jimmy to the park, where they got into a fight over who owned the family softball. At the park, their father gave each of his sons his softball mitt, picked up the softball from the green grass, and walked to the bleachers and sat down. With the softball sitting beside him, their father told them both to play ball. Both brothers looked surprised and mildly confused, and began to protest that they couldn't play without a ball. In the twinkling of the moment each brother looked at the other and both smiled. Their wise father had taught them about cooperation.

Fifty-four-year-old Danny and fifty-seven-year-old Jimmy had to make the funeral arrangements after their seventy-eight-year-old father died of a heart attack. These brothers were as cooperative in their grieving as in their softball playing. During the service Danny told the story of how their father had taught his two sons to cooperate and how they continued this lesson throughout their lives.

Their father taught them how to move from resentment to cooperation.

When you get beyond your resentments and look at your appreciations for your special peers, your pathway may clear up. Add up your resentments, both the small ones and the big ones, write them down, tear up the paper, and burn the strips. Add up your appreciations, write them down, and mail them to your sister or brother. Make a copy of your appreciations for your sisters and brothers and keep the list, read the list when you forget, and add to the appreciations list as time goes on.

Resentments are a part of life. The closer we are to our sisters and brothers, the greater the chance of resentment.

Appreciations are a part of life. The closer we are to these special people, the greater the chance that appreciation will appear.

## You Hate Them While Loving Them

Now admit that in the core of your hate is the seed of hurt delivered to you by one of these unique family members. Whether it was intentional or accidental, hurt is hurt. When you were a kid and were hurt by your sibling, you processed hurt by lying about it, hiding it, stuffing it, shifting it to anger, beating the offending sibling up or by simply stating, "I hurt." Healing begins when you diagnose hurt. If you remember how your brother or sister hurt you, look inside and try to see what caused it. Was your hurt of feelings, of body, or of mind? My brother is not responsible for what I *felt* when he ran over me with the tractor. He, unfortunately, is responsible for driving the tractor. He suffered enough for that!

Hate becomes ugly when it changes from a feeling to a fact. Most prisons have inmates who are model prisoners. Some of these model prisoners are inmates who have killed their brother or sister. The hate did not do the killing; the deed did the killing. Cain killed Abel. He could have hated Abel and left the deed out of their interaction. The first murder was a sibling murder. If we or our siblings nurture each other, then we are truly their keeper and we are truly kept by them.

## You Said Mom/Dad Liked Them Best

I don't recall now how I felt about my changing birth position so often. I was too young to notice the change. My wife's youngest sister was born ten years after my wife. When Annie was born an older sibling thought her name was a name to laugh at. Their parents opted for the name Annie instead of the name AnnaBelle. Her siblings agreed. These sisters had an impact on their parents and their parents chose to protect Annie from entering this family with a different name.

Parents may love all of their children, but not in the same way. Each sibling is unique. Parents have preferences. Some parents "fib" about the preferences. Some parents tell the truth about sibling preferences.

Parental preference can be based on: (a) birth order position, (b) gender, or (c) any other dynamic chosen by a parent.

Grey was the preferred sibling to his younger brother, Gerard. Their father had a special liking for his firstborn son that he never explained. The father took Grey on walks, on drives, to work, and frequently his father had Grey sit next to him. Gerard learned to live in the shadow of Grey and also learned to live in a world where he played with other kids. He gave up on his father's attention and continued to love his father, in spite of his father's lack of approval and recognition.

Gender can also be a determinant of parental favoritism. Allison is the firstborn of six siblings. Her two-years-younger brother, Bobby, was the preferred sibling. He received the accolades for being the firstborn male in the family. He was the "pride" of his mother and father. He was cute as a baby, handsome as a ten-year-old, and exceedingly good-looking as an adult. Older sister Allison at twenty-nine years of age had graduated from the university as a chemist, and later married a man who adored her. She had long ago given up winning over her parents. In her heart she knew that Bobby was not at fault. She forgave her parents for something that they denied. They did prefer Bobby over Allison.

Dynamics that include looks, resemblances, personality, abilities, color of hair, color of eyes, birth stories, intelligence, and any other trait that catches the attention of a parent may have an impact on parental preference for one child over another.

Third-born Cleotus was favored by his parents because he was born with a partial stomach. His older brothers were jealous of him and his preferred status with their parents. Cleotus grew up to become a many-times-married father of five children. He maintained contact with his parents and left behind his five children.

His preferred status with his parents undermined his sibling, marital, and parental relationships.

## Were You the "Nonpreferred" Sibling?

Nonpreferred feelings are common for most people. The facts about nonpreferred sibling status range from outright exclusion to mild discounting. Janelle was overshadowed by her younger brother James. He was cute, the athlete, the son, the parents' "hope," but he gave up preferred status to discover himself; he had been what his parents wanted him to be and not what he wanted for himself. Janelle, on the other hand, had nowhere to go but up. She got her parents' attention by putting herself at risk in relationships with men. She learned in her thirties that she could receive positive attention from other people and that she did not have to be at risk with men. She has been married for the past five years to Howard and she is happy with their marriage.

Many times a preferred child is chosen by the parent to fulfill a dream that the parent had for him- or herself. This is the stagedoor mother or father who has the child live out the parental dream.

Cardiac surgeon Christopher is the hero in his family. His father flunked out of his first year of medical school due to severe diabetes. Christopher, the youngest in this family of three children, was the "designated" doctor. His older brother and sister began calling Christopher "Dr. Chris" when they were children. Their father smiled, and each kid knew what would happen. Chris was monitored throughout his grade school, middle school, high school, and college years by their father. Chris's older sister and brother knew that they were left to be in the "audience" and not on the "stage" for this family drama.

Was Chris a doctor for himself or for his dad?

## Your Sibling Life Education is Ongoing

Another thirty-three-year-old client, Richard, recounted a recent awareness he had while having lunch with his mother, his stepfather, and his married thirty-one-year-old sister, Rachel, and her husband. During lunch, Richard observed a three-year-old girl, her five-year-old brother, and their father at the adjacent table. The three-year-old was attempting to get her father's attention. She was unsuccessful, and as a result she turned and struck her five-year-old brother. Her early training was to take her frustration out on her older brother. Richard pointed out to Rachel this scene as an example of their childhood relationship. Rachel saw the five-year-old brother as the instigator. Richard understood his feelings of being the nonpreferred child by witnessing the present-day scene. Rachel, however, continues to see Richard as the cause of their family problems.

## What Sibling Era Are You Experiencing Now?

Brother and sister life education has three eras: the childhood era, the adult era, and the elderly era. You can designate your own era's beginning and ending by your experiences.

Most likely your childhood sibling education was gained in close physical, emotional, and mental proximity. You shared the same house, the same parents, the same values, the same religion, the same food, the same conflicts, and created memories of the events.

Harlan was the oldest of four siblings, and his childhood era was filled with multiple family moves, changes in schools, changes in neighborhoods, and a general disruption of his family's steadiness. His steadiness was witnessed as his availability to talk with his younger sister and brothers. They learned to come to him when his parents were not available. This childhood-era steadiness gave them a sense of trust, reliability, and love. They looked to him. He has continued to provided adult steadiness, and most likely within five years when he becomes sixty-five years of age he will provide "elderly" sibling steadiness. His three siblings learned from his steadiness and they grew up to achieve steadiness of their own.

## In Your Childhood Sibling Era: What Were You Willing to Risk with Your Sibling(s)?

The risks involve asking your siblings about them, asking your siblings about you, asking your siblings about your parents, and asking your siblings about the world outside of your house. In adult brother-and-sister sessions, siblings reach into the childhood era, ask questions, give answers, and supply their perceptions about that time period. Johnny recalled that his remembrances of his childhood would make him crazy. His father was frequently gone and his mother lived most of the time in her bedroom, where her eating habits left her morbidly obese. When he was a child, his parents told Johnny that they had a happy family and that everything was fine. The adult brother-and-sister session reinforced for Johnny that his family had a craziness. His two sisters, Brenda and Louise, recounted this family craziness. The women were an uncovered resource for his understanding. This was a relief for him.

During her adult session, Ellen's brothers confirmed that their parents had a negative, somewhat violent relationship. This was not a blaming parents session. This was adult siblings sharing information that was helpful for each of them to understand more about their family. These unique historians assisted Ellen in understanding some of her unresolved conflict with her parents.

In my own childhood era, I risked my relationship with my siblings by asking safe questions and sometimes asking unsafe ones. A safe question has no "fallout." An unsafe question has fallout, but can still be worth the effort. Once the question is out, curiosity is altered in some fashion. Most of my childhood-era sibling questions were safe even though my brothers and sister would sometimes be critical about my "dumb" questions. I also sometimes criticized their "dumb" questions.

## In Your Adulthood Sibling Era: What Are You Willing to Risk with Your Sibling(s)?

Most of you reading this book are most likely in your adult era. You can still reach back to childhood. A lively discussion with your brothers and sisters may rekindle some early childhood memories.

This is the time when your sibling bond is stretched to permit you to marry, to have children, to work in your career, and to live in your community. You just don't have as much contact with your brothers and sisters as you did. They are still around somewhere. The bond is still present, only stretched.

When I encounter people who have had no contact with their sibling(s), I query their motive. Noncontact with a sibling requires an effort. Every day, the effort of keeping in contact with siblings is a small undertaking. Seeing a brother, talking with a sister, writing, e-mailing, all are there for the taking. I hope that my youngest brother is alive. Contact is both given and received and, if he is alive, he is not giving or receiving. Do you have noncontact with one of your brothers or sisters? What is the underlying hurt that prohibits your contact with them?

My paternal grandparents migrated from Tennessee and Oklahoma to California during the 1930s. My grandmother, the letter writer, kept in contact with her eight siblings, and my grandfather, the telephone caller, kept in contact with his five siblings. Here in California they had their children, their grandchildren, their great-grandchildren, and their great-great-grandchildren, and still they kept in contact with their brothers and sisters. My paternal grandmother, Eva (called Evie), was a twin. Her twin was named Effie. When the twins were nine years old, Effie died. During my childhood I had the privilege of hearing my grandmother's stories about Effie and Evie. My grandmother was a strong Southern woman with a quick wit, and her stories of Effie and Evie were a delight to hear.

My grandmother made her sister come alive to me. This was my great-aunt whom I never met and would not have known much about without my grandmother's stories. We may have relatives that we have never met, and yet they have an impact on us because they have had an impact on other members of our families.

## In Your Elderly Sibling Era

Eighty-two-year-old Helen was widowed after she spent fifty years with her husband, Charles. Two years after Charles's death Helen married eighty-six-year-old widower Bernie. Bernie had also had a long-term sixty-two-year marriage before his wife, Irene, died. Bernie had been single for over two years when his son, Leroy, introduced him to his former teacher and neighbor, Helen. Helen and Bernie hit it off, and within three months decided to marry. Helen requested that her eighty-four-year-old brother, Richard, give her away at this, her second marriage. Richard quickly agreed. Richard had also been best man at Helen's first marriage. Their brother-and-sister relationship is strong and the longest relationship for both of them.

In this elderly era, the presence of your brothers and sisters is unlike any other relationship. They have contact with you. It may be by letter, by telephone, by physical presence, or by the Internet. At this time in your life sibling resentments can be a thing of the past. Sibling appreciations are of the past, present, and the future.

Donald, seventy-six, and his sister, Louise, seventy-one, fought as children, fought as adults, and now fight in their elder years. Their fighting is based on a competition for parental love. In their family, love was scarce and the two of them never "figured it out." Their fighting created a pattern of negative stroking, created an unpleasant social "odor" when others were with them. Yet their sibling connection is strong because the cable between them has many more strands of negative strokes than positive strokes. Their resentments are not expressed but are withheld, and they build a case against each other. Their parents died long ago, yet these two siblings continue their competition for their parents' love.

Eighty-one-year-old Martha and her brother, seventy-seven-year-old John, have a strong sibling relationship because the cable connecting them has many strands of positive strokes and a healthy expression of both appreciations and resentments. Martha, who lives in Boston, was upset with John for his indiscretion in not sending her a card on her eightieth birthday. She promptly got on the telephone and told him that she knew he had inadvertently forgotten. He quickly apologized to his beloved sister and from his home in San Diego he went to the store, and picked out an "I love my sister" card. His message written in his own hand at the bottom of the card thanked her for reminding him. The next day in Boston, the United Parcel Service driver arrived with the card and a dozen white roses.

Resentments and appreciations are currencies exchanged during any sibling interaction. All people exchange currencies while interacting. Negative sibling interaction will most likely be traced to the siblings' relationship with parents. Parents who allow you and your siblings to work out your conflict are assisting you in the strength of your relationship. If you have some resentments you can release them. Look to your expressed appreciations to help you let go of your resentments.

### Brother and Sister Education Has Very Little Formalized Structure

The sibling classroom is steeped heavily in experiential behavior. The lessons are taught informally, accidentally, in both fact and fiction, biased, eye-popping, crude, enlightening, helpful for both the "teaching" sibling as well as the "student" sibling. I learned from my brother Stan not to leave his bicycle in the street, and I learned from him that when I was hurt he was supportive. I learned from my brother Chuck that I could ride on the tractor with him and that he would take care of me when I was hurt. I learned from my sister Marilyn that she could flip me on my back when we were kids when I was being a bully and that she would invite me to live in her house during my college summer vacation. I learned from my brother Jim that he could become grouchy when I was mean to him and that he continues to lend me his pickup truck for my weekend gardening chores. I learned from my brother Harold that being the youngest required him to be able to defend his position without being crushed, and his creative world of acting brought style into my life. He became an older sibling when he was onstage.

Siblings learn to fight with one another. However, when someone outside of the sibling world attacks, brothers and sisters support each other. When we are attacked by the Martians, all of the people on this planet become Earth siblings.

The sibling education has power, and that power influences choices.

# 4

*How Your Brothers and Sisters Influenced Your Choices*

Your brothers and sisters greatly influence your childhood and teenage years. You were persuaded by what they said, and by their experiences in and out of the home. They also often affected your choices of friends, where you went to school, your selection of a career, and even whom you married. You were influenced because you liked or disliked the other kids in your family and shared common experiences. Let me give you some examples from my own life.

When one of my brothers or sister got interested in something, I did too. I often modeled myself after my older brother; he played football, and in my freshman year, influenced by his example, so did I. I was the first to finish high school and went on to get a Ph.D. Inspired by my example, my forty-nine-year-old younger brother has gone back to college. My stepson, David, attended Mariemont Elementary School and El Camino High School. My daughter chose to attend Mariemont instead of a private school. She was persuaded by his example.

This chapter will help you to see, sort out, and examine how your brothers and sisters have influenced you, and furthers your understanding of what this means to you right now.

## By the Accident of Birth

Fifty-year-old Diane was brought to my office by her thirty-one-year-old son, Michael. Michael was a recovering longtime drug addict who had been through many drug-rehabilitation programs. I met Michael while he was an in-patient at the hospital. He attended my daily group-therapy sessions, and when he was released from the hospital, he asked to continue his therapy with me in my private practice.

When Michael appeared for his third session, his mother, Diane, came with him. He asked if she could join us because she had been his longtime supporter. Michael was a handsome man, and his mother was an attractive woman. They were both well dressed, simply, and both participated. I did not understand Michael's motivation. He didn't understand his own motivation where his mother was concerned. Michael's very successful father was disgusted with him. As a result Michael's father had written him off. I liked Michael and I liked Michael's mother. In the next three therapy sessions we focused on Michael's sobriety and his mother's support of this sobriety.

The fourth session took a new turn. Michael didn't show up, though his mother did. She asked to have the session even though Michael wasn't there. As Diane's story began to unfold, I began to glimpse how Michael had in his own brilliant way brought his mother to therapy. Michael had kept the focus on himself, partly by the use of drugs and partly by his early childhood intuition that told him that something was missing for his mother.

Diane's parents' greatest nightmare occurred when their first daughter, Diane, became ill and died of a childhood disease when two years old. Two years later, they named their second daughter Diane. Two years after that, the second daughter died. Approximately two years after that, the family had a third daughter. They were jubilant and also named her Diane.

These two sisters that Diane never met clouded the boundary that makes brothers and sisters into unique and distinct individuals. Look at this from a child's eyes: Is she Diane her oldest sister, is she Diane her middle sister, or is she Diane herself. Her parents, in their grief, most likely confused the distinction among their three daughters. They were three separate human beings, and to young

Diane she was them and they were she. In all other ways, Diane was a successful person—wife, mother, daughter, neighbor, and citizen. Michael's intuition told him that, but she had great difficulty overcoming her confusion. Michael's job of "saving" his mother was complete at this point, and he returned to his wife and son. Diane then returned to a better relationship with her husband. Unfortunately Diane's dead sisters influenced her choices, although she was unaware of their influences.

Loss of a child in the family is a tragedy that never completely heals. Helping a family with bereavement is crucial to family well-being. Because Diane's sisters existed for her parents, they existed for Diane in a way that influenced how she felt about herself and how she felt about her sisters. Her choices in her life were significantly influenced to the point that she lost sight of herself. She is a separate and unique human being. Once she understood that, she regained sight of herself.

## The Absence of a Brother or Sister

Donald and his sister Karen were both adopted from different parents. He grew up with her, loves her, and trusts her. Between the two of them they have six parents: Donald's birth parents, his sister's birth parents, and their two adoptive parents. Their birth brothers and sisters are not a part of their lives. Somewhere deep inside them, they know that these brothers and sisters have influences in their lives.

In childhood Donald dreamed of his "other" family. Absence becomes a sibling influence. Who are they? Where are they? How come I'm not with them? How do they feel about me? Do they want to find me? Do I want to find them?

Recently Donald learned of his birth mother. He has chosen not to meet with her for now. Donald's sister Karen has no interest in finding her birth parents. It is adoptees' right not to pursue finding a birth parent if they so choose.

Forty-seven-year-old Roger was six years of age when his family split up. He was placed in foster care with one of his brothers, where the two of them grew up. They were reasonably happy, knew they had other brothers and sisters, but didn't try to contact any of them. Recently Roger's long-lost sister Marlene tracked them down. and stunned her two brothers by telling them that their parents had given birth to a total of twelve children. After Roger came out of shock, Marlene proposed a reunion where Roger and John could meet everybody. Said Roger after the reunion in an interview with the *Sacramento Bee,* "It was amazing and wonderful. It opened up feelings that I had not felt for years. I keep trying to picture my brothers and sisters in my mind, and I can't do it."

Ilene became an only child the day her older brother died. Until his death, at nine years of age, Jerry and Ilene were inseparable. They played together, walked to school together, and confided in each other. Ilene idolized Jerry, and his death hit her hard. She withdrew from her friends, started having trouble at school, and kept to herself most of the time. She really missed Jerry. By the time she reached high school she had become a good student again, but had very few close friends. Even now, at thirty-nine, she can't say good-bye to her long-dead brother and embrace life again, even though she wants to.

A sibling missing from the sibling generation is deeply important. In childhood the ideal people to assist in grieving the death of a sister or brother are the parents. Unfortunately, they have lost a child. Their ability to grieve over their loss and assist in their children's grieving may be extremely difficult. Often grief counselors (clergy, therapists, concerned relatives, or trusted friends) can be extremely helpful.

In *On Death and Dying,* the pathway to "unstuck" flows through Elisabeth Kubler-Ross's stages of grieving the loss of a loved one. These are the dominant emotions most people feel when they lose a brother or sister:

1. Denial—Harvey's fifteen-year-old son killed himself. Harvey can talk of the tragic loss of his son, but his wife is unable to speak her son's name. The enormous loss for these parents and the two surviving sisters requires that they not speak the name of the dead son or brother with the wife and mother. Denial lives in that part of us that is overwhelmed with the brutal truth. The truth is that we are powerless to change the tragedy. The "stuck" place can last

seconds, minutes, hours, days, weeks, months, years, and in some cases forever.

2. Anger, sadness, fear—All losses contain elements of these feelings: anger, the injustice of the loss; sadness, the natural occurrence in the wake of the loss; and fear, What will happen to me now? We must express all these feelings to move to the next stage. Even when we move to the next stage, however, we will revisit these emotions periodically.

I am periodically angry at my youngest brother because he is in my mind and I am sad about this. Sometimes I am fearful that he is alive and thoroughly confused. Other times I fear he has died, but if he has died, when? Where? How?

3. Bargaining—"If I could only replay the event." This is a common reaction to the loss of a loved one. The scene is repeated many times, always with the same outcome. When sixty-two-year-old Ned was eight years old he was playing with a .22-caliber pistol in his bedroom and accidentally fired the weapon. The bullet pierced his bedroom wall and entered his younger brother's bedroom, striking his brother in the head. The shot was fatal. Ned has replayed the scene over and over ever since.

Ned has moved through the stage of denial and is emotionally "stuck" in the bargaining stage. No matter how many times Ned replays the scene, his brother is dead and gone; nothing will bring him back. Unfortunately Ned does not seek assistance by way of grief counseling. Bargaining is filled with "If only I . . ." This is self-torture.

Successfully moving through the bargaining stage requires Ned to forgive himself for this tragic, accidental loss of his brother.

4. Depression and despair—These result when no change occurs. Waiting for your brother or sister to change will lock you into this stage. You can make a case against your brother or sister. You can hate him or her. If you "disown" your sister or brother, you will remain locked in this stage. Lawrence disowned his sister, and never outwardly gave the reason. He lived in a world of excitement that distracted him from his depression. In his teenage and adult years, he lived in a world of sex, gambling, and drugs to distract himself from his depression. He believed that he "got the drop" on his sister for her wounding of him. She had said, done, or

had something that was hurtful to his feelings. He never forgave her, and sex, gambling, and drugs failed to carry him above this depression.

5. Acceptance—This is the stage in which one can talk about the loss. Whether my brother is alive or dead, he is lost to me at this time and had been lost to me during the last five years. I still have twinges of feeling when I think or talk about him. My feelings have mellowed and reality has set in. As I explained to a friend about the absence of my brother, I detected his surprise about the length of the absence, and he detected how willingly I could talk about it.

## The Senior Power of Siblings

The older child will always be older. The older sister will always have the benefits and the responsibilities of this position. The older brother may be looked at by his younger sister as a leader, a guide, a model, an advocate, and a protector. Whether this is a benefit or a responsibility will be determined by the power wielded by the older brother or sister.

My father was the geographical pioneer in his six-sibling family. He migrated to California during the dust-bowl times, and his parents and brothers and sisters followed. He continued in this leadership position by employing his brothers. My father had an ability to start a business and provide leadership in his business, and he also had a loyalty to his younger brothers to employ them when they were out of work. Their work with him was of short duration and frequently stormy.

Benjamin, a certified public accountant, is the oldest child in a family of nine children. He entered therapy at the age of forty-nine. Benjamin's father had died at the age of fifty, and Benjamin's concern was that he had to die before that age. This is a family "loyalty" myth. Benjamin addressed this myth in his therapy and came to realize that he created this myth in childhood. His "accounting" led him to understand and dismiss the myth of his loyalty to his father's early death.

The second myth in Benjamin's life was that he was and continued to be responsible for his eight younger adult sisters and brothers. The senior power of his birth order required him to remain loyal to this senior-sibling myth. To combat this Benjamin engaged in an exercise with therapy group members who represented each of his eight younger sisters and brothers. Benjamin gave his "goodbye, hello" sibling ritual to each of them: "I love you and I care about you and I release you to take care of yourself in the best way you can. I will continue to be your brother and I will continue to believe in our relationship."

Benjamin practiced the new relationship with his brothers and sisters and reported that he enjoyed their company in a fashion he had not experienced before.

Whatever your brother or sister myth is, it is likely not based in truth.

## The Junior Power of Brothers and sisters

Donna is the "baby" of the family. Donna is seventy-six years old, married, a mother, a grandmother, and a great-grandmother. She is the youngest of four children. Donna carried the title of "baby," and even in her adulthood refused to accept the responsibility of being grown-up. She looked grown-up, she did grown-up things, but she leaned heavily on others to take care of her dependent needs, and she refused the development of her own independent assertions. From the moment babies are born they begin growing. The junior-sibling power comes from the one-down position of remaining the baby. "Baby" requires others to take care of him or her. Babies also often transfer all responsibilities to others. At seventy-six , Donna is not a very cute baby.

The youngest sister or brother in the family can learn to stand with the other siblings as an equal. She can accept the privilege of being a grown-up and accept the responsibility of being a grown up. When a younger sister or brother takes the risk of making an informed decision about her- or himself and others, she or he can grow. Growing up means more and more opportunities to make a decision. Seven-year-old Pat, the youngest sister, chooses one scoop of her favorite, Jamocha Almond Fudge, at the ice-cream store.

Her smile signals her decision to be independent. Her three older sisters choose Mint Chocolate Chip.

My father's twelve-years-younger brother, the youngest in the family of five siblings, was introduced by my father as, "My kid brother." His brother remained a "kid" until his death at sixty-four years of age. This "kid" was a lot of fun, and my uncle J. T. told jokes, laughed, was popular, and had dramatically low reliability. Sometimes he borrowed a few dollars from me with the most earnest promise to repay the debt. I loved my uncle but he never repaid his debt. He was a dreamer, a storyteller, and a ladies man. As his nephew, I loved my uncle J. T., but learned to not count on his reliability.

Candice's sisters, Jennifer and Liz, waited on her hand and foot, did everything for her, and wouldn't even let her tie her own shoes until she was ten. When she was a teenager, they talked to her teachers anytime she had trouble and went out of their way to solve her problems as they came up. As a result, Candice felt almost helpless. It even became hard for her to talk to anyone outside the family. She simply didn't have confidence in herself. As a young adult she realized that if she was ever going to have a life she needed to take responsibility for herself. From that moment on she started declining the assistance of her parents and older sisters and began doing as much for herself as possible. She cultivated friends her parents and older sisters never met and moved to another city to be on her own. Once she took the responsibility of growing up, she began to feel more in charge of herself.

If you are the youngest in the family answer these questions:

*Are you known as the baby?*
*What are your drawbacks with this title?*
*What are your benefits with this title?*
*Are you willing to relinquish your title?*

## Parental Involvement

Sibling senior power begins as an accident of birth. Robert was the firstborn in his family of three children. He has a younger sister and a younger brother. All three were born within a five-year period. Robert would seem to have senior power as a result of the birth order; however, Robert's younger brother is named David Jr. The secret in this family is that David Sr., is not Robert's biological father. That another man fathered Robert is a secret no one discusses. David Sr., treats Robert as an outcast and undermines Robert's senior position. At one point Robert attempted to murder David Sr. Fortunately he failed, and at age fifty-nine Robert has been diagnosed as a schizophrenic and put on psychotropic medication. He now resides in a long-term board-and-care facility.

The parental involvement in this family drove a wedge between Robert and his two siblings. The wedge set Robert apart, and blocked a real family closeness—a real family tragedy.

Jim and Helen have two daughters who are three years apart. Amy is twenty-nine and Brenda twenty-six. Amy and Brenda have different biological fathers and the same "father in residence." Jim calls Amy his daughter, and Amy calls Jim her father, yet this relationship has created tension in the family, with Amy carrying the burden. She is identified as the family problem. The core of the problem in most family therapy lies in the marriage of the parents. In this family, Jim and Helen have unresolved conflict in their marriage and they have transferred their marital tension to their daughter Amy. Rather than examining the tension in their marriage, Jim and Helen terminated family therapy before opening their marital secret of different fathers, which would have greatly reduced tension in this family.

Parents are not to blame. Blame is the curse that keeps families unhealthy.

Parents, as guides, bequeath to their children the tools for living with brothers and sisters. The parental guide allows children to walk together on the trek and monitors their behavior on the trek. Susan encourages her two sons to trek together without her being involved too much or too little.

Susan allows her two sons to resolve their own conflicts. That's the healthy way siblings will interact when given conflict-resolution tools. But many parents become judge and jury, robbing their children of the experience of doing it themselves.

Look to your parents when as an adult you have unresolved conflict with your brothers or sisters; look for the answer. Sometimes even the deceased parent reaches back from the grave at the reading of the will. Forty-seven-year-old Jim, forty-five-year-old Barbara, and forty-three-year-old Kevin sit silently as their father's will is read: $499 to Jim, $229,365 to Barbara, and $499 to Kevin. Their disbelief, their disappointment, their anger, and their confusion create instant animosity between these two brothers and their sister. This parental involvement may keep the wedge between these siblings alive for the rest of their lives.

## Sibling Stroking Pattern

A "stroke" is a unit of recognition. The stroke can come in one of four forms:

1. Positive—"I like you."
2. Negative—"I don't like you."
3. Conditional—"I like you when you . . ."
4. Unconditional—Positive and Negative "I like you." "I don't like you."

The stroke may be conveyed by word, by touch, by gesture, by voice inflection, and by tiny nuances. The stroke begins as a stimulus and creates a response. In my family, my brothers and sister talked with and to each other, we hit each other, we gave the "look," we gave the pregnant silence, but most of all we did not ignore each other. We were not allowed to. Odds of five against one are hard to beat! Our sibling interaction as adults is a slight variation in that we are a bit kinder and gentler with each other.

## Psychological Hungers

Eric Berne, in his best-selling book about human behavior, *Games People Play*, identifies six psychological hungers: contact, recognition, incident, stimulus, structure, and sex. He placed recognition at the top of the list.

## Sibling Contact

Six-year-old David wanted to hold one-week-old Molly. I placed her in his arms and he placed her on the couch. He sat her up and then walked away. I touched her before she fell forward, and I informed David that she could not sit up by herself. His contact with her was short and sweet. Sibling contact is determined in large part by the interaction of parents. The boundaries between siblings are usually soft ones. With a stern look of disapproval on his face, six-year-old Arnie says to his mother, "He's looking at me." Five minutes later Arnie is eating ice cream out of the same bowl as his brother.

Physical contact across the gender boundary changes as sisters and brothers age. Six-year-old Melinda wrestles with her five-year-old brother, Mark. Ten year old Melinda wrestles with her nine-year-old brother, Mark. Sixteen-year-old Melinda does not wrestle with fifteen-year-old Mark; however, she does hug her boyfriend, Carl. Twenty-six-year-old Melinda hugs her twenty-five-year-old brother, Mark.

## Siblings Recognition

Recognition between kids is either positive or negative. The only thing worse than negative recognition is to be left out. Sisters and brothers rarely allow themselves to be left out. Better something than nothing! Assertive sisters get recognized. Passive sisters become aggressive. Dennis said what he wanted. Rachel held back. She was the "nice" girl, and she compensated for her passivity by being sneaky.

Boys and girls address siblings as a group. Each of the siblings have a name distinguishing them from each other. Pro boxer George Foreman has five sons. Each of his sons has the name George Foreman. How are they viewed by each other? They know that they are different people, don't they? How are they addressed when called by their parents? How are they addressed when called by another sibling? Over time each of these five sons most likely will develop a "title" that distinguishes one from another. They may become big George, George II, middle George, George IV, and little George.

Sibling recognition is fixed in one of two family traditions. The question is, Is there enough to go around for each family member? If the family tradition fosters an attitude of abundance then there is abundance. On the other hand, if the family tradition fosters an attitude of scarcity there is never enough to go around. Abundance and scarcity are attitudes, not fact.

The Cambridge family of nine children, Judy, Erin, Pat, Ed, Tony, John, Mark, Jim, and Lynn, have a spiritual belief that the universe will provide for their needs. All of the Cambridge children, while in middle school, high school, and college have part-time jobs mowing lawns, baby-sitting, helping neighbors, and other chores. In their home, each has responsibilities. Even with their spiritual beliefs they also have a strong work ethic. A Cambridge child's birthday is a celebration for the entire family. Their parents recognize each of these nine siblings as being separate and unique human beings. This family has an attitude of abundance that recognizes how each child deserves encouragement for being who he or she is.

The five Thompson children, Brendan, Louise, Kathy, Bernard, and Erica, eat hamburger. Their father eats steak. Their father was a wealthy man with an attitude of scarcity. He lived as if there was not enough to go around. Their father, Leonard, saw these five siblings as a group and not as separate individuals. Their mother, Donna, ate hamburger with her children. After twenty-five years of marriage Donna divorced Leonard and married a man with an attitude of abundance, a man who was willing to share equally. Donna learned to recognize that she was separate and unique and was able to convey this attitude to her children after they were grown.

The four Myer children shared equally in the family meals, the family work, the family play, the family conflict, the family vacations, the family home, and, later in their sibling life, they shared in the grief over the deaths of their mother and father.

## Sibling Interaction Creates Sibling Incidents

An incident can be positive or negative. Positive sibling incidents are interactions that bring a smile. Negative sibling incidents are interactions that bring a frown. In most cases brothers and sisters create incidents to ward off boredom.

An incident is something out of the ordinary that satisfies a psychological hunger. Remember when you picked a fight with your sister or brother or when your brother or sister picked a fight with you? The fight was secondary to the satisfaction of the hunger for an incident. Most sibling fights do not end with cuts and bruises or broken bones.

With youngsters, the "fight wounds" quickly heal and the child moves out of boredom to the next sister-or-brother experience. With older brothers and sisters the incident may cause a rift that is difficult to heal. Fifty-year-old Norita was afraid that her forty-seven-year-old-sister, Carolyn, would cause an alcoholic incident at Norita's daughter's wedding. Carolyn is a severe alcoholic with a long history of alcohol abuse. She has a history of getting drunk and "acting out" at family functions. Norita prevents a negative incident with Carolyn by enlisting her cousin, Robert, to stay with Carolyn at the wedding. Cousin Robert, a personable man, provides Carolyn with enough strokes through his talking with her, staying with her during the ceremony, getting soft drinks for her, and generally being a loving support for her. As a result, Carolyn did not have to "act out" with alcohol to receive strokes. This was a temporary solution to a more severe problem.

Recall your early and present patterns with your brothers and sisters.

*How did you and your sibling(s) feed your incident hunger as children?*

*How do you and your sibling(s) feed your sibling incident hunger as adults?*

*Were your sibling incidents positive or negative?*

*How did you appreciate your positive sibling incidents?*

*How did you resent your negative sibling incidents?*

*Do you have any "leftovers" from your sibling incidents?*

## Time Structure for Siblings

We hunger for structure in our lives. Without structure there is chaos and disorder. We all have twenty-four hours in our day. The framework of time structure can be divided into six component parts. For the purposes of this book time structure is divided by focusing on sibling interaction.

1. *Sibling Withdrawal.* John withdraws into his bedroom to be away from his sister, Marilyn. He physically withdraws. Marilyn withdraws into the comfort of her thoughts with her brother's absence. She mentally withdraws.

The forty-seven-year old conjoined twins Bill and James have opted *not* to have surgery that would physically separate them from each other. They have had this connection since their birth. They thought it over, and chose not to be apart.

Sibling withdrawal is a healthy reaction that assists in the development of individuality. Neither too much nor too little withdrawal is a formula for healthy sibling growth.

2. *Sibling Rituals.* When we were six young children living at home with our mother and father, we resided in a three-bedroom house. My mother and father slept in one bedroom, my sister slept in another bedroom, and my four brothers and I slept in the third one. This was our sleeping tradition. After my father left, my sister moved to our mother's bedroom. We then split the second bedroom between my two oldest brothers. My two younger brothers and I shared the third bedroom.

Sibling rituals develop over time and become the way of doing things. They are rarely questioned and lend a certain amount of comfort. Eleven-year-old Wayne followed the lead of his thirteen-year-old-sister, Polly. Polly stepped into the leadership role without question. Trouble brews when Wayne and Polly want to go to a movie of Wayne's choice, not Polly's. Wayne becomes successful in his choice when he convinces Polly of the benefit of seeing his movie: The leading actor in the movie is Polly's favorite. Wayne's assertion changes the leadership ritual in this sister-and-brother relationship.

Sibling rituals change over time, if questioned, or when someone offers an individual independence. James and Mark are ten years apart. Their childhoods were quite different due to their ages. Both brothers share the common ground of having the same parents, and when they participated in adult-sibling therapy at the respective ages of fifty-five and forty-five, they recounted some of the same rituals. Twelve-year-old James would reach out to two-year-old Mark. In the adult-sibling session, fifty-five-year-old James sat on my couch next to his younger brother, Mark. James extended his left arm around and behind Mark's back. James continued the ritual of reaching for Mark, and Mark was receptive to James's gesture.

3. *Sibling Activity.* Activity is a practice of behavior. Activity with a sibling will generate strokes. No activity, no strokes! In childhood, if you live under the same roof, the odds are against having no sibling activity. Sisters and brothers occupy space in the family, and in that occupation of space activity occurs.

Ricky would hide in the closet before his sister returned from school. She would walk into the empty house and call out Ricky's name. He would not respond, and she would then have a feeling of peace and solitude. Ricky would break her solitude by bursting out of the closet. Ricky stroked himself and his sister—his was mean and positive, hers scared and negative.

4. *Sibling Pastimes.* Siblings who spend time talking with each other provide a safe series of predictable and enjoyable stroking transactions. The topics of the talk are numerous and sometimes seemingly unending. I talk with my sister and brothers about "stuff." *Stuff* is the topic of the moment. It has no lasting consequence. This pattern of sibling stroking does not have a determined end point. At times the pastime fills in the gaps of life for siblings. Brothers have pastime-topic stuff with each other, sisters have pastime-topic stuff with each other, and brothers and sisters have the gender crossover pastime-topic stuff. My brothers and I talked about stuff without including my sister. Unfortunately she had no sisters; however, at my youngest brother's wedding, my *sister* served as his "best man," as she defined my youngest brother as the nearest thing she had to having a sister.

5. *Sibling "Psychological" Games.* In his best-selling book, *Games People Play,* Eric Berne defines "psychological games" as being "crooked" ways of interacting among people. This crooked

aspect of game playing is the result felt by each person at the end of the game. The shift, just prior to the end of the game, leads to confusion with the game players. Twelve-year-old Collin played "helpless" (psychological game) with his younger sister, Betty. He would lie and tell her that he needed help in loading the dishwasher and that he did not know how to start the machine. Collin then experienced glee at Betty's anguish when he laughed at her and told her how stupid she was for helping him do something he already knew how to do.

Sibling psychological games have the same elements described in *Games People Play,* with the uniqueness of brother-and-sister interaction. Thirteen-year-old Robert and his two brothers, Dale and Dean, play the psychological game of: "Let's pull a fast one on younger sister," seven-year-old Peggy. The game is played by the children to con Peggy into believing that her father does not love her. When Peggy cries, they laugh and tell her that her father does love her. Peggy is hurt and confused, the others are gleeful, and the intimacy among all four is undermined. They say, "No harm done." If Peggy plays the con role again she becomes a committed player in the game.

> *What were your sibling psychological games?*
> *Were you the initiator of the games?*
> *Were you the receiver of the games?*
> *Are you still playing the same sibling games?*

## Sibling Intimacy

Intimacy is psychologically game-free and is analogous to the sixth of Berne's psychological hungers. This is the delicate, warm, close association of a brother and sister that is spontaneous and heartfelt. All siblings have these moments. These intimacy times may last seconds, minutes, or sometimes hours. I remember the intimate moment when my brother carried me to my bed after I spilled scalding water on my feet. The intimate moment when my brother Charles was diagnosed with a mild form of polio when we were children. The intimate times at graduations, weddings, births of children, tragedies, and triumphs. Sister and brother intimacy is also shared at the memorial services for parents and other relatives.

Thirty-nine-year-old Sandy experienced moments of intimacy when her brother and sister agreed to participate with her in an adult session. From the time she was eight years old, she was not allowed to walk to the park with her older brother and sister. She convinced herself then that they did not care about her. Their desire to participate with Sandy in the adult session changed her early outlook from a feeling of distance to a feeling of closeness.

Intimacy is an "open" time, and this openness can be difficult to sustain over a long period. Brothers and sisters are human, and humans have difficulty with prolonged intimacy. Intimacy is the dessert of human interaction, and sibling intimacy is the dessert of sibling interaction. Parents at times want their children's intimacy to last. That is akin to eating dessert all the time, and eating dessert all the time becomes too sweet.

Seventeen-year-old Jenny was required to take her fifteen-year-old sister, Karen, with her when she went to a movie with her friend Kristin. Karen was then required by her mother to take Jenny with her when she went to the state fair with her friend Crystal. These sisters were not allowed to develop friendships away from each other. Their mother, an only child, imposed her own fear of being alone on her two daughters. The forced sibling participation eliminated the pleasure of intimacy that comes from choice.

## When a Parent Leaves

When a parent leaves, a gap exists in the family. Someone must step into the gap. Parents leave either involuntarily or voluntarily. The sibling who steps in can appoint him- or herself to fill that gap or be selected by the other siblings.

Here are some examples.

### Death

Dianna's mother appointed Dianna by saying, "Dianna, take care of your brothers and sisters if anything happens to me." Nine-year-old Dianna was given this task of taking care of her siblings when her twenty-nine-year-old mother died six months later. Fifty-seven-year-old Dianna has spent much of her life taking care of others. Unfortunately, her mother never told Dianna when her task was complete.

## Disease

Ten-year-old Carol has a father who is schizophrenic. As a result she becomes the self-appointed partner for her mother. Carol's mother refuses to leave her psychotic husband, who has resided for more than eight years in a state hospital. Carol wants to play with her friends; however, she is afraid to leave her mother alone. Carol's younger sister, Brenda, is afraid to be alone with their mother, and Carol's burden is to curtail her own friendships to take care of her mother and sister.

## Disability

Fourteen-year-old Carl had a father who was wounded in a war and has not recovered from his wounds. He is frequently hospitalized at a veterans' facility. Carl, with his two younger brothers and a sister, appoints himself to care for his mother and his siblings. His mother is an overly dependent wife and mother who never adjusted to the loss of her strong and determined husband. His disability was not in her plans, and Carl became the partner for his mother and the parent for his siblings.

## Incarceration

Nine-year-old Brendan is the oldest of three children whose father became a prisoner of war during the Vietnam War. Brenden was "other-appointed" by his absent father, his mother, his extended family, and himself. His six years of filling in the gap ended when his father returned.

## Abandonment

Eleven-year-old Kevin came home from the library in his small California town to discover that his father had left. This family had to adjust to their father's absence. Their lives had to go on. Kevin's older brother, Douglas, stepped into their father's gap. Douglas, never married and never had children of his own. He remained loyal to his mother and his younger siblings. Thirty-five years later their father was traced through a Social Security number and found to be living in New Hampshire. When Kevin visited his father, his father offered no apology and expressed no remorse for leaving. Kevin came away from the meeting sad and with a sense that his relationship with his father was over.

## Alcohol

Alcohol is a "glass shield" that separates parent from child. The glass shield prevents parents from having a loving, nurturing, and supportive relationship with their children.

Firstborn Ellen has a father who lives in the home with his wife and three children. He begins drinking on his way home from work, then continues his drinking at home, and the glass shield is firmly in place. Ellen steps into the gap and joins her mother in the parental generation. Ellen is robbed of some of the freedom and gentleness of childhood.

## Drugs

Whether drugs are prescription or street-acquired, they can become a glass shield. Tom's mother spent twenty years swallowing Valium pills. Initially they were prescribed to reduce her anxiety. The pills instead greatly reduced her participation with Tom and his brother. Their mother lived in her "cloudy" world in her bedroom, coming out only to use the toilet or obtain food. She neglected to pay her bills or buy groceries. Nine-year-old Tom stepped into the parental gap to care for his mother and three-years-younger brother, Eddie. Tom received his mother's monthly checks from her trust fund, deposited the checks in the bank, paid the monthly bill, bought groceries every week, and got himself and Eddie off to school every day.

## Work

Work never comes to an end unless (1) a parent puts a limit on it or (2) parents get too tired. Siblings find great difficulty in persuading a parent to come home from work. My six-year-old daughter came into the computer room, where I was diligently working on my paper. She said, "Isn't it time for you to spend some time with your family?" She was right, I set my upper limit by turning off my computer and joining her in the family room. Rarely do we hear the deathbed statement, "I spent too much time with my family." Most of the time the deathbed statement is, "I spent too much time at work."

## Dereliction of Parental Duty

Judy's mother was jealous of Judy. She resented Judy's conception, Judy's birth, Judy's school awards, and most of all she resented Judy in her life. Judy's mother provided food, clothing, and shelter. Judy became a serf to her mother and the parent to her parent in order to gain her mother's love and approval. When twenty-four-year-old Judy moved to a different location, she left the parenting of her mother to her younger sister, Thelma. Thelma is resigned to the fact that she will be her mother's partner. Their divorced mother never dates and has no friends. Thelma, a high school graduate, works part-time at a department store, never dates, and leaves the home socially only when she and her mother attend a movie.

## When a Parent Joins the Sibling Generation

Children do not want their parents to be their friends. The children want their parents only to be friendly. When my wife and I go out to dinner, I tell my daughter that she and her brother will not be going with us. She always protests loudly, and I tell her that she can go with us on the condition that when she goes out on her first date I will be invited to go to. She responds, "You and Mom have a good dinner."

Kay's mother and father have a "father-daughter" marriage. Her father becomes a single parent with four children. Her father has numerous affairs with many women, and Kay's mother has reacted by joining Kay's sibling generation. Her mother is childlike in her behavior and flirts with her children's friends when they visit. Kay and her younger siblings depend on their father and have given up on their mother being the parent they want her to be. Kay and her two younger brothers, Dan and Don, develop a habit of seeing their friends away from home.

## Disowned Siblings

In the movie *The Godfather Part II*, Michael Corleone disowned his brother by having him murdered. This is an extreme example of disowning. Siblings can be disowned for leaving, by violating a family rule, or by being excluded at conception.

Allen is a disowned sibling. He has three sisters he has never seen, and he doesn't know they exist. He was given up for adoption soon after his birth. Allen's mother, Barbara, was eighteen when she gave birth to him. She was a sexually active teenager with three different boyfriends at the same time. She was unsure which man was Allen's father and she never told any of the three that she was pregnant. Shorty after learning of her pregnancy, Barbara moved to a different town to live with her aunt. When Allen was born, her aunt arranged to have him adopted. Barbara chose not to see her son again. Four years later she married David, and in a five-year period she gave birth to three daughters. She has never told her husband or her children about Allen. Barbara's disowning comes as a result of her decision to cut him off from this family. Somewhere deep inside of Allen and his three sisters is an awareness that something is missing. His mother knows and chooses not to tell these four siblings, but keeps this secret to herself.

Sally Jessy Raphael, Maury Povich, Jenny Jones, Oprah Winfrey, Montel Williams, and others have television programs that help reunite lost brothers or sisters who were disowned by their parents. Because this reunion process is heavily laden with mystery, emotion, and curiosity, it makes for good television. The benefits to the reunited brothers and sisters would be a study worth pursuing.

## The Blended Family

All blended families have at least three parents and the possibility of four, five, or six. Children with the same parents are called siblings. Children with at least one of the same parents are called half brothers and half sisters, and children with four separate parents are called stepsiblings

I asked my eleven-year-old stepson what it was like for him to live in two separate houses, his mother's house and his father's house. He said that he has twice as many friends. In his father's house he is an only child, and in his mother's house he is the older brother of a sister. When I asked him about his fifth-grade classmates and their families, he said half of his fellow fifth graders live in two houses. With the high divorce rate in this country blended families are common.

Sibling influences in a blended family are largely based on the siblings' ages at the time of the blending. Grown children at the time of the blending have little influence on each other. Her children, his children, and their children may include siblings, stepsiblings and half siblings and can have significant influence on each other, again depending on their ages when the blending occurs.

Former President Clinton is ten years older than his half brother. Most likely they had little early influence on each other's lives. With the death of their mother, they may draw emotionally closer together.

Ellen, Rodney, and Roberta have the same biological parents. Their father died when Ellen was nine years old. Their mother married again to Harvey and they had a son, Bob. Bob's three older half siblings were required to call Bob's father their own. They addressed him as Dad and were not allowed to speak of their deceased father. All four of these children consider themselves siblings. Periodic tension occurs when they speak of either father, since both fathers are now deceased. The three older siblings have differing opinions of their fathers.

Some families can tolerate more than two parents. When the families will condone more than two parents, then sisters and brothers will most likely follow suit.

## Sibling "Gap" Order

A sibling with a disability will bring a "gap" influence. This subject will be further discussed in chapter 6. The age difference between each of my five brothers and sister is roughly eighteen months. My stepson, David, and my daughter, Molly, are six years apart. Sibling gaps are largely determined by proximity. The closer the sisters and brothers are in age the greater chance for sibling influence.

The sibling gap may result from the death of a sister or brother. The sibling gap influence is greatly determined by the age of the brother or sister when the death occurs. The younger the siblings the more influence the gap may have. The missing brother or sister gap is then filled with pictures, memories, anniversaries, and conversations.

The sibling gap may also occur when a family is forced to separate, such as in times of war. Or kids are forced to separate at the death of parents when they are parceled out to extended family members or parceled out to separate foster homes.

When the siblings' separation happens in the children's early life, they have less opportunity to exert an influence on each other. When the children's separation happens later in childhood, the sibling influence is profound. Sibling absence does make the sibling heart grow fonder.

Thirteen-year-old John lost his two-years-younger sister in an automobile accident. For eleven years of his life his younger sister influenced him with their sibling interaction. The death of John's sister will affect him for the rest of his life, and his life may be greatly impacted by his ability to grieve over his loss of her.

The sibling gap can be altered in many ways and yet it will always remain. Grieving over a sibling gap can complete the loss.

## Sibling Influences in an All-Brother Family

Thirty-nine-year-old Jim is the oldest of four brothers. He is not married, enjoys living alone, and loves to sit on his couch in his underwear, drinking and watching sports. He acquired this relaxed attitude from his family of origin. As children, he and his brothers felt at ease walking around their house in their underwear. Their mother, while respected by Jim and his brothers, was treated as a nongendered person.

Five years later, Jim takes his new wife, Sally, on a weekend outing with his three brothers and their wives. Later in the evening, as these four couples talk, Jim and his brothers begin cursing in a "boys' locker room" fashion. This is acceptable behavior for all four brothers. When Jim and Sally retire for the night, she lets him know this language was unacceptable. This begins Jim's training on how to successfully live with a "sister," something that is completely new to him.

An all-brothers family may *exclude* their mother from their "masculine club," if their father encourages this feminine exclusion; however, if their father *includes* his wife, their mother, as an "associate" member of the club then the brothers also include their mother in their club. The gender difference is respected and honored and the brothers become potentially good mates. Brothers often follow their father's lead in his relationship with the woman in his life.

Albert is the oldest of four brothers. All four brothers are gifted athletes whose parents are thoroughly involved in their son's activities. Their father, however, frequently neglects his wife to support his sons' athletic activities. This eventually leads to a divorce. Their mother loses the respect of her husband and her sons and she moves out of the home. These brothers may have some difficulty later in their adult lives in successfully interacting with women.

If these four brothers follow their father's example of relating to women, then the chances of their being successful in a relationship may be significantly limited.

## Sibling Influences in an All-Sister Family

Five-year-old Jeannie lives with her mother, her older sister, and her father. Jeannie enthusiastically picks up the rolled newspaper from the front porch every afternoon, proudly bringing the paper to her father as he sits in "Father's chair." She looks forward to sitting on his lap while he reads his newspaper. However, he does not offer his lap, but simply opens his newspaper and starts reading, and Jeannie walks away sadly. Her father is a "plastic prince" who demands that the three females in the family cater to him. He is from a family of three brothers and holds women in low regard.

Jeannie's family is a female "us" and a male "them." This cold-war stance does not lend itself to healthy conflict resolution, since Jeannie does not have a healthy masculine influence.

Later in life, forty-five-year-old Jeannie is divorced after an unhappy brief two-year marriage. She continues to be close to her older sister and her mother, who long ago divorced the father. Her mother has not remarried, and most likely Jeannie will not remarry. The same-gender sibling influence in their family is to stay distant from their father and other males in their lives.

Susan is the middle sister of Herbert's girls. They live with their father and mother. Herbert's wife, Elaine, loves her husband. Herbert loves Elaine and his family. The three sisters live in a home where there is enough love for the marital union and the parental union. No family member feels excluded. Their father is welcomed as an "associate" member of the "feminine club" in the family. He is the available masculine influence on his three daughters. Feminine and masculine conflict is resolved in a win-win technique.

The opposite-sex parent plays a key role in the same-gender sibling unit.

## Sibling Influences in a Mixed-Gender Family

John (age fifty-five), Eric (age forty-six), and I (age fifty-five) have been friends for over ten years. For many years we have met biweekly for a two-hour lunch. We are each in the human behavior–counseling arena. Our lunch-meeting topics are not focused on anything related to counseling. We enjoy one another's company, and our expressions of humor are frequent and sometimes contain a masculine bite.

John has an older sister, Eric has a younger sister, and I have a younger sister and two older and two younger brothers. This "sibling fit" for the three of us came about over time. Most likely our sibling influences in our mixed-gender families have had an impact on each of us that we were not aware of. In birth order, we are a youngest-born, an oldest-born and a middle-born, and this adds to our sibling fit.

In many families early-childhood sibling interplay is not based on gender difference. Sisters and brothers play well with each other. The gender differences begin to show up in early adolescence. Sisters join the girls' club and brothers join the boys' club. The physical, social, and psychological distance between mixed-gender siblings increases with the developmental stages. While I am driving my twelve-year-old daughter and her friend Laura to school, their conversation is open and animated. On the same drive with my daughter, her friend Laura, and my thirteen-year-old nephew, James, the conversation is more diminished. This is to be expected as boys and girls enter the teenage years.

*What is the sibling fit with your friends?*

## Sibling Influences in Lifesaving Pursuits

### Internal Sibling Lifesaving Pursuits

My thirty-two-year-old second cousin, Misty, has recently been diagnosed with leukemia. Her four older brothers will be evaluated for her bone-marrow transplant, and all four readily agreed to the procedure. The chance of a bone-marrow match is most likely with Misty's brothers.

Thirty-seven-year-old Linda readily agreed to donate a kidney for her older sister, Karen. Linda's kidney was compatible for transplant, and she never questioned whether to donate her kidney. It was never open to refusal. She gladly gave, and the gift came not only from her body but also straight from her "heart." Linda's kidney was removed and placed into Karen. From inside these sisters they are offering a lifesaving that is unique.

## External Sibling Lifesaving Pursuits

Twelve-year-old twins Samantha and Samuel were walking in the park when a car drove by and the driver hurled a racial epithet at them. Samantha, being aggressive, hurled a sexual comment about the occupants' mothers. The car turned around and headed toward the twins. Samuel realized immediately that the situation might be potentially life threatening and yelled to Samantha to run with him to safety. Thirty-two-year-old Samantha continues her aggression, and thirty-two-year-old Samuel continues to look out for her safety. This brother-and-sister pattern of protecting each other has extended into their adult years and most likely will continue unabated unless one of them changes. When Samuel marries, his new wife may be in competition with Samantha, and when Samantha marries her new husband may be in competition with Samuel.

When I was sixteen years old, I got off the school bus with my twelve-year-old brother, Harold, because he was afraid that he might be accosted by some bullies on his way to his after-school job. The bullies were boys who were angry at my brother for liking the girlfriend of one of them. I have really never enjoyed fighting. I've had three fights in my life, and won two and lost one. I did not want to be my brother's rescuer; however, I did not want him to be harmed. The bullies did not appear, but I was glad I made my brotherly effort and my brother was glad I made the effort.

Numerous radio, television, and newspaper stories describe sibling incidents of external lifesaving actions. Unfortunately, at times, the rescuing brother or sister gives his or her life in the process. Is this an example of the "greater love"? When interviewed after a lifesaving event, the sibling rescuer often describes his or her actions as not being open to question. "I didn't think about it; I just did it." Perhaps we are our siblings' keeper!

David Kaczynski had a most difficult decision to make. He concluded from his knowledge and intuition that his older brother, Theodore, was probably the "Unabomber" who was terrorizing this country. Three people had been killed and others had been wounded by bombs sent by the Unabomber. The evidence that led to David's conclusion about his brother's involvement with the bombings weighed heavily on his conscience and loyalty to his brother. David Kaczynski's sibling choice to connect his brother to the killings was influenced by David's hope that he could prevent possible further injuries and death to other people. David's intuition was correct, and authorities apprehended his brother and charged him with murder. David Kaczynski committed himself to placing the million-dollar reward with his brother's victims.

David Kaczynsky's brother loyalty was tested. His gut-wrenching decision violated the unwritten sibling rule that siblings must stick together. David faced the price of violating sibling loyalty and faced the consequences of sibling disloyalty.

Sibling influences begin in childhood, becoming a memory that continues throughout the rest of a person's life. The sibling-influences on sibling choices may range from powerful to pale; however, they always remain somewhere within each of us and within each of our siblings. You can fib about your sibling influence, but you know that it is not really true.

# 5

~

# How Brothers and Sisters Create Memories

1. **Memory** *The power or process of reproducing or recalling what has been learned and retained esp. through associative mechanisms.* (Merriam Webster's Collegiate Dictionary, Tenth Edition, 1993.)
    2. *You are my uncle who had a pillow fight with me and Tyler."* (Aaron, four years of age, 1998)

I did have the pillow fight with four-year-old Aaron and his five-year-old brother, Tyler, at my home sometime during 1998. They hit me, I hit them, they hit each other, and I attempted to set the boundaries of a safe "pillow war." Now each time I visit their home, they run into their bedrooms to retrieve pillows for all three of us. I have to decline most of the time, as the pillow wars create an atmosphere of chaos in their grandmother's home. Their grandmother is my sister, so sometimes she excuses our behavior.

When I was a kid we lived in a two-story house with the boys' bedrooms on the second floor. A slow Saturday or Sunday afternoon could lead to excessive amounts of free-floating sibling energy. One of us would make the statement, "Let's take it upstairs and settle it." No one ever said what "it" was. We took ourselves and that free-floating brother energy to the second floor. Rarely would our mother journey up the stairs to that domain. With pillows, bedding, mattresses, and energy we would settle it. After it was settled, there were no broken bones, rarely broken skin, some mild bruises, and a room in disarray but still standing. Our brother energy was dissipated and we became calm. This testosterone-laden activity was fun and had a life of its own. It did little or no harm, and we could laugh with one another after the event and even laugh much later in our adult lives as we relived the memories.

At my office I talked with two-and-a-half-year-old Trace while his mother held his six-month-old brother, Trevor. In response to my question, Trace said he has his own bedroom and his brother Trevor has his own bedroom. These two blue-eyed, blond-haired boys have a Scandinavian background. I asked Trace if he knew what Scandinavian meant and he said yes. I didn't pursue the subject. When I asked Trace for one of his Milk Duds, he held out his open hand with one Milk Dud. I thanked him and turned down his offer. I look to the near future when one-year-old Trevor will ask three-year-old Trace for a Milk Dud. They will then begin the process of creating brother memories they can share in their lives.

The neurologist can pinpoint the part of our brain that stores memory. That storage unit is large. Somewhere in that vast world, memory information is stored. The events themselves, with their smells, sights, feelings, tastes, and touches, are available at our call. Without brain injury or disease, our memories stay with us in the hard drive of our human brain computer.

If we liken the human brain to a computer, the mouse would be the agent for the recall of a memory. As you read this line, recall an event when you were five years old. Now be honest with yourself. You were five at one time. You don't have to stay too long in your memory; you can always return to it. You just made the journey through regression and reversion.

*Merriam Webster's New Collegiate Dictionary Tenth Edition* defines regression as a reversion to an earlier mental or behavioral level and reversion as an act or process of returning (as to a former condition).

In each adult brother-and-sister session we recall many childhood memories in exquisite detail. Fifty-four-year-old Randy recalled his fifty-six-year-old sister April's Asian flu episode of forty-three years ago. She was close to death and luckily survived. To this day, when he talks with her this memory brings tears to his eyes.

Everyone has a childhood. That is how we all started. Within that time we create memories, and those memories have a "psychological rubber band" connection to the adult present. Dr. Mori Haimowitz, a Chicago psychologist, used the psychological rubber band connection to help his clients understand some of their present-day dilemmas as having an origin in childhood.

Parent-child memories are created from the interaction of at least two generations. Parents, grandparents, aunts, uncles, other adult caretakers, are all seen by children as being one of those "other" people. The memories created between the two generations are memories made up of pictures, sounds, and feelings of us and them. They are the "big people," and siblings in the same generation, on the other hand, view each other as "one of us," the "little people."

Adult's memories carry the long-term history of both adulthood and childhood. Children on the other hand, carry a much shorter history of only childhood.

In June 1979 I invited my father to travel with me to explore his geographical roots. His first plane ride was a part of this journey. We met with his cousins—Lillis, from his mother's side of the family, and Pete and Jeff, from his father's side of the family. These cousins shared a childhood history with my father, so we can consider them semi-siblings. During our seven- day journey, these cousins/siblings shared many of the decades-ago memories of their childhood lives together. This connecting cord stretched over time and distance for them. Their conversations moved from the joy of happy times to the pain of family drama. Within each of them were the memories and their individual perspectives on their shared memories. They laughed and cried, and brought each other up to their differing perspectives on the same people, the same events, and the same times. I was the objective observer they allowed to glimpse their shared childhood memories. These were not adults I observed; these were children reclaiming that part of them that has passed and yet remains.

I stood at an intersection outside of Lexington, Oklahoma, the location of the 1930s gas station my grandfather, my father, and my father's siblings owned. Acres of farms surround this narrow intersection. Nothing was standing where the old gas station had been. On closer inspection, among the weeds we found the bricks that were laid side by side in the ground to support the old hand-activated gas pumps. We dug two up. My father held one in his hand and walked out to the middle of the intersection. There were no cars in sight. The clouds overhead turned gray and rain showers appeared to be near. For what seemed like a long time to me, I watched the expressions on my father's face. I could see his memories as if they were being played out on a large movie screen. He walked closer to me, and I asked him the question that pulled at my attention; "Dad, would you like to live here again?" His quick response was, "My home is in California."

We returned to our car and left Oklahoma the next day. We had created a new memory together that allowed me to be an observer of my dad's childhood. Up until my father's death in January 1996, he would periodically recount his childhood memories and our shared adult memories.

## Sibling Early Happy Memories

In the summer of 1954, we lived in a small house one-sixteenth of a mile from a major highway. The house was located in an agricultural field. We had acres of tomatoes growing on the front, side, and back of our house. The nearest neighbor was a quarter of a mile away. As you face our house, the right side has the Saikis' truck farm, and the left side a large, corralled ranch. To this day I do not recall the name of the ranch neighbors or ever seeing them. Their ranch contained in excess of twenty acres. They had one old horse that we were not supposed to ride.

At that time my mother attended Sacramento State College to complete her Bachelor of Arts degree and her teaching credentials. She was gone for most of the day and spent evenings studying in the library. We were "deprived" children—we didn't have a television! However, we had all the tomatoes we could eat. Occasionally a spontaneous tomato fight erupted among the six of us siblings.

A big weeping willow tree was located on the ranch property within a hundred yards of our house. That tree supported six siblings, lost many branches and untold leaves, and survived our raucous summer.

The old horse that lived on the property next to us was gentle and would readily walk when led up to the corral fence. We climbed the fence and mounted her. A gentle kick in the side and the nag would walk, not run. My cousin Gary was visiting on one of those hot summer days, and when informed of the nag he wanted to ride. I agreed and we mounted the horse. At eleven years old, I told sixteen-year-old, Gary to be gentle with the horse. I was sitting in front of Gary on the nag when Gary kicked the horse in a less than gentle manner. The horse's head dipped, and all I noticed was the ground coming up to meet me. We had been bucked off. Laughter followed after we checked for broken bones.

If I had a sixth sibling, that sibling would be Gary.

That house burned when I was in the fifth grade. No one was at home. Mrs. Saiki, our quarter-of-a-mile-away neighbor, looked up to observe our house fully engulfed in flames. Everything burned up. Later in the day, after the embers had cooled, we returned from school to observe what was left of our house in the tomato field. Since part of the structure still stood we walked through what we could. My mother found a handkerchief that had not burned. Printed on it was a picture of a man flushing himself down the toilet. The inscription read, *Goodbye cruel world*. My mother, who had a good sense of humor, told that story many times.

My mother taught elementary school at the nearby United States Air Force base, and we kids attended even though we were civilians. The day of the fire, those military people and my mother's fellow teachers collected money and provided clothing and lodging. The local newspaper published an article about how the military base had taken us under its wing, and my mother, a devoutly religious woman who always paid tithe, called our fire a blessing in disguise.

We siblings survived the fire, our family moved into another house, and, unfortunately, we bought a television. After that, however, if our television was not on, it was broken.

We had other sister-and-brother summers and other sibling times and more memories, and yet that summer sticks with me in a vivid fashion. It had a purity and ease that required us to provide our own sibling entertainment. We were and are siblings who do not lack energy or excitement.

Now to your early sibling memories! Imagine that you are seven years old.

*Where are you and your siblings living?*
*What are your happy sibling memories from this time?*
*When was the last time you revisited these early happy memories with your siblings?*

The memories fade with wrinkles and gray hair, but remain intact. Laugh a little and rekindle the joy.

## Sibling Unhappy Memories

"I wish you were dead" is a throwaway statement exchanged between two or more siblings. The wish is based on hurt and a desire to hurt back. The reality is that, left to their own conflict resolutions, siblings will send this line into the sibling dumper, never again to be seen. Seven-year-old Johnny and five-year-old Timmy's mother overheard Timmy saying, "I wish you were dead." She was shocked and sent five-year-old Timmy to his room. Johnny gets mileage out of Timmy's comment by siding with their mother about Timmy's "bad" language. By not reprimanding both, their mother undermined further closeness, driving a wedge between these two brothers. Are thirty-seven-year-old Johnny and thirty-five-year-old Timmy close or distant? Johnny is a recovering alcoholic, and as a part of his twelve-step program he is required to make amends for his actions. Over a dinner with Timmy, Johnny recounted the scene of thirty years ago. Johnny made amends to Timmy by apologizing for his behavior. The puzzled and surprised look on Timmy's face told Johnny that Timmy did not recall the scene. Both brothers laughed out loud. Johnny had carried the negative memory. Timmy said he would forgive Johnny if Johnny would pay for their dinner. These brothers hugged after their meal.

The death of a parent is one of the most devastating events and memories for a child. In Nancy Boyd Webb's book *Helping Bereaved Children,* she points out that the ideal person to help the siblings through the loss of a parent is the remaining parent.

Unfortunately, the parent has lost a spouse. Betty's mother died shortly after giving birth. Betty, the youngest of five children, carried the memory as told to her by her father and her siblings. Betty developed the childhood belief that she caused the death of her mother. Betty's childhood was then filled with foster homes, the care of relatives, institutional care, and a stepparent. Betty's father was not the ideal parent to help Betty and her siblings with their grieving.

Into her adulthood, Betty carried the responsibility for her mother's death. Deep down inside Betty lurked a pool of anger and rage that she couldn't express in a healthy manner. She turned her anger and rage inward and attempted suicide numerous times. Betty wanted to rid herself of her anger and guilt. The attempts were not successful. Her husband and grown children, however, were terrified that their behavior could trigger another suicide attempt. They tiptoed around her, which increased her anger, since she was not being treated honestly. Betty's breakthrough occurred when her therapist expressed anger directly to Betty about Betty's inappropriate behavior in a group-therapy session. Her therapist expressed the genuineness of emotion that enabled Betty to become "anger-friendly." Her therapist's example of a healthy expression of anger gave her permission to practice the same behavior. This tiptoeing had created a distance that prevented Betty from the sibling intimacy she craved. Her anger-friendly permission rekindled her brothers' and sisters' connections.

*What unhappy childhood memory keeps you disconnected from your siblings?*

*What prevents you from reconnecting with your siblings?*

## Sibling Memories Based on Fact

I grew up with my five siblings and they grew up with me. We lived in the same houses until my oldest brother, at age seventeen, left home to join the military. My second-oldest brother left our house when he was fifteen to live with our paternal grandparents. My sister left when she was sixteen to live with a cousin; his family provided child care for her. I left home when I was eighteen and went away to college. My youngest brother left home after high school graduation to enter the military, and my next-younger brother left our house to work. This created an empty nest for our mother.

The fact is that when we lived together in childhood, we loved, we fought, we played, we protected one another, we shared, we hated, we counted on one another, and we remained "lively" with one another. We were six individual characters, according to our cousin Polly. Around the Todd siblings was intensity—sometimes a bit too much for others and sometimes a bit too much for us.

John is sixty-five years of age and is the oldest of eight siblings. He has five living sisters and one brother. One sister died in her twenties. His parents died in their eighties and left their estate to their seven surviving children. During their childhood, John's father insisted that his children participate together in family meals, family vacations, family play activities, family work activities, family discussions, and other family activities. His father commented that spouses come and go, but siblings are forever.

During a discussion over lunch, John reiterated to me that every six months he and his siblings gather for a sibling activity. He has arranged for a one-day sibling activity this June, with all of them riding on a rented bus that will transport them to the various southern California locations of their childhood. They share this unique history and will enjoy reliving their experiences. One of their family traditions is to have a large brothers-and-sisters celebration when one of them has a birthday at the start of their new decade. Their next sibling birthday celebration will be the sixtieth birthday of John's younger sister.

John's sisters' and brothers' childhood memories continue to create sibling memories in the here and now.

*What are your sibling memories based on childhood facts?*
*Are you willing to check your childhood facts with your siblings?*
*What sibling memories are you creating in the here and now?*

## Sibling Memories Based on Fiction

When I was six years of age, my family and I visited Carlsbad Caverns in New Mexico as a part of our family summer vacation. I had a picture of the caverns in my memory bank. However, my whole memory was based on fiction. We did make the summer trip, but Carlsbad Caverns was not a part of the adventure. The "fiction" was pointed out by my brother and confirmed by my father. I love reading. I devoured the *World Book Encyclopedia* when I was a kid, and in the book of "C" was Carlsbad Caverns. The words, the pictures, and the vacation trip through New Mexico created my memory of the Carlsbad Caverns adventure. My brother filled in the blank that made this childhood sibling memory a fiction of my creative imagination.

In *Siblings—A Hidden Resource in Therapy* (1990), Karen Gail Lewis proposes that a vast resource of information is stored in the sibling memory bank. The information is there, and shared sibling memory bank information will clarify fact from fiction. Some sibling facts are the source of early childhood hurt, pain, and agony, and continue to the present. Some sibling fictions are the source of early childhood hurt, pain, and agony, and continue to the present. Separating sibling facts from sibling fictions requires risking, trusting, and a journey to the "sibling sources."

Fifty-seven-year-old Donald is afraid to invite his three younger siblings to his adult sibling therapy session. His fear is that they will turn down his request. Will he take the risk of asking? Will he trust that they will say yes? Will he be OK with their saying yes? How many sibling childhood facts will his siblings bring, and how many sibling childhood fictions will be uncovered? He knows how to handle a no. His siblings acquiescence to his request opens up this exciting and scary trek through their lives then and there and their lives here and now. Later in this book, we will share their trek.

Seventeen-year-old Robert is the oldest of four children. His father is in the United States Air Force and was recently given orders for his transfer to Germany. The transfer requires that each family member receive a U.S. passport. Prior to processing for the passport, the family tells Robert that his father is really his stepfather.

The sibling fiction becomes fact when Robert's parents reveal this family secret. Robert and his stepfather are close, and Robert must make an additional journey to discover his biological father.

When uncovered, the myth of sibling memories reveal the truth of sibling memories. Sibling perspective is a different view of the same memory. Sisters' and brothers' perspective may be different; the memory is the same. The sibling myth is an untruth. Sixty-four-year-old Arnold and sixty-two-year-old Larry have different perspectives on their father. Arnold's father is a saint and Larry's father is a jerk. Same father, different perspective.

*Are some of your childhood memories based on fiction?*

*Which of your childhood memories is based on different sibling perspectives?*

*Are you willing to risk the journey of asking your siblings?*

## Sibling Gap Memories

A sibling gap is that part of a memory that is incomplete.

Six-year-old Jeremy is riding on the train with his twin brother and his mother on their trip to Denver, Colorado. During the early-evening hours Jeremy falls asleep, and when he awakens, his brother and mother are missing. Jeremy is frightened by the gap in his life. His brother and mother are not there, even though they are only a few steps away in the rest room.

The firstborn in a family has no shared sibling experiences until the birth of the second child in the family. The firstborn's experiences are a gap for each succeeding sibling arriving on the scene. I was not a part of my two older brothers' experiences until I arrived. My younger sister and two younger brothers have a gap with the three older brothers' shared memories.

A gap means something is left out. Ann's foster sister participated in the adult sibling therapy session with Ann and her two sisters. In recounting their shared sibling history, Ann revealed that her foster sister was on the scene for only three years. The years before the foster sister came and the years after the foster sister went away left a very large gap. During the five-hour session, the sisters shared numerous memories. When Ann and her sisters shared childhood memories, their foster sister reclined in her chair. Weeks later, Ann indicated that she would not include her foster sister in the next session, since her sister did not have the time and distance as a sibling to be included in this unique sibling group.

Foster siblings, however, can be as involved as biological siblings, if the sibling involvement occurs early on, and over a significant amount of time with each other.

The strength of the sibling bond is determined in a large part by the participation of siblings with one another over time. The strength of the sibling bond between siblings who are reared in different families and locations is determined by the early years together. The shorter the sibling time together, the weaker the sibling bond. The longer the sibling years together, the stronger the sibling bond.

Johnnie was removed from his siblings' home shortly after his birth to join his adoptive family. Thirty-three years later he reconnected with his siblings. Their sibling gap can be filled only by a heartfelt discussion of their lives apart and now together. The possibility of filling the gap for all these siblings is determined by their desire, determination, and willingness to risk.

During the past five years I have had a sibling gap with the absence of my youngest brother, Harold. Prior to his absence I had a forty-six-year shared history with him. Childhood sibling influences are deep and wide. The early years contain the early seeds in our gardens. The growth of those sibling seeds in our gardens will always be with us, even though our siblings may be gone.

Karen's father married Irene when Karen was twenty-two years old. Irene has two grown children. Now that Karen is forty-seven years old, her two siblings share an adult life of siblinghood and a childhood gap of siblinghood.

Sibling gaps may occur from marital separation, divorce, illness, family trauma, or death.

> *What are the gaps in your sibling history?*
> *How did your sibling gaps occur?*
> *Do you want to fill in your sibling gaps?*
> *What have you done to fill in your sibling gaps?*

## Sibling Memories Created Together

*Simultaneously, concurrently, collectively, as one, side by side, jointly,* and *in unison* are words and terms that mean *together.* You can tell your siblings about the playground at the park, or your siblings can be with you on the playground at the park. Sibling togetherness strengthens the sibling bond whether or not the cables in the bond are created by positive memories or by negative ones.

Sibling loyalty underlies the decisions made in memories that are created. When my twelve-year-old daughter invites her twelve-year-old friend Laura to have an overnighter, Laura also invites her fourteen-year-old sister, Erin, to join in. My daughter enjoys the company of both girls. Brothers and sisters usually have a higher sibling loyalty than do friends.

The strength and uniqueness of the sibling bond underlies the "juice" in adult sibling sessions. Into this sister and brother session each sibling brings the luggage that he or she carries from the early-childhood memories, the adolescent memories, the adulthood memories, and finally the memories of later years in life. John has all the stages of sibling memories and continues in his later life to create more memories. The sibling juice is ever flowing and has the power of waves on one another's lives. The sibling wave action is perpetual. Imagine you are in a room with these people you have known all of your life. Now imagine what would make your sibling wave action stop. As a Chinese philosopher says, "If ten thousand waves wash over you, let it happen." This does not mean you can steamroll your siblings or they can steamroll you.

Thirty-nine-year-old Elke, her thirty-seven-year-old brother, Erik, and her thirty-five-year-old sister, Ulrike, explored their unique memories in adult sibling sessions. They shared their early experience of creating common memories. They now begin to explore their sibling memories, paying attention to both the history and the accompanying facts and feelings. Known sibling facts are exchanged through discussion and cross-checked for their individual perspectives. Elke's comment about this adult-session experience was that it gave her a way to gather more information and impressions about herself and her sister and brother. It allowed her to delve back into her past in a fuller way. It strengthened the bonds between herself and her brother and sister because she appreciated their generosity and love for her. Her sister said that she always thought of her childhood as happy. After the session, she started talking about her anger at their father much more than Elke had ever heard before. As Elke got to know her sister and her feelings about their father, more intimacy developed between them.

Other facts and feelings expressed by siblings in adult sibling sessions:

Claudia: "Familes stick together even if you have little in common."

Harry: "Work, don't relax too much, keep your feelings in."

Donna: "I understood them because my sister knew some history I did not."

Tracey: "I learned that my dad had cut off lots of relatives."

Doris: "I felt deep love and compassion as we shared hurts and pain."

Kevin: "I felt a great deal of support."

Caroline: "I was angry about the family situation. I was afraid of having blocked parts of my life out as the siblings brought out items I did not remember."

Rick: "I felt a lot of sadness and grief."

Louise: "For the first time I felt they understood what, when, and why I was the way I was."

Siblings in the session shared feelings that included anger, sadness, fear, and happiness. They also shared facts, both known and not known.

*Are you willing to participate in a Siblings—for Better or for Worse session?*

*Would your siblings participate with you?*

*Would you participate with your siblings?*

## Sibling Memories of Trauma

Trauma is defined as an injury to living tissue caused by an extrinsic agent or a disordered psychic or behavioral state resulting from mental or emotional stress or physical injury.

Freely translated, a trauma is a hurt. Hurt is a part of sibling life. If healing is also a part of sibling life, then the hurt can go away. Sibling hurt will return, and if sibling healing follows closely, the wound will be repaired.

### The Sibling Trauma of Miscommunication

Allison was born with her umbilical cord wrapped around her neck, but she survived. Her two older sisters were told to give Allison special treatment. This created resentment, which became a part of their sibling childhood and continued until thirty years later, when all three had a spirited discussion of the special treatment. Allison was confused over her outsider status, and her sisters were resentful.

When adult brothers and sisters have an opportunity for a full discussion of then-and-there as well as here-and-now sibling experiences, then misinformation may be corrected; more understanding of brother and sister behaviors, hopefully, will lead to forgiving each other's hurts. These are both the sibling hurts you received and the sibling hurts you gave. Be honest with yourself and these special people!

### The Sibling Trauma of Death

The death of a parent and the death of a sibling create memories that will remain throughout life. The movie *Ordinary People* is a drama of a family who lost their older son through an accidental drowning. The mother refuses to remove anything from her older son's room, and her seventeen-year-old younger son attempts suicide because he blames himself for his brother's accidental drowning.

Sibling death may be caused by illness or accident. Fourteen-year-old identical twins Barbara and Carol died of cystic fibrosis within four months of each other. Their three surviving older siblings have fourteen years of memories with Barbara and Carol, and the ongoing memory of their loss. Frank Deford writes of his daughter's cystic fibrosis and her early and untimely death in his warm and heart-touching book *Alex: The Life of a Child*. At the moment of his daughter's death he gives thanks that her suffering is over.

The universal rule is that parents are to remain alive until their children are grown and children are not to die before their parents. When this universal rule is broken parents experience their greatest nightmare.

Sibling birth order is forever impacted by a childhood sibling death and may also be forever impacted by an adult sibling death.

Joseph P. Kennedy, Jr., the oldest sibling in his family, was killed in World War II. His younger brother, John Fitzgerald Kennedy, followed in their father's desire to have a Kennedy in the White House. Both younger brothers Robert F. Kennedy and Edward M. Kennedy pursued the White House. Robert's pursuit ended in assassination and Edward's pursuit ended with Chappaquiddick. With the deaths of their older siblings, these brothers moved to the next oldest male sibling position in this family.

Richard, the second-born son in his family, was born dead. His five-years-older brother, Robert, had only the hope of what might have been, and unfortunately neither had the joy or pleasure of creating memories with each other. Robert had two younger brothers, however, who have given Robert the hope, joy, and pleasure of younger siblings.

Sibling death, as with all deaths, breaks the possibility of creating further memories. In a two-sibling family, the surviving sibling becomes an only child. In a three-or-more sibling family, a sibling death changes the birth order into senior or junior positions.

Trauma can impact siblings in the past, the present, or the future. The past is the history brought to the sibling. Meagan was born five years after the death of her brother. The present is the loss of a sibling in the here and now. Each of the seven siblings in the Conner family had activities and memories with one another. When their brother Randy died at age thirty-three, they experienced his death in the present. The future is then clouded by, for instance, the terminal illness of a sibling. Five-year-old Sidney has leukemia, and his older brothers know that he will pass away. They are obligated to do pre-grieving over the very strong likelihood that they will lose their brother.

*What are your sibling traumas involving death?*
*Is your sibling death trauma open to discussion in the here and now?*
*How did you and your family process your sibling death trauma?*

## The Sibling Trauma of Separation

Howard was separated from two older brothers and his younger sister when he was five years old. His parents' divorce changed forever this four-child family. Howard was sent to live with his aunt and uncle and was reared as an only child. His other siblings remained with their mother. In Howard's adult life, he married, and fathered three children. When his oldest child turned sixteen, Howard walked away from his family. Fourteen years after Howard left, his oldest son, Jack, tracked his father down, and discovered that his father had remarried and then died. Jack learned that his father had lived within a close geographical distance from his children. Jack's discovery of his father's death led to all the siblings' planning a memorial service to grieve over the loss of their father.

Did Howard's separation from his siblings in his childhood make it difficult for him to bond with others, even his own children? The risk of getting close to another human being is the risk of losing that other person. Losses of separation and death lead to grief. However, a process of saying good-bye leads to the process of saying hello, and most likely Howard did not have any help in saying good-bye to his sibling family and saying hello to his new family. Without assistance, Howard was stuck. Howard lived with his only-child family, got older, grew up, worked, got married, became a parent, and remained stuck in that emotional place that kept him from getting close to others. He also became an alcoholic, further preventing him from becoming close to other human beings.

Bobby was separated from his mother, father, and half sister five weeks after his birth when his mother and father separated and divorced. His mother moved out of state with Bobby's older sister, and shortly thereafter remarried her first husband. They had two more children. Bobby remained with his father's parents. Bobby has three siblings who grew up separated from him. His mother wrote him off. At age nineteen, Bobby visited his mother and his three siblings. These visits reconfirmed that he was not a part of that family. Twenty-one-year-old Bobby married Nancy, his twenty-year-old girlfriend, and they had a son, Douglas. Within two years of Douglas's birth, Bobby and his wife Nancy separated and divorced. Nancy and Douglas moved out of the state, where she married Keith. Keith completed a stepparent adoption of Douglas. Years later, forty-one-year-old Bobby was visited by his nineteen-year-old son, Douglas. They had not seen each other since Douglas was two years old. After their meeting there was no further contact. Fifty-three-year-old Bobby lives as a street person who will not allow himself to get close to anyone else. His childhood emotional wound has not healed, and most likely Bobby will die alone.

Bobby never learned or allowed himself to heal from his childhood and adult hurts. Hurts can heal only when allowed.

Sibling separation occurring before the child would normally leave home may cause a long-standing trauma. Siblings leaving home is a normal family turning point and usually is a welcome change.

I have been separated from my brother Harold since he left five years ago. This is a part of my adult life, and although I have a loving family, good friends, and a satisfying career, I still miss my brother. Harold is/was a fun-loving person who was routinely late in keeping commitments. I am a compulsive person who will show up five minutes early. Years ago I wanted to turn the tables on my brother. I committed to visit him in Monterey, California, on a specific day and at a specific time—two o'clock in the afternoon, as I recall. I purposely showed up at four. He was all over me for being late. I suggested that he is routinely late and he said, "Yes, but you are reliable." My wish is that he is merely late for this time in his life.

I do have the pleasure of my brother Harold's thirteen-year-old son, who is currently living with my family. He is a reminder of my brother, and I hope that I am a reminder of the fathering he received in the past from his own dad.

*What is your sibling-separation trauma?*
*What age were you when your sibling separation occurred?*
*What healing is required for you to complete this sibling separation?*

## Memories of Sibling Teaching and Sibling Learning

Ten-year-old Samantha has two younger brothers and two younger sisters. Their mother died unexpectedly at age twenty-eight. Samantha moved into the "mother gap" by reading *Casey at the Bat* to her younger brothers and sisters. Over and over Samantha read the poem that kept her brothers' and sisters' attention and ushered in their bedtime.

Samantha calmed them down with her voice, providing a predictable nightly activity, and creating safety for them to get to sleep.

When thirty-year-old Samantha's four children were too rambunctious, she read the Bible to them and then sent them outside to look for something. Her children soon returned in tears because the "outside" was scary. They were calmed down and ready for bed.

Once again Samantha's voice provided a calming and reassuring way to move her own children to a feeling of quiet and safety. They were able to sleep without fear.

Now fifty-seven-year-old Samantha, who resides on the West Coast, talks weekly on the telephone with her brothers and sisters on the East Coast. Rarely does she read to her siblings; however, her voice is still the music that teaches.

Samantha is a nurturing, loving, and trusting sister and mother. Her brothers and sisters love and admire what she has done for them. Her children also love and admire her. Her siblings don't always like her, and her children don't always like her; however, they all love her. Her calming voice created memories of tranquility in a sea of rough waters.

## Siblings Teach by Example.

Sibling examples are both good and bad.

The Collins brothers came from a family of limited financial means. Their father was a day laborer and their mother worked in a small factory. John, the oldest son, worked his way through college, finishing with high grades, and was accepted to medical school. After his graduation and his residency training, John entered a group medical practice. John's younger brothers, Erskine, twenty-two, and Larry, nineteen, asked older brother John for help for them to attend medical school. John agreed and helped Erskine select a medical school and complete the application with the type of summary needed, and arranged the financial means. Four years later John assisted younger brother Larry in the same medical-school process. Today these three physicians have a group practice together.

Maynard, the second-born of six brothers, is an anxious child and a rebellious teenager. Later, twenty-four-year-old Maynard is in jail for mail fraud. This is his third offense, the other two offenses being assault with a deadly weapon and armed robbery. His behavior is an example to his younger brothers of the type of behavior to avoid. When brothers and sisters experience pain and agony over their siblings' behavior it can be a valuable lesson, especially if they understand how to avoid repeating their siblings' mistakes.

Firstborn siblings and older siblings frequently become teachers because their behavior is an ever-present example to the younger children in the family. They are the pioneers. Parents usually give them great privileges and expect them to be better behaved. John is a good example to his younger brothers. Maynard is a disaster.

## Siblings Learn by Example

John's brothers learned from his example how to achieve their goals. With their own ambition and John's example they were successful in their pursuits. Maynard's younger siblings learned to walk the path they needed to walk in order to have success in their lives and to avoid Maynard's mistakes.

Younger siblings can also teach by example. Walter Toman's book

*Family Constellation,* identifies well-known younger siblings; Aldous Huxley, Ingmar Bergman, and Vladimir Ilyich Lenin. Each was a teacher and leader.

Frank J. Sulloway's scholarly *Born to Rebel* strongly suggests that the younger siblings set a tone of rebellion and often create a new status quo. These younger-borns question authority, ask "how come?" and walk a trail that often only they see. Charles Darwin, a later-born, is studied in depth in Sulloway's book. Darwin's *Origin of Species* work was developed partly because of his travels and exploration of the Galapagos islands. In part, Sulloway concludes that Darwin's rebellious nature made him a natural explorer.

With the younger brothers' and sisters' rebellious attitudes, their resulting behavior may set an example for older siblings to learn from.

### Siblings Teach with Activities

Ten-year-old Mark taught his five-year-old brother, Randy, how to throw a football. Forty-six-year-old Mark is teaching forty-one-year-old Randy how to ski. They are both comfortable in their teacher/student relationship.

### Siblings Learn from Activities

Five-year-old Calvin wanted to follow his two older brothers around and to be in the big-boys' club. He wanted to learn how to talk, how to walk, and what to do and not do. When he was an adult, these lessons learned from his siblings led him to accomplish much in his professional life. The rules of behavior he needed to learn to be in the big-boys' club also moved him from being a sibling follower to a sibling leader. Fifty-three-year-old Calvin is the vice president of marketing in a Fortune 500 company. He continues to practice the rules for success.

### Siblings Teach through Words

Five-year-old twins Mark and Mike speak a common language filled with large amounts of gibberish. They understand each other, and their mother also understands their gibberish. These twins taught each other their gibberish method of communicating. One year later, when the twins are in first grade, neither their teacher nor their fellow students understands what they are saying. In order for the boys to stay in school, this gibberish had to be translated into common classroom language.

Fifty-five-year-old Mark and Mike now speak a common language as executive officers in the banking business. They can both effectively speak "bank talk" in the banking community as well as "social talk" in their social community. To succeed, these two brothers had to learn a language beyond their comfortable childhood gibberish.

### Siblings Learn by Hearing

Most children are excited about learning dirty, bawdy, improper, racy, and foul words. When the older siblings risk this kind of language, the younger siblings learn, and parrot them. Three-year-old Johnny blurted out that the potato salad looked like "sh__." When his astonished mother scolded him, he told her he learned it from his seven-year-old sister, Belinda. Belinda was sent to her bedroom for thirty minutes to teach her not to use words like that.

Four-year-old Geoffrey uses his dirty words with his older brother and the neighborhood children in their backyard. In their house later in the day, Geoffrey informs his mother that some of the other kids are using the "F" word. Geoffrey has picked up sibling words from his brother and the other kids, and he learns that these same words are not acceptable in his parents' world.

*What were your dirty words?*
*What did you learn from your siblings about dirty words?*
*What did your siblings learn from you about dirty words?*

### Sibling Memories of Each Other and of Parents

Adult sessions, also known as Siblings—for Better or for Worse, are an idea I stumbled on fifteen years ago. In my counseling, it soon became apparent that the persons sitting opposite me bring into the room not only (1) themselves but also (2) a past history with parents and brothers and sisters, (3) a here-and-now presence with spouse or a significant other (i.e., a partner without the bond of legal marriage), children, the siblings from the past, and the parents from the past. Most likely these major family members will remain a part of each individual sitting in my office.

Forty-five-year-old Gordon is an only child, has consulted with me on numerous occasions, and is struggling with the difficulty of maintaining a healthy relationship with the woman in his life. Gordon's mother died from cancer when Gordon was twenty-two years old. One day Gordon announced that his eighty-eight-year-old father had just died and he needed to complete the funeral arrangements for his extended family. He asked me to be present at his father's funeral. My colleague Meagan Shertzer, an only child, had years earlier counseled me to act as a benevolent big brother to my only-child clients. Gordon asked and I became his benevolent big brother. I shared only Gordon's adult life, not his childhood, but his memories of his childhood became clear in my office. Gordon was the center of his parents' universe, and the bond that kept his parents talking to one another. This was a child-centered family, not a marriage-centered family. Gordon was the glue. Even though his parents are gone, and Gordon's glue is no longer needed for his family, he has not, as yet, learned to create a grown-up relationship with another adult.

Thirty-one-year-old Claudia and twenty-three-year-old Carol are half sisters. Half siblings share one common parent and two separate parents. These women had different fathers and the same mother. Their childhood was not *half*. From the time of Carol's birth they were together all the time.

Carol came into my office some months after she had seen me lead a counseling group. I have a knack for reminding some people that I am like a benevolent big brother or benevolent father. Carol's father had recently died and she was grieving over his death.

Shortly after Carol entered therapy, she referred her sister Claudia to my office. I was given the privilege of hearing their childhood stories. There were common stories with differing perspectives on family members and family events.

This was a first for me—an exciting first.

These two sibling historians had the elements of love, hate, envy, jealousy, rivalry, kindness, and respect for each other. Carol loved her father; Claudia resented her stepfather. I was intrigued how these two viewed themselves and their family. They agreed to meet together with me in a two-hour session. The room was tense when they came in together. This simple session created a strong impact—an impact that was even greater than the session itself. As I recall, both women sat opposite each other. The first thirty minutes was ordinary conversation about individual family members. As the session progressed, both of these bright, well-educated women began to discuss some of the conflict in their family, and toward the end of the session they both identified areas where they had significantly different recall of childhood stories and players.

Two hours into the session I had to conclude it, as our initial agreement was for only a two-hour session. However, I had the impression that many more sibling and family issues could be examined. I thanked them both for the opportunity to see them together, and they also thanked me.

In a later survey, Carol's responses to the session included:

"I . . . felt very tense; a little defensive."

"What a negative, somewhat violent relationship they [parents] had had, compared to the relative benign relationship I had with them."

"Families stick together even if you have little in common."

During the session Carol's responses to the survey question regarding her feelings were: ". . . more uncomfortable than distant."

"She [Carol's sister] seemed much more comfortable during the session than I."

"She [Carol's sister] had much more of a memory of my maternal grandmother and maternal relatives. We concentrated on more immediate relationships—She-I, mother-kids, and mother."

"Perhaps more honest." [Carol's relationship with her sister.]

"Mostly highlighted fears I had about exposing myself to family about feeling that love is scarce." [The session]

"There is a tremendous pool of information among siblings that's not always available from parents or my own recall."

"I am more honest in what I recognize about my mother, and more of my own person; I respect her more."

"Father is dead but my relationship to his memory is more honest."

I agreed with Carol's comment about the "tremendous pool of information among siblings." Two hours thus expanded to five hours to accommodate the pool of sibling information.

*What are your memories of your parents in your childhood?*
*What are your memories of your siblings in your childhood?*
*What are your siblings' memories of your parents in your childhood?*
*What are your siblings' memories of you in your childhood?*
*How willing are you to ask?*
*Do the memories differ? How much?*

Asking questions about the then-and-there memories with your sibling historians may clarify family misconceptions and family secrets, enhance your sibling relationship, and open new gardens for family growth.

A note of caution on this sibling journey—walk tenderly through this family maze. Carry with you the gifts of love, compassion, forgiveness, joy, shared tears, tenderness, and a desire to make your sibling relationship all that it may be.

On my numerous hundred-mile, nine-day treks through the gorgeous, rugged, challenging, and exhilarating mountains of northern and southern California, I had a guide, Curtis. I did the walking and Curtis led the way and provided the protection for a safe journey. As you trek your sibling mountains you may want a guide. Family therapists who have experience with adult sibling counseling are frequently excellent guides.

The journey is to reclaim sibling memories and understand their connection to your life.

# 6

$\sim$

# *Siblings With a Handicap*

## What Is a Handicap?

*The Twilight Zone* was a popular thirty-minute television program from the 1960s. The creator, writer, and producer of the program, Rod Serling, had a particular talent for viewing subjects from a unique perspective. One of my favorite *Twilight Zone* episodes took place in a hospital. The patients' face and head were completely bandaged. The doctors and nurses hovered about the patient, so the camera allowed us to see only the hands, arms, and uniforms of the doctors and nurses.

The plot is about a patient who has undergone plastic surgery to remove a facial handicap. The tension builds as the patient repeatedly asks about her progress and the doctors and nurses comfort her with the possibility of success. The moment of truth comes as the bandages are slowly unwrapped from her face and head. We watch the unwrapping, and as the last bandage is removed, the doctors and nurses gasp at the sight of the young woman's face.

As the camera allows, we see a gorgeous young woman with a movie-star face. The doctors and nurses console their patient that her surgery was unsuccessful and tell her there is a place for her to live with her "own kind." In the next scene, a handsome young man escorts this beautiful young woman to the place where she will live with her own kind. The camera then lets us look at the faces of the doctors and nurses. Their faces resemble pig faces, with curled-up lips, snouts, and ugly ears. They were the "beautiful people." The patient was the person with a handicap who was sent to live with her own kind.

I am a people person. My professional life is people focused. In my more than twenty-five-year career I have counseled people who are incarcerated, people who are mildly, moderately, and severely retarded, people who are mildly, moderately, and severely physically impaired, people who are acutely or chronically institutionalized in hospitals, and everyday people like you and me.

So what is a handicap? My thesaurus displays the words *impairment, disability, affliction, flaw,* and *limitation.* For those of us who have siblings with handicaps this chapter will help you understand and work through the feelings you have about them.

## Mental Handicap

The hope of every parent is that his or her child will be born "normal"—normal looks, normal intelligence, and normal health. Down's syndrome babies are born with "a congenital condition characterized by moderate to severe mental retardation, slanting eyes, a broad short skull, broad hands with short fingers and trisomy of the chromosome numbered 21." (*Merriam Webster's New Collegiate Dictionary Tenth Edition,* 1993)

The chance of having a Down's syndrome child increases as a woman ages. The four hundred or so eggs that a woman has are with her at her birth and age with her as she ages. The percentage chance of Down's syndrome is low when the woman is in her twenties, increases some in her thirties, and further increases in her forties. Down's syndrome occurs in a very small percentage of births; however, within every family the Down's syndrome child's birth is a loss of the hope for a "normal" child.

I have had the pleasure of and opportunity to work with families who have a Down's syndrome child, and other families who have had a child born with a disability. Most of these families have other children who are the siblings to this "special" child. In a not-too-distant past, these special siblings were placed out of the home shortly after birth. They were the family secret.

In 1961 President John F. Kennedy began to advance the idea that these special people were citizens who deserved all the rights and privileges everyone else had. His own sister Rosemary had a neurological impairment. The special people were brought out of the closet to become full members of their families. In my own state of California, the 1960s brought in the Regional Systems program that provided assistance for people with handicaps and also provided assistance for the families.

Down's syndrome people are loving, kind, thoughtful, love to touch, and don't seem to harbor some of our common quirks of resentment and jealousy. They *are* human beings with hopes, wishes, desires, and dreams who possess all the feelings that human beings have. They *are* loving siblings.

Billy is nineteen, has Down's syndrome, and is the youngest of four children. He has one older brother and two older sisters. Billy has lived with his parents and siblings in their home throughout his life. His father is an architect and his mother a teacher. Throughout his schooling, Billy attended special-education classes in his school district. He has participated in all of his family's activities, and has a loving and somewhat protected relationship with his older brother and sister. Currently he works at a McDonald's as the soft-drink dispenser.

Billy's family provided the possibilities for him to develop his talents. Billy is not a "forever child."

With all due respect to the parents, my experience in working with those who have a child with a handicap appears to fall into two distinct categories. Billy's parents and siblings were in the first category. They focused on assisting Billy in having the life he achieved. The second category are parents and siblings who focus on the child with a handicap as a "forever child." With some children born with a handicap their disability is so severe that they require extensive care and may need to be placed out of the home.

David is the oldest of four children and has two younger brothers and a sister. David was born with hydrocephalus, "an abnormal increase in the amount of cerebrospinal fluid within the cranial cavity that is accompanied by expansion of the cerebral ventricles, enlargement of the skull and . . . atrophy of the brain." (*Merriam Webster's New Collegiate Dictionary Tenth Edition*, 1993)

David's parents chose to keep him at home with his three younger siblings. David's body size did not grow beyond that of a young child. When David was sixteen years old his next-youngest brother, Michael, was fourteen. Their family had invited guests to dinner, and as family introductions were made, the family guest commented that Michael was the big brother in the family. Michael's quick reply was that David was the big brother in the family. When David was eighteen years old his parents placed him out of their home and into hospital care.

In her 1988 doctoral dissertation "Brothers and Sisters of the Mentally Retarded," Sonnee Weedn found that over fifty percent of people who have a sibling with a handicap work in the helping professions. Weedn further details a love/hate relationship with the brothers and sisters in childhood. She discovered that the love is common and that the resentment is a natural outgrowth of the sibling's handicap and subsequent "special" treatment required from siblings. Resentment is a part of the package of siblings living together. The sister or brother with a handicap increases both the love and the resentment. Self-forgiveness of sibling resentment paves the way for moving on without all the baggage.

## Physical Handicap

A childhood bicycle accident can cause an injury that results in a disability. This disability changes the children's relationship forever. In addition, a disease such as cystic fibrosis can also cause impairment in normal childhood development. The age of the sibling at the time of the accident will determine how the sister or brother relationship changes. Nine-year-old Allan, the oldest of three, was severely injured in a family automobile accident. Because of a severe spinal cord injury he will never walk, has limited speech, and is unable to care for himself. His two younger brothers are required to treat their big brother more as a little brother.

Sixteen-year-old Janet is the sixth-born. She has cerebral palsy and is confined to a wheelchair. She is of normal intelligence, has a bubbly personality, and is interested in boys. She has one older brother living. Janet has four older siblings who also had cerebral palsy, each of whom died in early childhood. Janet's oldest brother, along with Janet's parents, have provided loving and ongoing care. They are committed to providing the optimal life for Janet.

As with Weedn's point that sisters and brothers of the handicapped sibling may work in the helping profession, Janet's older brother, Arthur, attended medical school and later became a pediatrician working with the physically handicapped.

Fifteen-year-old Hal has two older brothers, a younger sister, and a younger brother. Hal was born with a severe hearing disability. All four of Hal's siblings along with his parents enrolled in signing classes at the local school district. Hal's brothers, sister, and parents routinely include Hal in the spoken and signed family. At times Hal's siblings will sign with each other rather than use the spoken word. Hal enjoys their humor. Hal is an insider, not an outsider, in his family.

As with mental handicaps, a sibling's development with a physical handicap will depend on (1) the severity of the handicap, (2) the age when the handicap occurred, (3) the siblings' and parents' responses to the handicap, and (4) the determination of the sibling with the handicap to live the best life possible.

Joe was born blind. His four sisters extended their hands, talked to lead the way, described what was happening at the movies and on television, read to him, helped him with the dishes when it was his turn, and helped him make his bed and wash his clothes. They also took him with them to school and made sure he participated in all activities. Joe now has a Ph.D. in clinical psychology and has a private counseling practice. Today he has developed his senses of hearing, smell, taste, and touch to the point that he can mentally see a picture of his client. As a child, Joe knew when his sister Candace entered his room. He knew when his sister Barbara left the house. He knew when his sister Bernice borrowed his shirt, and he knew when his youngest sister Karen whimpered.

Sight is only one of the five senses. Joe accentuated his other four to make his world one in which he could "see." His loving sisters lent him their eyes along with their love.

## Siblings with an Assigned Emotional Handicap

Susan has an emotional handicap: She is overly dramatic with her parents, her brother, her friends, her husband, and her children. In her childhood, four-year-old Susan got attention from her mother, father and brother when she played the harried actress. Without the harried melodrama, they rarely noticed her. Her brother, Steven, was the issue in this family. While Susan had the emotional handicap, Steven had the assigned handicap of being the family issue. The issue was that Steven caused problems. Unbeknownst to Steven, his problems were mainly normal childhood dilemmas. Every child in every family wants to give attention as well as to receive it. In this family there was not enough attention to go around. Susan provided the drama and Steven, unfortunately, began to believe that he was the family problem.

Later, thirty-two-year-old Steven entered psychotherapy because he has issues in getting along with his parents, his sister, and most other people in his life. His parents divorced about the time that Steven entered college. This family turning point exposed the parents' unhappy, miserable, and emotionally dead marriage. When Steven, the "issue," left, they had to look at themselves. Steven had long ago been given the assignment of being the family problem, and his younger sister had developed high drama to get her needs met.

Steven's work in therapy has given him permission to solve his interpersonal issues and to have loving and lasting relationships with others. However, within his family he has to continue to be their issue. With both his father and mother, Steven has limited his visitations. With his sister, Susan, who continues to dramatize everything, he limits his telephone conversations and his visits with her and is able to continue loving his family despite their craziness. They are his family. They will probably not change significantly. Steven can and has changed. His reluctance to be the family issue has, however, increased their craziness.

The "baby" of the sibling family can remain in a dependent position throughout life. Babies are beautiful, gorgeous, playful, vulnerable, soft, and innocent, and will grow physically, mentally, and emotionally into mature adults. Myra, the youngest-born child, is called the baby by her parents, her two sisters, her grandparents, and anyone else who spends time with her family. Five-year-old Myra, introduces herself as the baby. Six-year-old Myra enters school and for the first time she is called Myra by her teacher and classmates. Deep inside of Myra is a desire to be known as Myra, and an equally strong desire to be called "baby." The pluses of being called Myra in school are significant because she can be one of the kids. The minuses of being called Myra are that she will be expected to pull her own weight.

Myra's mother made the decision to withdraw Myra from the first grade, as the other children were mean to her. One year later seven-year-old Myra reentered the first grade. She is chronologically one year older than her peers. While others are still mean to Myra, she has developed some sophistication in setting the other children up against each other. She provides a "divide and conquer" mentality. The "bad" first-grade children are banished from her presence and the "good" first-grade peers are allowed to serve Myra. The "baby" has become more skilled at playing the baby game.

Twenty-five-year-old Myra marries "big daddy" Kevin. He is at her beck and call. They have a father-daughter relationship. Myra gives birth to their two children and at that point stops all attempts at parenting. Her husband thereby becomes a single parent. He does all the household chores, works out of the home, and gets tired, lonely, and depressed. Thirty-two-year-old Myra tires of her husband's moods and has an affair with her down-the-street neighbor, Rod. Rod, another "big daddy" type, and Myra, the baby, have a short fling. The fling ends when Rod becomes tired, lonely, and depressed with his relationship with baby Myra. Myra will look for a "real man" in her next encounter, but will find him only when and if she becomes a "real woman." Babies do not like competition.

Forty-five-year-old Myron is also a baby. His wife, Louise, is a "big mommy" who caters to Myron's desires. Myron's mother, father, and two older sisters are pleased with Louise when she makes Myron happy and they are equally critical when she makes Myron unhappy. They have no children because Louise knows she is married to a big, immature baby who wouldn't be a good father. His sisters secretly are happy that Louise is in the picture. They did plenty of parenting for Myron in their childhood. They both love and resent the baby who never grew up.

Not all youngest-borns become "forever babies." At times an older sibling can be assigned as the baby of the family. When taken to task, however, this sibling can develop into a mature adult and experience the joys and responsibilities of adulthood. Look out for the caretakers unless they are committed to a growth model of behavior.

Some assigned handicaps disappear when an event occurs. An event may be the death of a caretaker, the disability of a caretaker, or when the baby enters psychotherapy because the big daddies and the big mommies are turned off by the forty-five year-old baby. The effective psychotherapist lends temporary big daddy–big mommy stuff to this new forty-five-year-old baby client. In the therapist's mind is a picture of the baby growing into adulthood. If the therapist is ineffective, the baby will fire the therapist and look for a new big mommy–big daddy type. In the absence of change, the baby may become depressed to the point that he or she may leave the planet by his or her own hand.

> *Which sibling was the baby in your family?*
> *Were you the baby in your family?*
> *Were you the caretaker of the baby in your family?*
> *How old is the baby in your family?*

## Comparison Handicap

"Why can't you be like your brother, Kenneth?" "You are one of the Fallon brothers." "Billy, we expect a lot out of you. Your sister, Chris, was one of my favorites." *Cat on a Hot Tin Roof* is a play and a movie in which the younger brother is favored by their father, and the older brother "can't do anything right." The older brother is compared to his younger brother and always comes up short. The older brother attempts to please his parents, and this leads to his resentment of his younger brother. The older brother never quite makes the grade.

Some sibling comparisons begin very early in life. Sean, Kevin, Colleen, Douglas, and Lindsey were easy pregnancies, according to their mother. Third-born Leonard was a difficult pregnancy and he continued to be a difficult child. He had to live up to being difficult. Out of his awareness, he is being compared to his mother's other pregnancies and he resents the comparisons. He is not able to live beyond being difficult. He was not responsible for his mother's difficult pregnancy, and unfortunately the story was told and retold until it became a fact. Leonard's breakthrough occurred when his own wife gave birth to their first child and he assisted in the birthing process. He came to realize that the story told about him was never about him; the story was about his mother's pregnancy. His realization began his change from being difficult to being an easy husband, father, son, sibling, coworker, neighbor, and friend. He gave up his handicap.

Some sibling comparisons start with gender differences. "Brothers are like that" or "Sisters are like that" are common refrains in some families. Whether the refrain is a benefit or a drawback depends on the family.

Eugene's wife, Marsha, has one brother and four sisters. Marsha's brother is given special consideration in their family, and Marsha transfers that special consideration to her husband, Eugene. Eugene is allowed to mess around with other women in his married life. Marsha doesn't like his behavior; however, she believes that "Brothers are like that."

Fourteen-year-old Carla is a math wizard and an accomplished gymnast. Her twelve-year-old brother, Carl, is a singer who reaches those high notes, captivating his mother and father and his audiences. Carla's mother demonstrates how to be the "wife behind her husband," and she subtly and firmly moves Carla to be "the sister behind her brother." Carla resents this and begins to gain recognition away from math and gymnastics. She gains parental recognition by stealing money from them. She does not want the money, she wants their undivided sibling attention. She does not want to be the way a sister is "supposed to be." She wants to be herself, with all the privileges and responsibilities.

Brothers and sisters are much more alike than different. Some families and some cultures favor brothers over sisters. I attended the funeral of Byron. He was the third-born, thirty-year-old only son in his family. He has two older sisters, and at the funeral service the official identified Byron as the long-awaited brother and son. The long-awaited son had ended his life by his own hand. He was not able to live up to the expectations that were determined by the accident of his gender. Byron was ruled by his handicap. His depression was severe and his handicap became his life's slogan: "I never measured up." He was compared to the brother image, and deep down inside he felt the pain and the disappointment of the other family members.

## Famous Siblings

Lyndon Johnson had a younger brother, Sam Houston Johnson. Jimmy Carter had a younger brother, Billy Carter. Both presidents Johnson and Carter were firstborns who set an early path in their lives of success and prominence. Lyndon B. Johnson was a teacher, a congressman, a United States senator, a U.S. Senate leader, vice president, and president of the United States. His younger brother was rather a ne'er do well. Was the sibling comparison too much for Sam Houston Johnson? Jimmy Carter was a governor and later president of the United States. Billy Carter was an alcoholic who later became sober and had some business successes.

## Infamous Siblings

David Kaczynski is the younger brother of serial bomber and murderer Theodore Kaczynski. David has countered comparison with his brother by being the person who informed the Federal Bureau of Investigation of his suspicion that his brother, Theodore, was the the Unabomber. He further countered comparison by donating the million-dollar reward to the victims of his brother's deeds.

Most siblings are ordinary in that they are not compared to the famous or infamous siblings. There is a normal comparison of siblings in each family. However, when the pluses and minuses of each sibling are recognized, then sibling comparison has no validity. Melinda and Melody's parents realized that their daughters had differing intellectual abilities. When Melinda, a math wiz, received an A, she was rewarded with a dollar. When hardworking Melody received a B-minus in math she was given a dollar. These parents were wise in the ways of identifying sibling differences. Thirty-nine-year-old Melinda is a university math professor, and thirty-seven-year-old Melody owns her own interior decorating business.

> *Are you the sibling who is compared?*
> *Has your model-sibling comparison caused a handicap for you?*
> *What is your handicap?*
> *Are you the model sibling your siblings are compared to?*
> *Has your being held to sibling comparison caused a handicap for you?*

## Loser Handicap

Thirty-two-year-old Shirley is a loser. In childhood she always lost out to her younger sister, Dolores. Dolores was cute, precocious, and bright. Shirley was the ugly duckling. Deep down inside Shirley was the beautiful and sophisticated swan that was not allowed to fly free. Shirley is a real success with her children and her career; however, her husband demanded that she remain an ugly duckling. Her husband, Don, is a rescuer of women. He sees them as inadequate, and when Shirley reaches some level of success he points out what she has not accomplished. She will remain an ugly duckling with Don until he gives up his role of rescuer.

Kevin is a jewel thief. He is the fourth-born of seven children and is a loser because he always wanted the "big fix." As a child he was given the distinction of being the clever brother who could figure out the legitimate cop-out every time. He was tired, hungry, sick, or cute, and would fascinate his parents with his stories. He is now a forty-seven-year-old adult who has spent seventeen of his adult years in prison. He continues to look for the big fix. His older brother Dennis is a police officer, and his other five siblings are law-abiding citizens. "Cute" Kevin continues to be a fascinating talker even though his parents are dead and his fascinating talk will not remove him from prison. Kevin's sibling handicap was his core belief that when he talked himself out of his chores he was a winner. As yet, he has not realized that he is really a loser.

Loser siblings do not set goals for achievement, or they do set a goal but proceed to undermine the effort required to complete the goal. The sibling loser handicap can be eliminated by achieving a goal. With a new attitude of success, coupled with work, no sibling comparisons, and encouragement from others, they can begin the process of positive change.

Twenty-five-year-old Linda, the younger sister of twenty-eight-year-old Bernard, is a single mother with two young children. She has been supported on Aid to Families with Dependent Children since the birth of her first child, six-year-old Brian, and later with four-year-old Lee. Linda has had numerous psychiatric hospitalizations during the past five years. Her hospitalizations became a revolving door of a few days in to a few months out. Her outpatient therapist urged Linda to give up her sibling "loser" handicap. Linda was intrigued. Her older brother was the success in the family and Linda was the loser. The therapist encouraged Linda to create a goal for success. She decided her goal was to remain out of the hospital for a year, although she continued in outpatient therapy for support.

Linda completed thirteen months and twenty-seven days without being hospitalized. She was hospitalized for one weekend after reaching her successful goal. Upon discharge her therapist asked her what she had learned by being once again hospitalized; she quickly replied, "There was nothing for me there." The stuff of success was now inside Linda.

*Are you the loser-handicap sibling in your family? How come?*

*Does your family require a loser-handicap person? How come?*

*Is your sister or brother the loser handicap in your family? How come?*

*What is your relationship with this loser-handicap sibling?*

## Siblings with a Winner Handicap

Winners set goals and achieve them. A "real" winner is allowed to enjoy the joy, exhilaration, confidence-building, and satisfaction of attaining the goal. Billy, a moderately mentally retarded youngest brother, participates in the Special Olympics. His event is the hundred-yard dash. He and six others complete the race. At the awards ceremony, Billy proudly stands with his fellow racers as each of them receives his or her award. Billy is an authentic winner who revels in his efforts.

Siblings with a winner handicap have to win. They don't get to enjoy their wins, since there are never enough. Their need to win becomes a handicap. The need-to-win sisters and brothers frequently carry the hopes and dreams of the parents—not the hope and dreams of parents for their children, but the hope and dreams that their parents were unsuccessful in achieving for themselves.

Is Michelle an actress by her own choice? Or is she living out the dream of her stage mother? To her sisters Michelle is a winner. In her own life Michelle wonders if she is playing the piano or if she is sitting at a player piano.

Fifty-three-year-old Gerald, the oldest brother, is an orthopedic surgeon. His father was an orthopedic surgeon and his grandfather was an orthopedic surgeon. Gerald finished college in three years, spent the required four years in medical school, and completed five years in residence in orthopedic surgery. He has a successful medical practice, and is wealthy and well respected in his medical community. He has married three times, divorced twice, and has four grown children. His fast track to success requires him to be *driven* rather than to *drive*. On paper he is a winner. His winner handicap, however, prevents him from living the life he craves. He won't give it all up to have what he wants.

The front of his tombstone will read: *Gerald_____,M.D. I lived the life of success.* The back of his tombstone will read: *Gerald_____, M.D. I forgot who I am.*

Gerald's two younger sisters are proud of Gerald, although deep down inside each of them knew that he was living a winner-handicap life.

*Are you the winner-handicap sibling in your family? How come?*

*Does your family require a winner-handicap sibling? How come?*

*Is your sibling the winner handicap in your family? How come?*

*What is your relationship with your winner-handicap sibling?*

## Siblings with a Scapegoat Handicap

According to *Merriam Webster's New Collegiate Dictionary Tenth Edition,* a scapegoat is one that bears the blame for others or one that is the object of irrational hostility.

Janice had the sibling scapegoat handicap in her family. Unfortunately, Janice was conceived two months before her parents marriage and bore the brunt of blame for the "interruption" of her parents' lives. Janet's mother was angry at herself and her husband for getting pregnant, and Janet's father was angry at himself and his wife for her getting pregnant. Neither parent would take responsibility for their anger and instead laid it on their daughter, Janice.

Anger is born of an injustice, and Janice was simply an innocent bystander. Her parents had two other children after their marriage, and Janice's younger brother and sister were welcome additions to the family. Janice's brother, Arthur, and sister, Laura, knew Janice was being treated unfairly, yet they also treated her as a scapegoat. Janice developed a system in which her primary recognition came from taking on the anger of others. She is blamed for her own, Arthur's, and Laura's mistakes, errors, omissions, and accidents. For a sibling, that is better than no recognition at all. From prior to Janice's birth to the day she turned thirty-seven, her parents and then her siblings, her husband, and her own children treated her as a scapegoat.

Janice entered therapy to help her unhappy husband. She was convinced that she was the cause of his unhappiness. The magic of therapy is the reality of what is. Janice has lived a life of semiconsciousness about responsibility. She carried the handicap of being overly responsible for others and that of her loved ones for being underresponsible for themselves. Her therapy was a mirror for her to reflect the truth about responsibility. She was able to reach into her depths to retrieve the *rage* she carried. In little bits and pieces she released her anger and rage for the injustices visited upon her. She discovered that she didn't deserve the blame. She was *not* responsible for her parents' unhappy marriage, she was *not* responsible when her siblings did their dirty deeds, she was *not* responsible for her husband's unhappiness, and she was *not* responsible for her children's unhappiness. She had only the responsibility to be the best parent she could be.

To paraphrase Dr. Jerome Lackner's idea: remove a scapegoat and view the family craziness. The family is changed when you place the responsibility where it belongs. Janice is a loving daughter, loving sister, loving wife, and loving mother. She has questioned the family loyalty that locked her into being the family scapegoat. Family craziness creates a dangerous balance. Change creates an unbalancing. The family unbalancing most likely then leads to a balanced and healthy family. For the individual family members change is not easy, and resistance to change is a by-product of change. With effort over time and with encouragement, Janice will throw off her scapegoat yoke.

Walking without a yoke takes time. The yoke is well known to the wearer, and the sensation without the yoke requires adjustment.

*What caused the sibling-scapegoat handicap in your family?*
*Which kid in your family was given the scapegoat handicap?*
*Were you given the scapegoat handicap?*
*Are you still carrying the yoke of being a scapegoat?*

## Identified-Patient Handicap

Marty is fifteen years old and the fifth-born of eight siblings. He carries the label of being the "identified patient" in his family. The identified patient is the troublemaker. He looks normal to you. He walks and talks normally. But he does have a great big chip on his shoulder with a little sign that reads, *Go ahead and try*. He is failing in school, has experimented with drugs, and annoys his siblings, parents, and anyone else in his vicinity.

I liked Marty because he has loads of energy, a sharp wit, and a sharp tongue to match. Into my family therapy office marched Marty, his seven sisters and brothers, and their parents. The chairs in the room were arranged in a circle, and each family member took a seat. Marty was the first one to speak as he sat on the edge of his chair with his fists clenched. He resented being there, and yet he was the reason that his family came for therapy.

As I was the expert in the room, Marty was ready to battle me because he had battled everyone else and they had given up the fight. Right away he challenged my authority by asking, "Who do you think you are?" I answered that I was the family therapist and that I would require his assistance in helping his family. Marty was mildly surprised; his hands were now unclenched. He reclined in his chair. Marty let out a sigh, and deep down inside him was a budding awareness that his identified-patient sibling handicap status might change.

Marty is the tip of the family iceberg. He is the visible trouble above the surface and he protects the ninety percent of the family iceberg below the surface. As with many family iceberg dramas, the trouble is in the core of the parents' marriage. Marty's mother and father do not fight with each other. They are both terrified of their anger and they early on put a lid on it. Seeping at the edges of this family is husband and wife anger. This is normal. However, anger is not allowed in any outward form. Sensitive Marty intuitively accepts the anger. He takes pressure off Mom and Dad's marriage, and acts out their anger. He has elements of being a fifteen-year-old undereducated family therapist.

I require seven family sessions to identify the generational boundaries in this family. Marty is moved from the parents' generation back into the child/sibling generation. He greatly reduces his acting out and begins to have healthy interaction with his siblings and his peers at school.

The eighth family session is a marital session without the eight children. I introduce Marty's mother and father to that region in their marriage where conflict is seen as normal, and feelings such as anger can be experienced and expressed in a refreshing, clean manner. Thirteen additional marital sessions lead to Marty's parents learning to fight fairly with one another. Marty occasionally puts his two cents' worth into his parents disagreements and they forthrightly invite Marty to butt out.

Leslie is a twenty-two-year-old diagnosed schizophrenic older brother. He has been in psychotherapy treatment for over two years with Dr. J., who believes in the "wellness" of people. Dr. J's. view of the world is that everyone comes from a family. The family may be traditional—mom, dad, and children—or some other variation, e.g., stepparents, single parents, an institution. Dr. J. knows that Leslie has crazy behavior and stable behavior. Dr. J. focuses on Leslie's stable behavior, and Leslie's stable behavior outdistances his crazy behavior. Leslie can identify the crazy from the stable and acts accordingly. Unfortunately, Leslie's family needs a crazy person to deflect the "infection" in the parents' marriage. Neither one of Leslie's parents would even hint that they had a problem!

Leslie's Thursday family session includes Leslie; his younger brother, Robert; Leslie's parents, Arnold and Louise; and Dr. J. In the last minutes of the family session, Dr. J. directs his comments to Robert within earshot of the parents. Dr. J. informs the family that Leslie is able to continue living on his own in his apartment and can continue his work at the local factory. He further says that this family needs a crazy person and, looking at Robert, he says, "You are selected to be the crazy." This is an advocate statement in support of Leslie's wellness and a statement of awareness of the family craziness. With Dr. J.'s continued support, Leslie becomes a former identified-patient sibling. Robert and his parents are left with the job of finding another person to occupy the crazy identified-patient role in this family.

The identified-patient sibling is highly sensitive to the family disharmony, and yet lacks the skills to move a healthy distance from that disharmony. The boundary that distinguishes each family member as unique and different is blurred. This family lacks awareness in determining what is "mine" and what is "yours." This family has not traveled through the valley of "separation" and the valley of "individuation." These two words mean "we are related and we are different."

Sally is the valve on the pressure cooker of her family. When things get too tense in Sally's family, Sally does the "acting-out dance." She is willing to sacrifice her well-being for her mother, father, and four brothers. She acts out, they blame her, and this releases the tense steam from the family pressure cooker. All is once again temporarily calm, Sally is "wounded," and her "wound" keeps the family from solving their own problems.

In families, calm is interrupted by conflict. Conflict is a given in any relationship involving two or more people. "Where are we going on our next vacation?" moves the family from calm to conflict. Mountains or seashore? If Sally's family has the tools for effective conflict resolution, then a family vote leads to negotiations, which lead to compromises, which lead to resolution, which leads to a happy vacation.

In the absence of tools for conflict resolution, conflicts leads to anxiety, which leads to tension, and Sally and her family can handle only so much tension, which results in the identified-patient sibling having to temporarily reduce the family tension by sacrificing her own "wellness." Sally's family drama may play out in seconds, minutes, hours, days, or weeks, but will most certainly play out. Sally may be hospitalized, incarcerated, or engaged in unhealthy behavior without her full awareness of why it happens. She actually believes that she is the cause. She is burdened with guilt, blame, shame, and a whole bag of not-OK-ness. The "danger" of therapy is that Sally may discover that this family drama is not all about her. Then she will need support in the process of letting herself know what is hers and what is not hers. This will result in an unbalancing, and the family forces committed to the balanced disharmony most likely will test Sally's resolve.

The identified-patient sibling unfairly bears the weight of the family disharmony, which may be lifelong in duration, may end with a suicide, may end with the natural death of family members, or may end when the family gets well with healthy separation and individuation.

*Does your family have an identified-patient sibling?*
*Are you the identified patient?*

*What is your family's necessity to have an identified-patient child?*

*What is required to cure your identified-patient person?*

## Unlucky Handicap

Fourteen-year-old Rodney is a "dumb" kid. He has an older sister, Billie, a younger brother, Herbie, and a younger sister, Lizzie. Rodney's IQ is 117, a little above normal. Early in life he was given a mythical jacket that read in bold letters, *Hi, I am Rodney and I am unlucky.* Billie is sophomore-class president, Herbie is captain of his soccer team, and Lizzie has the lead in her elementary school play. Rodney and three of his classmates fill balloons with water and toss the balloons into the girls' bathroom. When the hall monitor appears, only Rodney is left with wet hands and holding three balloons. He spends two days of suspension in the principal's office. Billie, Herbie, and Lizzie "pull a fast one on him" when they tell him that the neighbor girl, Candace, likes him. Rodney visits Candace, who won't even give him the time of day. The father's attempts at playing catch with Rodney end when the ball bounces off Rodney's forehead. His father's only comment is that Rodney is all thumbs.

Twenty-four-year-old Rodney lost his $5,000 investment when his best friends moved to Europe without telling him. Married thirty-four-year-old Rodney is served with divorce papers by his wife of six years, Pam. Thirty-eight-year-old Rodney files for bankruptcy after his business fails. Rodney is now tired, depressed, and fed up with being unlucky.

Change comes for Rodney when he participates in a course called You and Luck. His course identifies removing his unlucky jacket as one of the tools for his success and creates for him a support team. Rodney moves into a pattern of setting realistic and attainable goals and begins to enjoy his wins. His internal attitudinal shift is away from unlucky and toward lucky. Rodney's new luck is filled with mental, physical, and emotional sweat. He changes his own unlucky jacket to the lucky one, and the muscles at the corners of his mouth pull in an upward direction.

Rodney reenters his brother's and sisters' lives with his stories of wins and losses. His siblings are now required to play with Rodney as a winner and not an unlucky loser.

Unlucky stuff happens. Rodney required assistance in learning that a shift in his attitude leads to a shift in his behavior, which leads to a shift in his life's direction away from an attitude of unluckiness, to a grateful attitude of luckiness.

*Was there a child with an unlucky handicap in your family?*

*How was that unlucky jacket given to that child in your family?*

*Was the unlucky jacket removed from you or your sister or brother?*

## "You Resemble" Handicap

You may look like, you may imitate, you may favor, or you may suggest—they all mean that you resemble someone or something. The resemblance may be your walk, your talk, your smell, your behavior, or your looks, and you may not even understand or know that you have a handicap. Your resemblance is a reminder of someone or something. That someone or something may be an unforgiven incident, action, word, or deed.

Fourteen-year-old Callie is the third-born sibling in her family. Her sister, Carlene, and her brothers, Richard and James, live with their mother. When Callie was seven years old, her father was caught by her mother molesting Callie. Her mother intervened and banished her husband from the family. Unfortunately Callie did not receive supportive counseling from her mother or anyone else. Callie's siblings never learned of their father's violations and they knew only that he had left all of them.

This set Callie apart from her siblings with the handicap of reminding her mother of the loss of her husband and the loss of the children's father. Even though Callie's mother knows she did the right thing, she has not been able to get beyond her resentment. Callie's siblings know that somehow Callie is different, but they have only a hunch about the origin of the difference.

Eventually the truth will come out about Callie's resemblance handicap. The time is not yet now.

Beverly is the only sister in a family with three boys. Her father, Daniel, had a premarriage girlfriend who was also named Beverly. Lo and behold, at the birth of their daughter, Daniel suggested to his wife, Kathy, that they name their daughter Beverly. Dad's previous girlfriend was unknown to Kathy until Beverly was a year old. The secret came out in a heated argument between Daniel and Kathy. Beverly was innocent and yet she reminded Kathy of the other woman.

Fast forward to a Gestalt therapy session in which Kathy imagines girlfriend Beverly sitting in one chair and daughter Beverly sitting in another chair. When Kathy addresses imagined girlfriend Beverly, she says, "You are my husband's former girlfriend," and she says to her daughter, "You are my daughter and I love you because you are your own person." Kathy shifts her attitude about her daughter's name and her husband's former girlfriend.

In a later conversation with her husband, Kathy comments on her Gestalt work. In surprise, Daniel tells her that his favorite fourth-grade teacher was named Beverly and he liked her and the name. They have removed daughter Beverly from her resemblance handicap.

If the resemblance to a person, event, or time is positive, then the resemblance is only a pleasant reminder for the sibling.

*Is there a sibling resemblance handicap in your family?*
*What is the resemblance?*
*Who knows about the resemblance handicap?*
*Are you the sibling with the resemblance handicap?*
*Do you know which one of you has the resemblance handicap?*

## Secret Handicap

The book and movie *The Thorn Birds* depict an Irish family that migrates to Australia to start a new life. The family consists of both parents and seven children—six grown brothers and one younger sister. The family settles on a ranch in the countryside, and each of the family members works in running the ranch. The firstborn son has an antagonistic relationship with his father; he simply cannot do anything right. In a heated argument between father and son, the father blurts out, "Bastard." The secret is revealed! The firstborn son was fathered by another man when his mother was sixteen years old.

The stepfather and mother both knew the sibling secret, and once the secret is out, the reason for the negative family behavior becomes clear. The oldest sibling in this family was weighted down with a "secret sibling handicap."

Sibling secrets are known to at least one family member and can be a shared secret with two or more people in the family. Charley is a thirty-one-year-old married man with two younger brothers. Charley has two daughters and he carries a secret sibling handicap. He didn't know that he was adopted until his four-year-old daughter, Alisa, was diagnosed with leukemia. In an extended family session with his daughter's oncologist, Charley's parents revealed that he is adopted and that Charley's brothers most likely would not be a blood match for his daughter's needed transplant.

Charley's top priority is finding a suitable donor match for his daughter, and that takes the vast majority of his time and energy. Exploring the revealed secret will come later.

Darlene, a thirty-one-year-old woman, lives with her husband and daughter in a small Midwestern town. Twenty-eight-year-old Douglas, an architect, has a younger sister, Wanda. Douglas and Wanda live in southern California near their parents, Sam and Diana. Darlene, Douglas, and Wanda are sisters and brother. None of the three of them know the sibling secret. When their mother, Diana, was fourteen, she became pregnant after her first sexual encounter with her boyfriend. Diana's parents were adamant that her child be given up for adoption. Fourteen-year-old Diana complied. Six months in a maternity home, one day in the hospital to give birth, and two additional days to complete the adoption process, and Diana was on her way back to her home in southern California.

Diana has grown up to be a successful professional, a loving wife, and the mother of two more children, Douglas and Wanda. Diana has shared her secret with her husband, Sam. Diana, Sam, Diana's now-deceased parents, and Darlene's adoptive parents share this sibling secret. Siblings Darlene, Douglas, and Wanda are unaware of the threesome of their secret sibling handicap. Not knowing the secret becomes a sibling handicap.

The truth will set you free! However, the truth can, at times, be very difficult to reveal. With the Fillmore family everyone knows that Larry has a different father from his sisters Louise and Linda; however, the subject of Larry's paternity is never open to discussion. This well-known sibling secret makes free and open family discourse difficult.

*What is the sibling secret in your family?*
*Who knows your family secret?*
*How does your family sibling secret cause a handicap?*

## Beyond the Sibling "Handicap"

A final note: All handicaps have an accompanying attitude. The attitude is either growth producing or growth inhibiting. I admire the families who take the challenge of viewing the sibling handicap as growth producing, and I am committed to assisting families in their move from sibling growth inhibiting to sibling growth producing.

# 7

*When Brothers and Sisters Fight*

## The Narrative of Warfare—"I Am Right; You Are Wrong"

What would your family be like if every sibling were a clone? There would be no differences in each sibling from the other, no separate individuals, no conflict, no fighting, no disagreement, no back talk, and one *big* boring sibling group. When you look in the mirror, is that you or your sibling? You think alike, you choose the same clothes, the same classes, the same friends, the same tastes, the same sights, the same smells, the same touches, and you see everything the same. Sounds dreary!

If you and your siblings are clones then this chapter would be one sentence long, and it would read, "We are right!" Fortunately you are not a clone, and your sisters and brothers are not either. This leaves you with the problem of differences, distinctions, variations, characteristics, dissimilarities, contrasts, clashes, brawls, diversions, and trouble. I had a fight with one of my siblings when I was twelve years old. I had fighting "afterburn." Lying in bed that night I decided that I would be perfect and not have any more fights. I would go along with each of them and I would not be a problem. I woke up at eight A.M. refreshed and ready to start my new perfect sibling life. I was successful until nine-thirty A.M. Neither my brothers nor my sister would cooperate and I returned to my old ways. I liked my fighting stance, and I retired my perfect sibling life to the Edsel/Thomas Dewey museum.

What is happening when siblings fight? It is not about fighting. It's about staking a position. The younger the siblings the less they are tied to their right position. Alone in their bedroom, four-year-old Scott and three-year-old Nathaniel fight over who will turn the radio knobs. They say angry words, give each other slight pushes, and agree to take turns.

Brother and sister fighting provides two benefits: (1) distance is created between each child and (2) each child receives strokes. As discussed in chapter 4, a sibling stroke is a unit of recognition, and these strokes come in four different forms:

(1) positive—"I still like you even when we fight,"

(2) Negative—"I don't like you and no one else in the family likes you,"

(3) Conditional—"I like you when you say you're sorry," and

(4) Unconditional positive—"I love you" or unconditional negative—"I hate you."

Some siblings are "stroke starved." Strokes are the psychological food of life. When the children's food is not plentiful, then sibling fighting may take place. Better to receive negative strokes from your sisters and brothers than to be ignored.

Three-year-old Jeannie knows how to provoke her nine-year-old brother, Daniel. She removes his Nintendo video game from his room and places it squarely on her bed. Daniel looks around for his game, presumes his sister took it, and the battle begins. Jeannie says indignantly that she doesn't know how the video got into her room. Daniel's face reddens, and he moves slightly toward Jeannie. He stops and calls her a liar. "Am not, am not, am not." Daniel makes a mental note of how to repay his sister at another time. He retrieves his video and stalks away.

Daniel and Jeannie have exchanged more than twenty strokes apiece, and both feel great. There is no stroke starvation here. Some minor afterburns remain, and then the afterburns disappear to the same place where the one missing sock resides. Neither child will ever retrieve the afterburns or the socks.

Most families have at least two and sometimes three or more generations in the same house: children, parents, and sometimes grandparents. The family usually makes clear distinctions between the child generation and the big people generations. The extent to which the big-people take care of themselves and of the children influences how siblings fight. Self nurturing parents who also nurture children create a stroke-rich family.

*What was the stroking pattern in your family?*

*How often did you pick a fight with your sister or brother to obtain strokes?*

*How often did they pick a fight with you to obtain strokes?*

## Fighting Is Natural

"She's looking at me." "He's looking at me."

Healthy sibling fighting requires rules. The big kids can't beat up on the little kids and the little kids can't provoke the big kids. Boxing has the Marquis of Queensberry rules: Go to your separate corners, no hitting below the belt, three-minute rounds, one minute between rounds, listen to the referee, and fight fair. No Marquis of Queensberry rules exist for sibling fighting.

Brother-and-sister fighting rules are based on:

(1) healthy parental instruction,
(2) unhealthy parental instruction,
(3) absence of parental instruction and sibling trial and error,
(4) winning fighting experiences, and
(5) losing fighting experiences.

Four-year-old Aaron and three-year-old Linda fight in their bedrooms, in the kitchen, in the living room, in the front yard, and in the backyard. Their mother, Inez, has one rule for these two fighting siblings: They must report to her how they made "friends" with each other after their fights. Aaron and Linda love telling their mother how they made friends. In addition to their normal fighting they also each pick fights in order to get their mom's recognition for their brilliance in making friends. Fifty-four-year-old Aaron continues looking for the path to making friends with his wife after their arguments. Winning the argument is secondary to making friends with his wife. Aaron learned this experience with his sister. Now Aaron fully understands that when he makes his wife wrong in their conflict he sacrifices closeness with her.

Parents who (1) give permission for healthy sibling fighting, (2) practice healthy marital fighting, (3) provide safety for healthy brother-and-sister fighting, and (4) develop their own Marquis of Queensberry rules are parents who practice what they preach. The siblings in this family develop an attitude of win-win, not an attitude of win-lose. No sister or brother likes to lose. The kids' win-win attitude assists in the removal of shame and assists in the benevolence of saving face. When your brother helps you to save face you owe a debt. When your sister doesn't rat on you to your parents you owe a debt. Siblings have to keep in mind their own level of integrity, and not sacrifice that even for a sister or brother.

I did slightly compromise my own integrity when I was thirteen years old and attending the same school as my sixteen-year-old brother. I saw him smoke a cigarette at the café across the street from our school. When we made eye contact, I walked out of the café. The truth was out! He was smoking and I was disappointed. Some days later our mother asked, "Does your brother smoke?" I looked at him and looked at her. Many thoughts went through my thirteen-year-old mind, but the words out of my thirteen-year-old mouth were, "No, he does not smoke." I was still in the brother loop and one foot into the fibbing to our mother. I survived and he later mustered the courage to tell our mother that he did smoke. She didn't confront my brotherly fib and I never brought it up.

My twelve-year-old daughter will sometimes commit a sibling fib to protect her eighteen-year-old brother. This requires a certain parental flexibility on my part not to allow too much or too little in the sibling fibbing business.

Brian's parents preach fair fighting to each of their four children. Yet they practice swearing, hitting, shouting, lying, and cheating on each other. They say, "Do as I say, not as I do." This high drama marital family system has a reverse effect on eleven-year-old Brian and his three sisters, ages nine, eight, and five. They have lived with this family drama for their entire lives. In their sibling generation they profit from their parents' mistakes. They have become the parents to their parents and sacrifice much of their childhood joy and happiness. The children are overresponsible to compensate for their parents' underresponsibility. Their sister-and-brother bond is strong because they survive together.

A recent television program featured a family with twin six-year-olds. The exasperated parents tired of the twins' fighting and concluded that they would allow the twins to literally slug it out. Arms, legs, and fists flew. Unfortunately or fortunately, the parents videotaped the fight. As it happens, the videotape became public and the parents had to answer to the authorities. These parents permitted the twins to physically harm each other, and the lesson taught by the parents and practiced by the children is to solve their problems with violence.

M. Scott Peck's book *People of the Lie,* recounts a story of parents who gave a rifle to their fifteen-year-old son for Christmas. That same rifle had been used previously by their nineteen-year-old son to commit suicide. Dr. Peck did his best to convince the parents of the implications of this gift. They were not convinced, and Dr. Peck found an alternate living arrangement for this fifteen-year-old. These parents were giving a message to their son that he could use the rifle as his brother did. Dr. Peck's book is about overt or covert family lying. These parents most likely were sending a covert message to their son.

Children are brilliant at figuring out parents. Siblings share with each other and, if need be, they will form a committee to protect their parents. They have a vested interest in keeping parents healthy and in preventing themselves from becoming orphans.

Back to sibling fighting. Absence of parental instruction frequently leads to a sister or brother practice of trial and error. Some parents don't care. They don't care because of alcohol, drugs, depression, desertion, their own deprivation, their own immaturity, or any reason that prevents their tracking their children. Children hunger for a healthy family structure that moves from chaos to calm. All siblings have conflict, and this conflict leads to fighting. Siblings teach each other, and their teaching may be positive or negative. However, young children do require ongoing parental supervision. When siblings borrow parental supervision their fighting can be fair and satisfying. The Burton siblings, Irene, John, and Barbara, have an absent father and an alcoholic mother. Their next-door neighbors, the Templetons, have five children, and the Burton siblings adopt their sibling fair-fight rules. The Burton children watch, listen, and learn, and like those of the Templetons, their fights are short and fair.

J. C. Bennet, in *Psychological Reports* (1990), addresses how nonintervention in sibling fighting becomes a catalyst for younger sisters and brothers to learn helplessness. Siblings know what is fair; however, the practice of sibling fairness can run aground when parents don't track their children. Fifteen-year-old Randy is a bully. He bullies his sister, Brenda, and his brother, Darryl. Randy physically hits, curses, and belittles his two siblings. They cower in his presence and have the bruises to reinforce their learned helplessness. No parent or parent figure intervenes on behalf of the younger children, and they learn how to *not* defend themselves, thereby learning the practice of helplessness.

Forty-five-year-old Randy is in prison for murdering his girlfriend, and his siblings, Brenda and Darryl, are on supplemental social security disability. Randy, the older brother "bully," continued being the same type of bully with his girlfriend as with his sister and brother. He escalated his rage and killed his girlfriend in a fight. Brenda and Darryl continued to experience themselves as helpless people who were not able to care for themselves.

## Winning Sibling Fighting Experiences

When children start fair fighting early in childhood then the outcome of disagreements is a win-win. They can walk in each other's shoes. This is sibling empathy. Twelve-year-old Bernice fights with her ten-year-old sister, Karen, anytime she wants. But when their twelve-year-old neighbor, Leonard, fights with Bernice, then Karen is on her sister's side. Sibling blood is thicker than friendship water. You and your sister can fight, hit, and be ugly to each other, but no one else can do it with either of you. Friends come and go; siblings remain forever. The winning sibling fighting experiences add one more strand to that cable. During the fight your brother is a schmuck and you are a schmuck, and when this fight is over your brother smiles to signal the end of this round.

## Losing Sibling Fighting Experiences

Cain killed Abel. The first killing in biblical history is a brother killing. Homicide is the extreme example of a losing sibling fighting experience. I have felt homicidal toward my sister and brothers at points in my life; luckily I did not act on my feelings. Remember when you had the same kind of feelings? What was your behavior?

Losing sibling fighting experiences may lead to a brother or sister cutoff. Lawrence disowned his sister, Chris, when he was unsuccessful in bringing her around to his way of thinking. He psychologically killed her, made her no longer exist, and refused to utter her name or allow anyone else in his family to say her name in his presence. Lawrence not only killed off his sister, he kills others who won't come around to his way of thinking. He is neither a happy brother nor a happy person. The front of his tombstone will read, *I was treated unfairly,* and the back of his tombstone will read, *I killed my sister and many other people.* Lawrence never learned how to fight fair with his sister to create a win-win attitude and practice.

*What were your healthy parental instructions in childhood fighting?*

*What were your unhealthy parental instructions in this fighting?*

*What were your trial-and-error experiences in sibling fighting?*

*What were your winning sister-and-brother fighting experiences?*

*What were your losing brother-and-sister fighting experiences?*

## Hurts

"She hurt my feelings." "He took my scooter."
Hurt is universal. Sibling hurt is unique in part because this relationship is the longest relationship (see chapter 9) most of us will ever have. This longest relationship gives us many opportunities to both inflict and receive sibling hurts. From the time we first snatch a sister's sandwich or have a sister grab our food, the hurting starts. Hurt is a part of the game of sibling life. We can be self righteous in inflicting brother and sister hurt, and we can be the target of their hurt aimed in our direction.

Keeping a sibling scorecard of hurts would prove how bad the others are, and if you want to make that point, then there is enough evidence to convince others of how badly your siblings have hurt you. Your sibling scorecard of hurts will have to be tossed out, however, when you look in the mirror and recognize your part in inflicting pain.

Three-year-old Conrad blames his older sisters for the broken catsup bottle. He cries, pouts, acts like a hurt jerk, and puffs up his chest in righteous indignation. His father sends his sisters to their room. They protest all the way down the hallway. Little prince Conrad has won an empty victory. He broke the bottle and his sisters paid the consequences. Conrad loses his three-year-old integrity and his sisters' kindness.

### False Sibling Hurts

These are a play for sympathy, most likely, aimed at parents. Five-year-old, Jennifer blames her brother, John, for what he said about her leaving his bicycle in the driveway. He hurt my feelings is the message conveyed to Jennifer's mother. Jennifer left out the part about leaving John's bicycle in the driveway. Her pouty, curled-up lip is a sign that something is amiss in this sibling drama. Jennifer's mother is a schoolteacher who points out to Jennifer the gift of personal responsibility. Jennifer is responsible for leaving her brother's bicycle in the driveway and she owes him an apology, and John is responsible for what he said and he owes her an apology. What John said to Jennifer was hurtful and what she did with his bicycle was hurtful.

## True Sibling Hurts

These may also be a play for sympathy or a simple request for redress of a grievance. Giving the death penalty for jaywalking is not a part of the penal code. Any legal or code violation has a minimum and a maximum penalty. In the sibling code, a small hurt could be a request for the perpetrator to be banished from the home. Eight-year-old Laura took her older sister Betty's favorite teddy bear to school. When the truth came out later in the day, Betty was indignant at this offense. Betty suggested to her mother that Laura be sent away to a foster home. The mother's cooler head prevailed. Laura was forced to return the teddy bear and write a note of apology to her sister.

Sibling apologies can be as difficult as extracting an impacted tooth. Twelve-year-old David says to his younger sister, Danielle, "Mom says I have to say I am sorry for taking your candy." He repeats his mother's words without taking responsibility. David's mother, an attorney, congratulates David on his skillful maneuver, and informs him that the apology must come from him. David's reconfigured apology is said with a smile and a tinge of humility: "Danielle, I am sorry for taking and eating all of your candy." Part of his penalty requires him to use his allowance to purchase candy for his sister. Sister Danielle is humble in accepting her brother's apology, and she later shares the candy with him. She knows that sometimes she is wrong and will also have to humbly apologize to him. This wise young girl understands that with her and her brother, what goes around, comes around.

*What are your leftover sibling hurts?*
*Which sibling hurts did you receive?*
*Which sibling hurts did you give?*
*Which of your hurts are you holding against your siblings?*
*Which of the hurts are being held against you?*

## Tools for Reconciliation—Removing the Judge and Jury

*Penitence, atonement, penance,* and *remorse* are words that can describe the pathway to sibling reconciliation. Reconciliation is waiting around the corner when the journey begins. Early in childhood, reconciliation is easy, quick, and always available. Young children are bright enough to know that to get along with each other, there is a give and take. As former speaker of the house Sam Rayburn was fond of saying, "To get along, you must go along." His words of wisdom helped keep him in the speaker's chair for nearly forty years. Siblings intuitively adopt a variation of his words of wisdom. They say, "I will show you mine if you will show me yours." What children show is their innate ability to let go of stuff.

Enter the judge and jury. The judge and jury may take the form of a parent, a teacher, a neighbor or anyone else who really knows what to do. If the siblings give in to the judge and jury system they then give up their native ability to solve their own differences.

Parents, teachers, and other big people who take the position of mediator with siblings should not take sibling sides. A mediator says to each child, "You are right" and "You are wrong." Young sisters and brothers get it. Each sibling then releases the case he or she has constructed against the other.

### Sibling Distance

The absence of sibling reconciliation is brother-and-sister distance. The distance may be physical or emotional.

### *Sibling Physical Distance*

Robert's answer when asked by a fellow student at his fortieth high school reunion, "What happened to your brother Donald?" is "I have not seen or talked with my brother for forty-two years." Both Donald and Robert live in the same moderately sized Midwestern town. The chasm was created when younger brother Donald asked Robert's former girlfriend, Carolyn, to the junior prom. Robert never forgave Donald, and he never told Donald what he had done to hurt his feelings. The truth is that Robert's feelings were hurt and Robert did not muster the courage nor take the risk to express his feelings. Donald also has responsibility for the brother-brother distance.

## Sibling Emotional Distance

Fifty-four-year-old Georgia and her younger brother, fifty-one-year-old Henry, worked together thirty-two years ago in Georgia's small department store. Back then, twenty-two-year old Georgia worked fourteen hours a day to make her business successful. Nineteen-year-old Henry enjoyed his fun and didn't like to work more than five hours per day. This sibling critical-mass point came when Henry did not appear for work on a spring day in 1967. When he returned the next day, Georgia laid into him for being irresponsible and immature. Henry's blood pressure increased, his face flushed, and he walked out of Georgia's store. Their sibling relationship was dealt a semifatal wound.

Georgia and Henry continued seeing each other at their family gatherings during the past thirty-two years. They barely acknowledge each other and usually sit far apart. Neither will speak of their problem even though their parents' fondest wish is for them to bury the hatchet.

In adult sibling sessions, the willingness of a brother or sister to participate is a strong strand in the fabric of their reconciliation. The unknown, unexpressed internal statement about siblings is crucial to reconciliation. Down deep inside of each person is the statement, and bringing the statement into the here and now will free the energy for reconciliation.

A healthy dose of humility is required to crank up the engine of sister and brother reconciliation.

*Who was the judge and jury in your early years?*
*Who is the judge and jury in your adult sibling years?*
*What unresolved hurt is standing in the way of your reconciliation?*
*What would you have to give up to forgive your brother or sister?*

*What would you have to give in order for him or her to forgive you?*

*Are you willing to be forgiven by your siblings?*

*What would your sister and brother relationship be after forgiveness?*

## Resentments—Holding on for Self-Righteous Dear Life

Resentments are a fly in the ointment of sibling relationships. From the beginning, genetic differences, gender differences, birth order differences, or behavior differences may become the source of that resentment. Whether resentments are known, unknown, or openly experienced and expressed, they are a source of tension. Sibling tension hangs around when resentments are not expressed in a healthy manner. My mother compared my younger sister's early school accomplishment to mine and I came out the winner. I received a genetic talent for being bright. My sister is a master's-level teacher and school administrator. My mother, although an extremely nurturing person, inadvertently caused a resentment.

Sibling resentments, whether known or unknown, may carry elements of anger, animosity, huff, spite, grudge, ill will, or maliciousness.

Forty-five-year-old Thomas was resentful of his younger brother, Kenneth. Kenneth was his mother's favorite, and from childhood on, Thomas was unable to get his mother's favor. This created a tension between Thomas and Kenneth that they wouldn't discuss. Their mutual resentments, Thomas for Kenneth's favored relationship with their mother and Kenneth's resentment that he was the object of Thomas's resentment, prevented these two brothers from being sibling friends. Each one's resentment was unknown to the other. Their resentments existed in the "let's not think or talk about that" world.

Known sister-and-brother resentments exist within each one's resentments and are either

(1) not expressed,
(2) expressed without forgiveness, or
(3) expressed with forgiveness.

Sibling resentments come from actions taken or actions not taken. A brother resentment from action taken is when twelve-year-old Brian steals his brother Rodney's girlfriend. Rodney does not express his resentment. A brother-and-sister resentment from action not taken is when twenty-seven-year-old James did not participate in an adult sibling session with his sister, Eunice, after he had agreed to the session.

Sibling expressed resentment without forgiveness leaves a wound that festers. A sister's expressed resentment with forgiveness heals the wound. Sixty-four-year-old Sheryl never forgave her sister, sixty-eight-year-old Brenda. Twenty-eight-year-old Brenda did not ask twenty-four-year-old Sheryl, to be maid of honor at Brenda's wedding. Sheryl's expressed resentment, without forgiveness, forced Sheryl to keep an emotional distance from her sister. Sheryl's forty-year-old unforgiven resentment leaves a big internal soreness and a big external self-righteousness. Sadly, Sheryl will most likely die with her sibling unforgiveness.

Hal and Leon worked together in their family business, and after their business was sold to an outsider, Hal was required by the new owner to fire Leon. Leon was bitter, disappointed, and resentful. Within two years, however, Leon tired of his unforgiven resentment and concluded that it wasn't worth it. During the last twenty-seven years of their relationship both of these brothers continued a strong relationship. Hal died at seventy-seven, and Leon was grateful for their years together.

*What are your known sibling resentments?*
*Which resentments are yours?*
*Which resentments are held against you?*
*How could your unknown sibling resentments become known?*
*Have your sibling resentments been expressed with forgiveness?*
*Have your sibling resentments been expressed without forgiveness?*

## Relationship—Positive or Negative— the Bond that Will Never Break

The opposite of sibling love is *not* sibling hate. Love and hate are on the same continuum. Continuum is a long line with love at one end and hate at the other end. Love and hate continue to be the connection. Sibling indifference would be the ability to wipe out all childhood history. Imagine being detached from all your activities from the time of your birth until you become eighteen years of age. Sibling activities create memories, and memories are the threads in the bond between these people.

Mary Gullekson's dissertation, "Am I My Brother's Keeper?," explores the topic of people with a mentally ill sibling. When a brother or sister has a mental illness, the sibling bond can be stretched to the point of exhaustion. This bond, however, has the elastic quality of being malleable, expansive, resilient, pliable, and flexible. The bond is never broken. The sibling bond can only be denied.

When the sibling bond contains more negative than positive energy, look to the parent generation. After an argument and a fistfight, forty-seven-year-old Ernie and his brother, forty-one-year-old Timothy, raced in separate cars to their parents' home to plead their case of being the righteous victim. Unfortunately, their parents played the psychological game of "Let's you and him fight." Their fighting provided a great deal of family drama. The drama was played out on a stage with the brothers as the actors and the parents as the audience. With the addition of alcohol addiction, the family drama is played out to death for fifty-seven-year-old Ernie in a single-car accident and an alcohol-related death for Timothy at age sixty-four.

When the sibling bond has more positive than negative energy it is usually the result of healthy rules set forth by the parents. Six-year-old Elizabeth and five-year-old Samantha plead the cookie case to their mother: "Sam ate more than I did." "Liz ate the most!" Their wise mother sends them both to the living room to negotiate a description of the cookie truth. Five minutes later, Liz admits she ate the most, and Sam defends Liz's actions based on the fact that Liz is older and can eat more. Their sibling bond becomes stronger.

The sibling bond is significant because the sibling relationship within the family is unique. These early years, prior to schooling, are when sisters and brothers share the most time together. Jalong and Renck (1985), in their review of childhood literature, suggest that the early influences of siblings will impact later relationship with others. When children begin school their bond changes.

Tisak and Tisak (1990) asked 126 children in grades two, four, and six about the parents' rights to prohibit outside friendships. They asked, "What should you do when your brother or sister defies your parents' order to stop being friends with someone?" Most said they would keep the sibling secret. This suggests an early loyalty bond within the same generation rather than between the parent and child generations. The sibling snitch is not a jacket worn well.

*Currently, do you view your sibling relationship as mostly positive?*

*Currently, do you view your sibling relationship as mostly negative?*

*How did you view your relationship in your childhood?*

*What has changed your view about your relationship in the present?*

*What makes your sibling relationship positive or negative?*

## Squabbling—Then and There and Here and Now

Describe your sibling squabbling back "then and there." Was it a disagreement, altercation, argument, battle, brawl, challenge, combat, discord, dispute, feud, fight, fracas, hassle, rift, scrap, scuffle, spat, tiff, or war?

Describe your sibling squabbling in the "here and now." Is it a disagreement, altercation, argument, battle, brawl, challenge, combat, discord, dispute, feud, fight, fracas, hassle, rift, scrap, scuffle, spat, tiff, or war?

Sibling squabbling is as common as Mother, apple pie, and television, and at the Todds', childhood squabbling came mainly in the form of loud arguments. Shouting was the fuel that fed the squabbles. We were loud and mildly pushy, and frequently went off in a huff to drain the squabble. My mother's frequent quote was, "You kids will be the death of me yet!" We never killed her and somehow she survived.

In the here and now, in middle age, we Todd siblings have developed a sophistication that makes squabbles into sibling disagreements and sibling disagreements into differences and sibling differences into acceptances. We have a shared sibling history for a long period of time and we are different. However, we are a sensitive lot, and over the years we have developed a sense of how not to set each other off and instead how to say the words with kindness.

First-degree squabbling involves words only.

Second-degree squabbling involves words and actions.

Third-degree squabbling involves actions only.

The degree of sibling squabbling ranges from 1.0 to 3.0. My own childhood sibling squabbling would most likely range from 1.9 to 2.1. When you check the range with my siblings they may slightly differ in their interpretations of the range of our squabbles. Even though my nine-year-old brother ran over me with a tractor, he did not have malice aforethought.

First-degree sibling squabbling was featured on television programs of the fifties, sixties, and seventies. *Ozzie and Harriet, Father Knows Best,* and *The Brady Bunch* were mild depictions of sibling squabbling. David and Ricky Nelson disagreed, but not too much. Kathy, Bud, and Princess listened to their father's wisdom on *Father Knows Best,* and the three sisters and three brothers in *The Brady Bunch* disagreed, but not much.

Larson (1989) studied sibling disagreement by analyzing the nature of sibling interaction on three prime-time family situation comedies. A total of 1,354 sibling interactions from shows taped during 1986–1987 indicated that there was more positive sibling interaction than negative. Most television sibling squabbling is talk only.

In reality, first-degree—talk only—sibling squabbling is more fantasy than fact.

Second-degree sibling squabbling falls in that large middle section of the bell-shaped curve: some heated words, some hitting, and some intense anger. Second-degree sibling squabbling may be hidden because the parents demand that the kids be nice to each other. In hidden sibling squabbling the fighting is underground. Six-year old Melanie hits her five-year-old brother, Zach, when no one is watching. Zach hides Melanie's Rollerblades in the garage. Both Melanie and Zach put on a happy face for Mom.

Open second-degree squabbling requires rules. You can shout at your brothers or sisters, but not too loud. You can hit them, but only softly and only in the safe spots, and you can use words with them, but not too many of the mean, nasty, rotten, or tasteless ones. When you cross the boundaries of fair squabbling with your siblings, then you are forced to offer the apology of, "I really did not mean what I said. I'm sorry."

Third-degree squabbling may result in bruised or broken skin and broken bones. Cain and Abel from the book of Genesis had a third-degree brother squabble. Abel's skin was broken and he died. Third-degree squabbling is a result of an extremely chaotic family system. Whether the chaos is above the surface and open or below the surface and closed, the chaos remains.

In Dennis Wholey's, *The Courage to Change*, Jerry Falwell re-counts the relationship between his father, a small-Southern-town bootlegger, and his father's younger brother. In a sibling dispute, Falwell's father shoots and kills his younger brother. Because Falwell's father was a "power" in the community, it did not bring charges. In the book and movie *The Godfather Part II*, younger brother Michael Corleone has his older brother Fredo Corleone killed when Fredo reveals internal family business to a non–family member.

Fortunately, third-degree sibling squabbling is a rarity.

Then-and-there childhood sibling squabbling many times is the precursor for here-and-now sibling squabbling, and most likely is a precursor for squabbling in other areas of life.

If you have sisters or brothers then you have sibling conflict. Seven-year-old Marguerite hits two-year-old Cheryl on the head with a ruler for two reasons: The first reason is that Cheryl had the audacity to bump Marguerite out of the youngest-sibling position in the family, and the second reason is that Cheryl took Margarite's coloring book. Marguerite hits Cheryl on the head behind her mother's back because Marguerite is a "nice girl." Marguerite has little or no awareness or understanding of Cheryl's birth-order bumping. The head hitting is in Marguerite's awareness.

Sibling conflicts create the opportunity for sibling negotiation. Helen, a wise and loving mother, allows eight-year-old Scotty to pour the remaining lemonade into two glasses, one for him and one for his younger brother, Philip. This wise mother tells Scotty that Philip gets the fullest glass. This gives Scotty an opportunity to learn sibling compromise. As it turns out, the glasses contain the same amount of lemonade. Scotty has moved through the stages of sibling conflict, negotiation, and compromise, and finally to sibling resolution.

Sibling conflict resolution leads to closeness. The tools of conflict resolution in the then and there frequently lead to sibling conflict resolution in the here and now.

> *What was your degree of squabbling in the then and there?*
> *What is your degree of squabbling in the here and now?*
> *What were tools for resolving your squabbling in the then and there?*
> *What are tools for resolving your squabbling in the here and now?*
> *What are your leftover squabbles from the then and there?*
> *Do you want to resolve your squabbles from the then and there?*
> *Do you want to resolve your squabbles from the here and now?*

## Closeness and Distance—"I Thought You Didn't Care"

Ask yourself this question: "Would my siblings take part in an adult sibling session with me if I asked?" Now reverse the question: "Would I participate in an adult sibling session with them if they asked?" When I ask the first question, the frequent answer is, "No, they would not attend an adult sibling session." When I ask the second question, nearly everyone answers "Yes, I would." The perception of siblings' closeness appears to be much stronger in how a person feels about sisters and brothers than how that same person views how a sibling feels about him or her.

Sibling closeness and distance are determined by the amount of time siblings do things together. My California grandmother, Evie Landress Todd, was a lady of Southern grace and humor who stayed in contact with her siblings in Texas through her eloquent letter writing. She wrote to them regularly from the time she left her home state of Texas in the 1930s until her death in the 1970s. As long as one of her nine surviving siblings was living, my grandmother kept in contact. On one special occasion, her two sisters, Hattie and Florence, both in their sixties, visited Grandmother in California. My grandmother was also a twin, but unfortunately her twin sister, Effie, died at nine years of age. My grandmother prized her one picture of Effie.

My maternal grandfather, William Moody, was born in far northeastern California. Shortly after my grandfather's birth his mother died, and he lived with his father. His father later remarried and had another son. Then my grandfather and his brother were sent to live with different families. They never had contact again, and to my grandfather, his brother was only a distant memory.

My grandfather was short, quiet, bald, and fun-loving. He liked to say that we grandchildren were sticks in the mud. I didn't know what that meant, but I knew he enjoyed saying the words. Unfortunately, when my grandfather was seventy years old and on his ten-block walk downtown to join his friends, he stepped out from behind a parked car and was hit and killed by a passing car. The tragedy was further complicated because the driver of the car was a longtime neighbor.

My grandfather's brother came to town after reading about the death of his brother. I was fourteen years old, and as I walked into grandmother's house to meet my great-uncle, I was struck by his strong resemblance to my grandfather. At that moment I experienced déjà vu. He was short, bald, and had a humorous twinkle in his eye. Without knowing it these two brothers had lived within three hundred miles of each other for years.

Sibling closeness and distance wax and wane over the years.

The sibling waxing is fueled by participation, and waning is fueled by sibling nonparticipation. The sibling bond remains forever.

*How close did you feel to your siblings when you were a child?*
*How close do you feel to your siblings now that you are an adult?*
*How distant did you feel from them when you were a child?*
*How distant do you feel from them now that you are an adult?*
*What was the level of your participation with your sisters and brothers in childhood?*
*What is the level of participation with your sisters and brothers now that you are an adult?*

## Forgiveness—"Maybe He/She Is Not So Evil After All"

You squabbled, you fought, you disagreed, you hit, you said bad words to your siblings, and they, in turn, fought back. The sibling distance created by conflict and squabbling is sometimes emotional and sometimes physical. The siblings rubber band can be stretched to great lengths and always returns. Sibling forgiveness, after the conflict and squabbling, eases the distance and moves them to you and you to them, and the sibling band is back to its resting place.

Forgiveness can repair the wound that has created extreme sibling distance and nurture the seed of sibling closeness.

*What is the conflict you are holding toward your sisters or brothers?*
*What is the conflict that they are holding toward you?*
*What is required of you to forgive them?*
*What is required of them to forgive you?*

# 8

*Siblings Working Together*

## Permission

You do not have permission to pick your siblings. As children you have permission to fight with your brothers and sisters, you have permission to include your brothers and sisters in your activities, you have permission to exclude your brothers and sisters from your activities, you have permission to love them or hate them, and they will remain your siblings. Your parents probably told you that hate is not nice, and yet if you are honest, the permission to hate your siblings runs through your insides. Childhood sibling hate is short-lived. Every moment of your life as a child helps create a brother-and-sister history. You have permission to participate with them by virtue of living under the same roof, and yet you have little awareness of the impact the developing lifelong siblings' history will have.

My brothers and sister were not a part of my childhood; they *were* my childhood. We were—and are—separate individual human beings. However, sometimes I experienced my brothers and sister as being a part of my own being. The extent to which I am a separate human being from all five of my siblings is guided by a permission to experience myself. The paradox is that the more permission we have to be separate, the greater the likelihood that we will be close.

As children, we reluctantly worked together in cleaning the

kitchen, cleaning the living room, cleaning our bedrooms, and working in the yard. Our work together was based on a permission given by our parents to work together. As adults, we do not work together in our career fields. My siblings and I took significantly different career pathways. My oldest brother works as a diesel mechanic, my next brother is in the retail merchandising business, I am in the human behavior field, my sister is a teacher, my other brother works in the postal service, and my youngest brother is also in retail merchandising.

During the past fifteen years, my brothers and sister and I worked together for the care of our elderly mother, who had Alzheimer's disease. Most recently, after our mother's death at age eighty-four, we worked together to arrange for the funeral services.

As sister and brothers we have worked together at various times in our lives, but our work together has never been career work. I love them and yet I know that I would not be able to work in a career field with them. I believe they would say the same about me.

Permission for brothers and sisters to work together comes in two forms. The first form of permission is internal permission and the second is external. Internal permission means that you have an agreement with yourself to engage in work with your sibling. External permission means that someone, your sibling or someone else, gives you permission to work with them. When the external permission is stronger than the internal permission then sibling dissatisfaction results. When internal permission is stronger than the external permission then sibling dissatisfaction results. When internal and external permission are a match, that results in high sibling satisfaction.

Imagine that these kids who shared your bedroom, shared your kitchen, your living room, your bathroom, your childhood, and your parents, are now the people who share your workplace. Sisters and brothers in the workplace share a past from their childhood, share a present from adulthood, and most likely share a future in their work together.

*Did you choose to work with your sisters and brothers or was the choice made for you?*

Forty-one years ago their father gave permission for sixty-year-old Malcolm and his fifty-nine-year-old brother, Maynard, to work together in their father's furniture store. From the time the brothers were eighteen and nineteen years of age, their father insisted they work in the family furniture store. At the time they joined the store, the family furniture business started by their father was twelve years old. The two brothers were reluctant to work together. Then their father died fifteen years ago and willed the store to them.

Since their father's death, they have continued the family furniture business with Malcolm as president and Maynard as the chief financial officer. They have a forty-one-year sibling working relationship, and the ghost of their father continues to keep them in a career that they both resent. Neither Malcolm nor Maynard discusses his resentment, as that would be disloyal to their father. The external permission given by their father overran the brothers' internal permissions to have different careers. Malcolm and Maynard have purposely steered their children away from the furniture store.

Early in his life Malcolm wanted to be a civil engineer. He applied and was accepted into the University of Maine. His younger brother, Maynard, dreamed of becoming a professional musician and planned to attend the Julliard School of Music. Both brothers agreed with their father's external permission for Malcolm and Maynard to work, learn, and eventually own the family furniture store. They allowed their professional dreams to go the way of what might have been.

As if to live out his unmet career dream, Malcolm's older son, Hiram, became an architect, and Malcolm's younger son, Willard, became a civil engineer. The unmet professional dreams of parents may be reincarnated by their children.

Maynard's daughter, Alisa, is a radio disc jockey, and Maynard's son, Leon, has become a band manager. Did these four adult children, Hiram, Willard, Alisa, and Leon, give themselves internal permission to choose their careers, or were they influenced by the external permission of their fathers?

Malcolm and Maynard never spoke openly of their professional dreams. They are financially successful, have an ongoing, mild irritation with each other, and rarely spend time together away from their business. The ghost of their father is the bond that binds these two together. Their own sibling bond has been stretched out of vitality. Because Malcolm and Maynard did not fully and successfully express their internal permissions, they were condemned to unsatisfactory careers.

Siblings who work together in an established business have to ask the question, Who are they serving? Are they choosing to work together to please themselves or to please someone else? Malcolm and Maynard worked together to please their father.

When siblings enter an established work environment:

(1) The brothers and sisters must be able to distinguish their sibling relationship prior to the business.

(2) The sisters and brothers must now be able to distinguish how their sibling relationship will function within the established business. Sibling personal boundaries and sibling working boundaries require knowing the behavior allowed in each setting. At the family picnic they may not be allowed to talk business, and siblings who work together may not be allowed to talk about their personal lives at work.

Forty-five-year-old Iris is married, plump, and well-groomed. Her smile radiates her personality, as do her colorful words. She is firm in her independent decision making, has a ready wit, and is quick with stories that put others at ease.

Iris's forty-three-year-old brother, Kenneth, is married and the father of two. He is frumpy, bald, intelligent, and a dependent follower who always listens to Iris's words of counsel. Kenneth's wife, June, is a firstborn like Iris. June provides leadership for Kenneth on the home front. Kenneth is also as much a follower with June at home as he is at work with Iris.

As children, Iris was the leader and Kenneth was the follower. In their early adulthood, after college, they both worked together in their family produce business. Iris made the decision to do this, so Kenneth quickly followed suit. They are the third generation in the family business. Their three cousins, Leonard, Carl, and Diane, and their uncles, Leo and David, also work there. Iris is a college graduate with a master's degree in business administration, and

Kenneth is a college graduate with a degree in marketing. Both Iris and Kenneth chose to work together. In this family business, the boundaries and responsibilities are well-defined and well supported. Iris is the comptroller and Kenneth is the marketing manager. Conflicts between Iris and Kenneth are quickly resolved because they have developed a win-win philosophy. Iris has always treated Kenneth in a maternal way, and Kenneth trusts that she is interested in his well-being. They look toward fair business negotiations and agree on compromises and satisfying resolutions that lead to a sense of closeness. They employ a management negotiator when their business conflict becomes stuck. The management consultant enables Iris and Kenneth to get unstuck from their business impasse.

Apart from work, Iris and Kenneth do not discuss business. They talk about spouses, kids, vacations, and any other nonbusiness subjects of their choosing. Iris and Kenneth employ the same win-win philosophy when personal sibling conflicts arise.

Iris and Kenneth have expressed internal as well as an external permission to work together.

Their relationship will change the business somewhat, and the business will change their relationship somewhat.

## Safety

Siblings who work together require safety that comes about because of their shared reliability, trust, history, and a willingness to protect each other. This is a mutual protection society that protects each sibling at work and away from work.

Tommy and Dick Smothers are well-known sibling entertainers who have brought music and laughter to us for more than thirty years. One of their comedy lines is, "Mom always liked you best!" It gets us to laugh. The energy flow between these two brothers onstage and on the screen is pleasant to watch and entertaining to experience. They let us in on their sibling relationship onstage. Offstage their personal sibling life is their own business. Each of the Smothers brothers has individual businesses apart from his onstage and on-screen business.

Tommy and Dick provide safety for each other with their acceptance of each other's differences. While much of their act is their sibling shtick, they display a sense of pushing each other to acceptable limits. They never get too mean.

The Marx brothers, Groucho, Harpo, Zeppo, and Chico, provided zany entertainment in their many movies. Their movies continue to be classics in their use of humor and seduction. They pushed the boundaries of behavior and made the audiences laugh. The Marx brothers also had success apart from their work together. Groucho had a very popular television program, *You Bet Your Life,* as a single performer. None of his brothers appeared on the program with him.

The Magliozzi brothers have a weekly call-in radio program entitled "Car Talk," broadcast on National Public Radio. They invite callers to ask the brothers any questions about cars. These brothers combine a superb knowledge of cars with a hilarious brand of humor. The well-educated Magliozzi brothers can laugh at themselves and each other and can laugh with the callers while simultaneously giving out information about cars. The chemistry between the brothers is refreshing to the listener, and the brothers seem to be enjoying their work together.

Forty-two-year-old Phillip and thirty-nine-year-old Raoul are family-practice physicians who share a combined medical practice. They frequently work out together at the gym during their lunch hour. Both are excellent physicians, good husbands, beneficial fathers, grateful sons, friendly neighbors, responsible citizens, and otherwise ordinary human beings. Their sibling bond enhances their work space and benefits their patients. Phillip and Raoul created their own sibling business relationship out of a desire to be physicians *and* to be brothers working together in their professional lives.

Phillip and Raoul's sibling safety is guided by:

(1) their individual professional goals,
(2) their combined professional goals,
(3) their trust in the reliability of each other,
(4) their ongoing discussion about conflict,
(5) their willingness to employ a win-win strategy when conflict occurs,

(6) their willingness to forgive and move on when feelings are wounded.

Phillip and Raoul's sibling safety exists within each of them and exists between each of them. Their sibling safety permeates their medical office and provides a family-friendly atmosphere.

Even though at various times in my father's life he worked with his three younger brothers in the businesses of house moving, truck and tractor parts, and recycling of secondhand materials, they did *not* have sibling safety. Their sibling relationships were fraught with:

(1) unresolved conflict,
(2) verbal fighting,
(3) physical fighting,
(4) alcoholism.

My father could provide business leadership, but he and his brothers were not able to create a safe sibling working structure. Their joint sibling business ventures were short-lived and had an afterburn of bitterness and resentment. To say the least, they were not successful working in the same business.

The chemistry of siblings in successful businesses is one based on a growth model. The growth is for the business. A sibling growth model requires safety. Without safety growth does not occur. The planted seeds must be protected from elements of the weather—heat, cold, moisture, and too little moisture—and be given the right combination of plant food.

## Strength

Strength is a requirement for a successful sibling business. In the movie *The Godfather,* brother Fredo did not possess the strength to be in the family business. He was a passive man who never fully understood the rigors of the mafia business. As much as a chain is only as strong as its frailest link, then a sibling business is only as strong as its frailest sibling.

Strength in business is based on four conditions.

## Ability of the Frailest Sibling to Be Compensated by the Strength of the Others

In the 1970s Karen and Richard Carpenter were a very popular sister-and-brother singing duo. They had many popular songs that were million-copy sellers. Unfortunately, Karen Carpenter battled with bulimia and, ultimately, the condition took her life. Richard Carpenter was devastated over the loss of his sister, and her death ended their very successful duo career. Richard has never able to compensate for the loss of his sister.

Initially the Pointer Sisters, a well known singing group, sang together until one of the sisters opted out. The three remaining sisters continued to sing as a group. The absence of one sister did not stop this strong sibling group from achieving success. The Pointer Sisters sibling compensation was successful.

## The Strength of the Sibling Relationship Is Greater than the Sum of its Parts

All siblings who enter or start a business must:
a. share a history of growing up together,
b. understand each other's strengths and weaknesses,
c. have an effective means of communication,
d. share a common loyalty to each other and their business,
e. have business and professional talents to support the business,
f. share common business goals.

The combination of these six conditions lend themselves to success in the business.

## The Business Was Created Prior to the Siblings' Entrance

Louise and Richard finished college, and after much soul searching both agreed to work in their father's automotive business. Louise possesses the strong business mind of her father. She is decisive, bright, articulate, and loves the business spotlight. She does commercials for the business, is the general manager, and has assisted her father in his semiretirement. Richard is an offstage, loyal, and effective younger brother complementing Louise's flamboyance.

Louise and Richard continue their father's strength in this very successful automotive business, and their sibling participation in the business adds to the ongoing success of the business.

## The Business Will or Will Not Continue after the Siblings Are Gone

No one can substitute for the Marx brothers, no one can substitute for the Smothers brothers, and no one can substitute for Karen Carpenter. These sibling businesses expire when one of the participating siblings leaves. Any attempt to continue these sibling businesses would fail. These businesses are unique and are based on the talents of the siblings.

Warner Brothers movie studio is one of the most successful businesses in the Hollywood world. The brothers started their business in the early days of the movie entertainment era. The brothers, of course, are long gone, and yet their business continues to this day. It has outlasted the brothers because of the strength created by them and has continued with effective management after the Warner brothers died.

Permission, safety, and strength are the conditions required in a successful sibling business.

*How did you and your sibling receive permission to enter business together?*

*What safety did you and they require to be in business together?*

*What strengths did you and they bring to your business?*

## Leadership

Whether we like to admit it or not, some lead and some follow. The king has his court, the queen has her court, the president has his cabinet, the chief executive officer has his staff, and the godfather has his capos. Leadership can be dictatorial, democratic, autocratic, or any number or variations. Leadership is required to run the business, and how the leadership develops may vary with the sibling combination.

Frequently, sibling leadership in business is based on primogeniture (firstborn). The firstborn child in the royal family becomes king or queen. The firstborn (see chapter 1) through an accident of birth is given a senior position from the start. The senior position most likely will remain in effect throughout the sibling-created business. This is an old familiar history of leaders and followers.

A second possibility of sibling leadership is a third-born. At times the second-born is skipped over due to a desire to stay in the second position. Twenty-seven-year-old Sybil successfully writes books on gardening. Her three best-selling books created a cottage industry, allowing her to hire her older brother, Darryl, and older sister, Louise, to manage the business. She is the entrepreneur and they are the managers. As Harvey Mackay writes in his best-selling book *Swim with the Sharks without Being Eaten Alive*, don't have entrepreneurs managing and don't have managers entrepeneuring.

Sibling business leadership does not have to be based on senior or junior birth order. The sibling business may have to be managed by an outsider if the siblings do not possess the skills of successful business leadership. Such is the case with the three Thompson brothers, forty-seven-year-old Michael, forty-five-year-old John, and forty-three-year-old Garth. They are wealthy farmers who love to farm. They don't have a clue about managing money, ordering seeds, ordering crops, buying farm equipment, or investing their money over time. But they know how to farm. Twenty-three years ago, the Thompson brothers hired Michael's best friend from high school, Joseph McClarty, to manage their farm business. Joseph is a hotshot with money and organization skills, and knows how to create successful working structures. This is a Thompson sibling business and a Joseph McClarty success structure.

The leadership in a sibling business either comes from the siblings or from someone out of the sibling loop. The leadership in a sibling business may come through trial and error, by sibling selection, or be an accepted dynamic at the start of the business—by acclamation and without protest, one of the siblings has the talent and desire to lead.

Thirty-nine-year-old Calvin Lobus and his thirty-three-year-old brother, Louis Lobus, are attorneys with a small practice. Calvin specializes in bankruptcies and civil litigation. Louis specializes in patent law and entertainment contracts. They are successful in their practice and neither one wants to assume leadership. The leadership has fallen to their paralegal, office manager, party organizer, and all around Girl Friday, Nancy. She tells them when to and when not to. She doesn't take any guff from either of the Lobus brothers. She is the boss and there is no doubt in her military mind who is in charge. The sign on the office door reads, *Lobus and Lobus, Attorneys at Law,* and in the very, very small, almost unreadable print below their names, it reads, *Run by General Nancy.*

The most responsible person in the kingdom is the king, the most responsible person in the queendom is the queen, the most responsible person in the presidency is the president, the most responsible person in the company is the CEO, and the most responsible person in the mafia is the godfather.

Sibling leadership requires a most responsible person to bind the sibling business relationship.

*Who is the leader in your sibling business?*
*Is the leader at the front of the business or is she or he leader in name only?*


## Siblings in, Siblings out

Ernest and Julio Gallo are the only brothers in their wine-making business.

The Kennedy brothers, John, Robert, and Edward were in the business of politics. The Kennedy sisters in this same generation were supporters of their brothers.

Brothers and sisters are either included or excluded in a sibling business. When they are included, how was the decision for this sibling inclusion made? When a sibling is excluded, how and who made the decision?

The siblings included in businesses have jumped through the hoops of:
(1) same professional training,
(2) same business training,
(3) same family business, or
(4) a mutual desire to work with one another.

The Andersons—Allison, age thirty-eight, Howard, age thirty-three, and Neal, age thirty-one—are all physicians who practice medicine in a medium-size Midwestern city. Louise, the Anderson siblings' office manager, is the mother hen who admires, protects, manages, and sets them straight when they stray. Their straying may include petty or major conflicts. Louise requires that the Anderson kids fight fair with one another and enter the arena of a win-win-win conflict resolution.

Candy, age thirty-three, is the office manager for her dentist sister, Elaine, and their dentist father, Harvey. This long-term sibling and family practice provides a comfortable office atmosphere that lends itself to happy, smiling patients.

Twins Craig and Carl are certified public accountants who attended the same schools—elementary, middle, and high school, as well as college and graduate schools. They never considered not working with each other. Their wives quickly learned that when one of the twins complained about the other, the wives could not take sides. The twins had a style of complaining about each other to their wives that was only a debriefing. The twins did not want a change. They enjoy their successful sibling business and their successful and mutually supportive relationship.

Siblings who continue working together in the family business may not consider leaving unless

(1) they become dissatisfied with their role in the business,
(2) their role in the family business is in name only, or
(3) their role in the family business becomes extinct.

Such is the case with Michael. His management style, in his family and sibling business of retail marketing, no longer reaches the successful levels of corporate management. In a corporation board of directors meeting, Michael was booted upstairs to oversee the family corporation endowment funds. He was put out to pasture while his two brothers and sister remained in their corporate management positions. This created a tense relationship between Michael and his siblings. He is still their brother, but knows that he is out. In a fit of anger Michael resigned his position with the family business, took his stock and other investments, and now refuses to speak to the other family members.

Michael left his home on the West Coast and moved his wife and children to Florida. The geographical distance does not create the emotional distance he wants. He hurts and he knows he hurts. His hurt begins to heal, however, when his three siblings fly out to visit him in Florida. They talk and he listens, and he talks and they listen. The sibling cutoff fades and the positive sibling bond begins to reappear. Michael knows that he is out with his siblings in their retail marketing business and he also knows that he continues with them in their sibling relationship. Very little in their conversation will address the sibling retail marketing business. Sibling forgiveness can move the sibling bond from a theme of negative to a theme of positive.

Brothers Thomas and Randall inherited over $2 million from the estate of their uncle Harrison. Thomas and Randall pooled their inheritance and invested in a trucking transportation business. From the time that their sibling business venture started these brothers fought. They fought about money, time, planning, investments, and management styles. Their ongoing business conflict ended with a gunshot. Randall in a rage ended his brothers' life. In a subsequent trial, the attorneys portrayed Thomas as the "aggressor" sibling and Randall as the "passive" sibling. The jury sided with Randall and found him guilty of sibling involuntary manslaughter. Within three years, Randall was free on parole.

The question is, Who was the judge and jury when siblings Thomas and Randall were children?

Most people who leave a sibling business leave on less dramatic terms than homicide. Leaving a sibling business may cause some lasting hurt feelings that most likely will take years to heal. The closer the sibling business the deeper the hurt and pain from leaving.

Were you an "in" sibling in the business or were you an "out" sibling in the business? What determined your "in" or your "out" status? If "out" is voluntary then most likely little or no hurt is involved. If "out" is involuntary then most likely you have hurt and resentment. Hurt and resentment can lead to a sibling cutoff. You can be out of the business, but you cannot divorce your siblings. You can divorce your spouse, but the relationship with your siblings is long-standing and forever.

## Work

Alan's parents gave five-year-old Alan the job of protecting his three-year-old brother, Gerald. The parents encouraged the sibling protection "job," and Alan and Gerald accepted the idea. Gerald felt the presence and protection offered by his older brother. These two brothers, from a close-knit, ethnic eastern European family, remained close throughout their childhood, adolescence, and adult life. They both attended college and both majored in financial management. They each married, had children, and continued to live within close proximity of each other.

Now forty-five-year-old Alan owns a small investment company, and fifteen years ago Alan invited his brother, Gerald, to join the company. During the past fifteen years they have had a successful sibling business relationship. Gerald attributes much of their success to his trust of Alan. From childhood, Gerald has trusted Alan's counsel and leadership. "Alan looks out for me" is Gerald's statement of how he feels about the strength of their sibling bond.

Within the structure of their business, Alan has successfully structured a division of labor that is acceptable to both of them. Alan is the leader and Gerald is happy following his brother's direction. As you enter their office, you feel the warm, friendly family atmosphere. Their five staff members, in addition to the brothers, greet each person by name. Alan also has a knack for remembering the small things about clients.

Away from work and at a family gathering, Alan and Gerald are gently chastised by their mother when they begin business talk. Alan and Gerald have a younger sister, a veterinarian, who does not work in their business or in their career field.

The atmosphere in a sibling business will be defined by the strength or weakness of the sibling relationship.

Areas of sibling strength are:

1. a mutual desire to work together,
2. talents that are utilized in a spirit of cooperation,
3. acceptance of a leader who will support the sibling relationship,
4. a clear plan for the care and feeding of the business,
5. an ongoing structure that leads from conflict to mutual resolution,
6. a winning attitude of each sibling about life and the sibling business,
7. suitable personality development of each sibling,
8. a willingness to support the business above individual ideas,
9. a willingness to work in an interdependent role.

Areas of sibling weaknesses are:

1. working together to please someone else,
2. ongoing and unresolved conflict,
3. collected hurts and resentments,
4. lack of mutually interdependent talents,
5. a contaminated communication system,
6. blame and character defects,
7. substance abuse,
8. the lack of awareness about individual desires.

Ask yourself if you and your sibling have more strengths than weaknesses. The joy of siblings working together is threefold: (1) familiarity, (2) desire, and (3) mutual and interdependent talents. The agony of siblings working together is threefold: (1) familiarity is not translated to the workplace, (2) there is a clear lack of sibling desire to work together, and (3) there is a lack of mutual and interdependent sibling talents. You do not have to work with them; however, if you and they make the choice, be prepared to honor your sibling relationship at work as well as away from work.

# 9

## *The Longest Relationship*

We're all familiar with this scene: The talk-show host introduces the guest, Rachel, a middle-aged woman with slightly graying hair. In a halting voice she tells her story: Her father died shortly after she was born. Her mother simply couldn't support the family of four children. Her mother tried. She took a job as a waitress, but they couldn't live on what she made. They often missed a meal or two every week, and the family fell behind in the rent.

Finally the mother gave up. Two of the children went to live with relatives, the oldest boy went to a friend, and she, the youngest girl, stayed with her mother. In the beginning they kept in touch. Then over the years they lost track of each other. When Rachel was eighteen her mother died and she was on her own.

Rachel went to college for a while, then married an engineer she met at school and raised two children. Despite the fact that she now has a good life, she couldn't forget that she had two sisters and a brother out there—somewhere. It nagged at her until she started making inquiries. She found the relatives who had taken one of her sisters, but they hadn't heard from her for years. She couldn't find the other sister, and she had no idea how to start looking for her brother.

On her thirty-fifth birthday she hired a local private detective— still no luck. That was when she responded to an appeal from one of the television talk shows for brothers or sisters looking for lost relatives.

Here she was on the show. She still had no idea whether they had found anyone or not. She listened as the host told the story of her search. Her heart stuck in her throat as the host said they had found her brother.

Her brother! She was going to see her brother! There he was— a tall, stooped-shouldered man with graying hair. He was wonderful.

Then they were hugging, tears pouring down her cheeks. Her brother—at last she had found her brother. After that they spent the weekend catching up, and over the next year they found the other two sisters. Now they stay in constant contact.

Over the years all of us have seen this scene repeated dozens of times. Detective agencies can tell you that finding lost relatives is often a good part of their business.

Why?

Because the sibling relationship that begins at birth and ends at death is frequently the longest and sometimes the most complicated of all relationships. And even when they don't have contact for long periods of time, the ties between brothers and sisters are strong. In short, there is simply nothing like it.

## Natural Bonding

The bonding between siblings occurs naturally. When children are close in age they face everything together and share the experiences. When a child starts school it's a lot easier if he or she has an older sibling to rely on. A brother who stands up for a younger sister or brother and helps when other kids tease her or him creates a strong bond.

In one case there were three children in the family, two boys, twelve and fourteen, and a younger brother, nine. The younger brother had classes after school every day, which required him to come home in a special bus. Unfortunately one of the older boys and his friends kept harassing the younger child, throwing his lunch box off the bus, or taking his hat and mittens and playing keep-away with them. Almost every day for a week, the younger boy came home in tears.

The second week, the two older boys met the bus at the tormentors' stop, grabbed them and left them bound and tied to a telephone pole. They were severely reprimanded, both by the school and by the parents, but the bullies never bothered the younger brother again. We often see this kind of bonding among siblings. Another example we are all familiar with is the older brother who worries about his younger sister dating someone the brother doesn't approve of.

This participation during childhood and adolescence creates a strong bond. In many cases the more participation with each other, the greater the bond. We all know of siblings who fight constantly. An outsider might say that the children hate each other. But let the outsider interfere and they will defend each other vigorously.

In another case, a family of three boys and two girls played on the same softball team. In the summer two of the boys went to camp together; so did the two girls. The girls often shared secrets with each other. They complained about the younger brother spying on them and often got mad at the older boys for teasing them. Sometimes the fights got furious, but so did the friendship and the love. In the end they became confidants and good buddies. As they found out, there is excitement in belonging. Often actions speak louder than words, and participation within a family creates a bond that is hard to break.

As the children grow up and leave home this early bonding creates a long-term fallback relationship that often lasts until death. In reality even though families may lose track of one another and decide not to participate, siblings in the long run cannot divorce each other. No matter what happens, they still have brothers and sisters out there until they die.

## Parental Interference

When we were born, our parents were already adults and became our teachers, our guides, and our protectors. Remember how your parents read your favorite book to you every night? When

178 ～ LINKED FOR LIFE

you learned to ride a bike, they ran alongside to make sure you didn't fall, and whenever you got hurt, Mom was usually there to kiss the hurt and make it better.

All of this attention helps internalize the relationship both verbally and nonverbally, creating an emotional and physical bond between parents and child. When parents give training in conflict resolution, then the siblings become very good at working out their differences and learn to resolve conflicts in a healthy way.

The Chorlings, a family of eight, encouraged the children to solve their own problems rather than running to one parent or the other. In the beginning, when there was a dispute the mother sat down and had the children explain their points of view. Then they were asked to give their solutions. Four-year-old Cindy suggested that she and her brother Nathan take turns on the rocking horse. Whenever they couldn't agree the one who was riding had to give it to the other.

If the parents do too much or too little, it creates problems between the siblings. When there is negative bonding you can usually look to the parent as the source of the problem.

For instance, sometimes the parents will dote on one child, or give that child special privileges because of his or her health.

I had one female client who almost died at birth, causing her parents to insist that the others give her special care and consideration. The other children had to do the vacuuming and fill the dishwasher. If they didn't get their jobs done they were punished. The parents insisted the youngest daughter was too fragile to do any of that. The sister got into the habit of grabbing the toys from the other children. When they grabbed back, she screamed her head off and the parents came to the rescue. Often when the other children had plans they had to cancel them to take care of their sick sister. This caused them, in later life, to essentially cut her out of their lives.

Other times the parents are busy and just treat the children differently, especially if there is an age gap. If the brothers and sisters are close in age, the bond will be strong, either positively or negatively. When there is an age difference of more than seven years, with no brothers or sisters in between, the bond loses strength.

I have, as clients, two brothers, forty-five and fifty-five, with a ten-year difference in age. Because of the age gap, these brothers had a significantly different childhood. John, the older brother, received a great deal of attention from his parents, who read to him every night. When he started school he did well. He also participated in activities such as the space club, scouts, school district writing contests, etc. When John was ten, his brother Bill was born. Bill was a surprise to his parents, who were now extremely busy and had little time to give him extra attention. In school, instead of excelling as his brother had, he did just enough work to get by. Outside of school he spent most of his time in his room watching television. He was especially tired of teachers who kept comparing him to his brother. As Bill grew up there was little interaction between the two brothers, and as a consequence only minimum bonding. As adults they had very little contact with each other. I find this to be true of almost all siblings with this large an age difference. They have characteristics more like those of only children than those of younger brothers or sisters.

In this case, when John and Bill's parents died, and their children grew up and left home, these brothers turned back to each other. They are now reexperiencing the memories that they once shared, to the exclusion of everyone else. Once these brothers came back together and began living an active sibling relationship, the misunderstanding disappeared and joy returned to their lives. In many cases, what appears to be the weakest of bonds between siblings has surprising strength.

## Cutoffs in the Family

Families affect the relationships between the siblings in many ways. One of these occurs when a family member cuts off an uncle, aunt, grandparent, or other relative. Molly, a high school teacher, had gone through a divorce and bankruptcy and had many unresolved issues about her family.

She had a crazy aunt who periodically went in and out of the state hospital. When Molly was a small child the family cut the aunt off. They wouldn't see her. "We don't talk about Aunt Mary," they told her, "and we don't want you to see her." Cutoffs are based on unresolved hurt and they take energy. In this case, this turned out to be a grieving problem. Molly still grieved the loss of her aunt and hadn't resolved it. As I often do, I suggested that we call on the resource of her siblings and try to work through this problem together. Unfortunately we had a problem, since Molly and I were in California and the sisters and parents were in Tennessee.

It was obvious from the beginning when they walked in the office that they were glad to see one another. Then the session started, and a number of secrets came out. The oldest sister confessed that as a child she felt suicidal. She felt isolated, and for a while just wanted to kill herself. Molly thought that this sister had had it made.

Marsha, her other sister, acquired a different perspective on their father. She was sure her father didn't care about her. The other two said no, she was all Dad talked about.

All three thought the others didn't care about them as individuals. They were wrong. Sibling relationships are not only the longest, but often surprisingly strong.

In the middle of this, the parents flew in from Tennessee. They were afraid my therapy would isolate them from their children. In this case it allowed the children to see things from everyone's prospective and brought them closer together.

## Alcohol and Drugs

When a parent has an alcohol or drug problem, or if one or both of them is a workaholic, the bonding may be only partial and the children themselves often assume an additional burden.

Doris, for instance, was the oldest of four brothers and sisters. Her mother worked most of the day, then came home and spent the rest of the time drinking in her room. When she wasn't there, she was usually out getting drunk with her boyfriend. This left the rearing of the family to Doris. She got them up in the morning and off to school and was there when they came home. When they had trouble at school, she talked to the teacher in the place of her mother. Doris managed to attend high school and get reasonably good grades, but she did not have time for after-school activities. Her dream was to become a cheerleader; instead she had to meet the bus and walk her younger sisters home. While the children developed a close relationship, they hardly realized their mother was in the house.

Parents who are alcoholics also often affect the sibling bonding through mental or physical harassment. Marilyn and her brother and sister grew up in a family where the father continually threw tirades and ranted and screamed at the kids. He was Japanese, a music teacher in the local high school, and highly educated, and he stressed education for his children. Unfortunately he felt he was the absolute ruler of the household. He was also an alcoholic, and when he drank he was especially abusive and made the children feel like nonpersons. "You can't do anything right," he would yell at Marilyn.

Instead of breaking the children apart, it brought them closer together. They supported one another and each warned the others of their father's moods. They also kept secrets from him that they thought would bring out his ire. When one of them didn't do quite as well on a test as the father expected, they tried to make sure he never found out. When these children became adults they saw very little of one another. "I felt terrible anger at my dad for mistreating me," Marilyn confessed, "and some resentment at my brother and sister for not helping me more."

At age forty, Marilyn came to me as a client because she had recently divorced her husband and was seeing another man who cheated on her. Her eight-year marriage had ended and the new relationship was already in trouble. She was bewildered.

I always do some work on the family of origin, because I often find that this is where the problem starts. There is always a rubber band connection between here and now and then and there. If the facts and feelings around an issue were settled in the family of origin, there is no connection; if not, it is connected in the now. Unfortunately people are not aware of this.

My experience told me that we needed her brother and sister as hidden resources, so I told her that I wanted her to ask her brother and sister to come to therapy. She rejected this at first, since she knew they would turn her down anyway.

"What would you say," I asked, "if one of them asked you to help them. Would you do it?"

"Of course."

Both of them came, and the fact that they were here spoke louder than words. On the board, I started to visually detail their genealogy for three generations starting with the parents. I put on the board the mother and father, the three children, and then their children. In this case, despite the fact that their father was cruel to them, they were still grieving. I got out the blankets and put a pillow down to represent their dad and told them to say whatever they wanted to say to him—to express their sadness, anger, fear— to let their feelings flow. They all burst into tears simultaneously.

It turned out that Marilyn and her brother looked upon their dad as cruel and unjust. The sister said that she always thought of her childhood as happy. As the three of them talked, Marilyn began to get angrier and angrier at her father. Their father had died years ago, yet his treatment of them almost tore them apart. None of them had really grieved, and all were still angry. It also emerged that Marilyn had been the clown, with her dad as her best audience. The feeling in the room was that their dad had just died. This is what siblings can do as a resource. After all, they are our longest and strongest relationship. And no matter what the problem, most really care about each other.

In this particular family system, love was conveyed by actions, not words. But in the therapy session, the more exposed their emotions, the closer they became. About a year after this I received a wedding announcement from Marilyn; she was marrying a new man. She had now taken charge of her life, resolved the conflict with her father, and was a completely different person.

Parents can also affect the adult sibling bond far into adulthood in other ways. I had a client, the oldest sibling, whose sister and younger brother were at odds with him. His first wife had committed suicide. His new wife didn't like her mother-in-law. As a result his mother went to the other two and helped start a fight with my client. It was clear to me that if the mother would stay out of it, these three could work out the issues. Unfortunately, she wouldn't hear of it.

When the three showed up for a session in my office, the mother came along. When I asked to talk to her adult children by themselves she refused to let me. The real issue here was that the older ones were protecting their mother. Finally, I conducted the session with her in the room. I then promised I would help her handle this if she would call me. She did, and that allowed me to take her out of the loop. Unfortunately, without help, and with mother egging both sides on, they simply couldn't resolve the conflict.

I also recently worked with a client in his middle forties whose brother felt that my client, the older brother, was too critical of their mother. Unfortunately, the mother wouldn't stay out of it, and I was unsuccessful in getting them to see that this mother was causing their long-standing conflict.

## Divorce and Remarriage

Sometimes divorce and remarriage can be catastrophic to the relationship between two brothers. I brought together Henry, forty-eight, and his brother Bob, fifty-eight. Their father died and their mother remarried. From the beginning, it became clear that these two had very different stories to tell.

Henry had bonded with his stepdad; Bob hadn't. When Henry was six his brother, who was sixteen, left and went out on his own. Henry puzzled over this for years, and still didn't understand when he came to me.

As Bob told it, he and the stepdad had a number of fights. His stepfather didn't like Bob's friends; he didn't like the way Bob kept his room; he didn't understand why Bob didn't get better grades. There didn't seem to be any love between the two anywhere. When Bob turned sixteen, he came to breakfast one morning and his stepfather told him he had to leave; there was no longer anyplace for him in the family.

This astonished Henry, who remembered the stepfather with affection.

Even with these differences, the relationship between the brothers was strong. When they came to the session Bob sat with Henry and put his arm around him on the back of the couch.

In my family, while we were close, I have to say we actually raised each other. My father was gone much of the time and my mother worked outside of the home. This left us to our own devices. But my brothers and sisters really came through and made us closer.

In my practice, I am surprised to find how many people are disturbed at being emotionally separated from their brothers and sisters. Often when adults reach middle age and are separated from their siblings by problems that keep them apart, they begin to feel something is missing. That's when I see them in my office.

Ben, one of my clients, grew up feeling that he was alone, even though there were four siblings in the family. All members kept secrets from one another, and the sisters formed a cliquish group that excluded Ben.

Closeness in a family, as we have seen before, results from participation within the family and for respect for each person as a separate and distinct individual. Unfortunately, this participation and respect weren't present in Ben's family. This distance between the sisters and brother bothered him for years; then he, with hesitation, asked them to join him in therapy. Together they discussed the problems they had as children. As they began to talk of the hurts and pain, Ben began to experience a sense of deep love. This often happens because brothers and sisters in a family share an extended history not matched by any other relationship.

## When It's Time To Leave the Family

In a close family, the biggest problems occur in the teen years, when children are trying to become independent but don't know exactly how to go about it. This is a time of turmoil in a lot of families. The parents still have rules and the typical teenager thinks they're all unfair.

The real problem for the parents at this time is to teach the kids how to leave and be ready to become competent adults.

Permission to leave is twofold. It comes from both the parents wanting to help launch their teenager into the world and from the teenager telling his or her parents it's time to leave.

For instance, parents often help their teenagers to plan for college. When the time comes they frequently drive their child to school, meet the child's dorm roommate, walk around the campus, and say good-bye. This launches the teenager on a new adventure. Or the teen and the parents talk for weeks about work, and the parents help emotionally as the teenager looks for a job. Or the parents see their teen off to join the military. If young adults feel okay about leaving home, they stay close to their parents the rest of the parents' lives because they know that their parents love and are concerned about them. When a child wants desperately to get away from the house, there is much more love and action outside. Everyone knows of at least one teenager who marries a boyfriend or girlfriend just to get away. Frequently, however, this takes them from one relationship they don't care much for to another one that's not completely positive, a relationship that often ends in divorce.

The relationship between parents and children, whether positive or negative, ends with the death of the parents, although the memories linger for the rest of the child's life and always affect the way brothers and sisters treat each other.

Because the sibling relationship begins at birth and ends at death, it is frequently the longest and sometimes the most complicated one of all. However, in many cases the problems can be solved by discovering any third-party interference then resolving the problem between brothers and sisters themselves.

## When Marriage Intervenes

We never have a choice about who our brothers and sisters are, but we can choose our marriage partner. Unfortunately, we don't always make wonderful choices, but when we marry and divorce, our brothers and sisters are often there to support us. This makes them, in many ways, a safety net for a marriage ending and often a safety net for some of life's other problems.

Research has shown that families often cling together even after a marriage. Sometimes there are huge gatherings at holidays with whole families flying in from all across the country to be together.

My wife comes from a family of seven children. She has five sisters and one brother, all still living. These siblings all have second marriages and live all over the country—Virginia, Washington State, Colorado, New Mexico, and Arizona. They are close to each other, support each other, and are on the phone with each other all the time. While we have a good marriage, her brother and sisters form a very important support group.

Even when we don't have contact for long periods of time with our siblings, the ties between our brothers and sisters are always strong, either negatively or positively. The sibling relationship, which begins at birth and ends at death, is frequently the most complicated of all relationships. But most family members agree, there is simply nothing like it.

# 10

~

# When You Retire

Tuesday, October 29, 1991, seventy-two-year-old Nebraska farm boy Robert L. Harrison retired from his second career. His sister Eloise was seventy-five years old, his sister Winnifred seventy-four, his brother Paul sixty-nine, and his brother Henry sixty-seven. Robert's sisters and brothers are married with a total of seventeen children among the five, twenty-eight grandchildren and four great-grandchildren. All are married, and only sister Winnifred is widowed.

In 1942, twenty-three-year-old high school graduate Robert left the Nebraska family farm after being drafted into the army. Robert was sent to Fort Leonard Wood, Missouri. This was Robert's first trip away from the family farm and out of the state of Nebraska. The draft board deferred Robert's two younger brothers from the draft in order to let them continue work on the farm.

Robert never returned. After he'd successfully completed his basic training, his company commander chose Robert for pilot training in the army air force. After completion of that training Robert was stationed in Great Britain and flew a troop transport between the United States and Great Britain.

During the war Robert kept in contact by way of a weekly letter to each of them. They in turn wrote him weekly. Robert's graphic weekly letters during his wartime experiences and travel painted a picture of a bigger, wider world than their world of farming. Six months after the end of World War II, discharged from the army, he now faced the prospect of what to do with his life.

Back at the farm, the family discussed his future. All knew he was not cut out to remain on the farm. His sister Eloise brought up the subject. From his letters, the family began to realize that their son and brother was bitten by the travel bug. With his parents and the others at rapt attention, Robert explained that the United States Army would allow him to reenter the military and attend the University of Iowa to complete a degree in aeronautical engineering. At the completion of his university training he would once again rejoin the active military with a promotion to captain.

Moments of silence for the Harrison family.

In two weeks Robert would be on the campus of the University of Iowa to begin his training. The Sunday dinner ended and Robert retired. Bright and early the next morning, as is customary on the farm, all the family members shared a five A.M. breakfast. Robert looked around the table at his family and did his best to keep the tears from running down his face. Robert was leaving his family, never to return as "one of them." He drove away with their waving arms outstretched. In the car, Robert let tears roll down his cheeks.

On the campus of the University of Iowa, sophomore Robert met Carmen. They were married one year later in the church in the small town near his family's farm. Robert's brothers and his sisters were attendants. Carmen's sister was the maid of honor.

Fast forward to his first retirement and sixty-two-year-old Robert. Robert retired from the military with an honorable discharge and many ribbons. His two adult children, Brendan and Lacy, are grown; they moved away from home to attend college and are now married with young children of their own. His second career and next adventure began as a deputy probation officer in a midsize California city. He and his wife, for the first time in their marriage, lived for ten years in one home. No traveling except to visit his sisters and brothers in Nebraska twice per year, once in the winter and once in the summer.

The time had now come, and seventy-two-year-old Robert decided that he wanted to retire again and spend time fishing, working in his yard, playing golf with his friends, and enjoying retirement with his wife.

Later that summer, around the Nebraska family dinner table with his sisters and brothers, Robert could look into the faces of each of them and see the kid there. They had not aged; they were just older. The joy of their relationship was wrapped in tears, laughter, and sweet memories. Once again Robert announced that he and Carmen had decided to remain in California. His brothers and sisters were mildly disappointed and yet supported their brother. The Harrison sibling bond had stretched around the planet and across the country and remained strong.

Through frequent letters, telephone calls, and visits, the Harrison kids never lose contact.

It requires energy to nurture any relationship. The sibling relationship is no different. Notice what energy is required to nurture your unique relationship. Sisters' and brothers' relationships are never status quo; they either increase in strength or decrease.

The Harrison family kept in contact, and their contact made their relationship strong and ongoing over time and distance.

## Parents Are gone

My eighty-four-year-old mother died three weeks ago. Her death came two years and thirty-three days after the death of my eighty-four-year-old father. That generation for me and my sister and brothers no longer exists. We can no longer look up to that parental umbrella. We are now the seniors and we are on the edge of becoming the elderly. I don't feel like a senior, and I don't see the elderly in my brothers' and sister's faces. We are just older.

None of us has retired. My oldest brother is fifty-nine and my youngest brother is fifty-two. Retirement time awaits around the corner. We now look to each other with only the memories of our parents' participation in our lives. We knew that this time was coming, and now that it is here we view each other with a shared lifetime of parent and sister and brother participation and now the shared loss of our parents.

Rarely are your retirement years spent with your parents. Unless you retire young and/or your parents live into their eighties and nineties, your retirement years will be spent without them.

In the past ten years I have attended the funerals and memorial services of my two parents, two aunts, and three uncles. These were the parent umbrella of my siblings and cousins. With the death of these parents, my family has withdrawn to a family reunion based on our own children, our same-generation family members, and our cousins. Cousins are the "siblings" who bring up the second tier.

So look around at your own retirement years. Will your parents be gone? What are the strengths of your sibling bond? What are the weaknesses of this bond? Keep in your mind that the essence of love is participation. Participation can take place through the spoken or written word and the magic of being in the presence of your brothers and sisters. What essence of sibling participation is present for you and what essence of sibling participation is absent for you? Sixty-eight-year-old Armondo and his four brothers and two sisters live in a small town in southern Oregon, and each Sunday after Mass they all, with spouses, children, and grandchildren in tow, enjoy a late-afternoon potluck lunch. Lunch is always at sister Gloria's house. This Sunday family ritual is more than twenty years old. No one remembers when and how it got started. Now that you are retired and your parental umbrella is gone, where are your siblings in your life and where are you in their life?

Nonparticipation is the ritual of brothers Leonard, seventy-five, Jim, seventy-three, and Barry, sixty-nine. They send a card at Christmas and that is all.

Sisters Karen and Frances, age sixty-plus, live in Philadelphia. Their other sister, Barbara, lives in Palm Springs, California. Karen is widowed, has children and grandchildren, is retired, and lives alone. Frances is divorced, has children and grandchildren, and has never worked outside of her home. However, her divorce settlement allows her to live an affluent life. Barbara is divorced, never had children, is attractive, is working, and is mistress to her married lover.

Their parents are dead, but Karen, Frances, and Barbara have each other. Their sister bond has increased and strengthened over the years because each reaches out to the others with the telephone, letters, and frequent visits. Deep down in their gut they know that each of them is responsible for maintaining this loving relationship.

Brothers Dennis, seventy-five, and William, seventy-two, have not spoken to each other for over forty years. Their seventy-year-old sister, Carmen, speaks to both the brothers and both of her brothers speak to her. Dennis never asks Carmen about William and William never asks Carmen about Dennis. When these two brothers were in their thirties, Dennis took offense when William was incarcerated for embezzling money. Dennis never forgave his brother, and William never forgave his brother for not forgiving him. These brothers were both hurt by each other's actions and they both chose to stay emotionally stuck. Dennis and William are both retired and enjoying their individual retirements. They will continue to rob themselves and each other of the pleasure of each other's company in their retirement years.

Sisters Karen, Frances, and Barbara have chosen to continue participating in one another's lives. On the other hand, brothers Dennis and William have chosen not to be involved with each other. They both remain hurt, unforgiving, and lonely for each other's company. If and when these two brothers reach into the room of personal humility they will be able to forgive themselves and each other and forget the actions that divided them. Reaching across their brotherly divide, they can reclaim the joy of their relationship. They could express their appreciation of each other and talk about their resentments without criticism and blame.

There is no magic in maintaining a sibling relationship. Blaming them never heals the wound, and the siblings who falsely maintain that they are right, remain stuck. They haven't learned that you can be right or you can be close. You can't have both.

Have you chosen to be right or have you chosen to be close with your siblings? It's your choice!

## Appreciation of Parents

At a quiet time after a singer's rousing version of "Amazing Grace," forty-two-year-old Marlene spoke soothing words at the memorial service for her father, Willis. With a smile and an occasional tear, Marlene was the spokesperson for herself and her brothers and sister. Her eloquent words reflected what they felt about their father's involvement in their lives. At the service, Marlene recalled a time when they were skiing and their father remained on the deck at the lodge. In full view of his children and the ski run, he watched over them. The theme in this family was that all four of them appreciated their father's watching over each of them in their childhood and adulthood, and in Marlene's closing words she looked upward and said, Dad, I know that you are still watching over me and my brothers and sisters.

These family members are grateful for the many appreciations between themselves and their father.

In these, my preretirement days, I am grateful to my father for teaching me the value of mentally, physically, and emotionally having the courage to take calculated risks. I am also grateful that he instilled in me a willingness to work, of putting in effort over time, and of being able to laugh and enjoy humor.

In these, my preretirement days, I am grateful to my mother for giving me the gift of learning. The expression on her face when my sister, brothers, and I learned something new reflected a soft glow and a warm smile. When I went away to college—my first time away from home—her weekly letters were of encouragement, support, and a rundown of what her five other kids were doing. Her letters, and the many other family letters that I received, helped me through my valley of loneliness.

My mother was truly a teacher, both professionally as well as personally.

*In these, your retirement years, what do you appreciate about your parents?*

Appreciations have to be expressed. Holding your feelings within yourself robs both you and your parents. Thinking about how you appreciate is not enough. You like people to tell you they appreciate you, if you are truly humble enough to accept. Your expressed appreciations to your parents will soften them. If you look closely, you will see the kid part of them on their faces. It is hard to realize that your parents were also children at one time.

## Resentment of Parents

Forty-eight-year-old Ronald never married. He has never had children and he has always lived near his parents' home. From the time he was a child, a mythical promise was made that his parents would take care of him and that when they died, he, along with his brother, would inherit their wealth. Unfortunately, at their father's death the lifelong mythical promise was broken when father's estate was disclosed to have many debts and few assets.

Ronald was furious and blamed his brother, Arnold. Ronald was the loyal child. Arnold had created a life with his wife, Irene, and his four children, a life away from Ronald and their parents. Ronald raised his shield of resentments to his brother Arnold, and Arnold was unable to convince Ronald to drop it.

Most likely a bitter and resentful Ronald will go to his grave with a wound to the brother bond that he will not allow to heal. These brothers' retirement years will be spent with Ronald replaying his hurts and proudly displaying his resentment shield. Most likely on the front of Ronald's grave marker will be written, *My brother treated me unfairly*. On the back of Ronald's grave marker will be written, *I treated my brother unfairly*.

When siblings do not resolve conflict, they need to look at the parents' generation. By nature, early in life, sisters and brothers learn to resolve their conflicts out of necessity to reduce the tension. Children are brilliant at figuring out solutions to problems. Parents set the rules, much as in professional boxing, the Marquis of Queensberry rules allow for a boxing match and not a chaotic fight. Some parents encourage chaotic sister and brother fights for their own ulterior reasons, frequently to satisfy a need for recognition.

Linda was a chaos-loving parent. She still functions as a wife to her husband, Bill, and as a mother to her two children, Ellen and Robert. Linda has been moderately depressed since childhood, due in part to her father's alcoholism and her mother's domineering behavior. Now, at age ninety-one, Linda is still moderately depressed, and her two retired children, seventy-one-year-old Ellen and sixty-nine-year-old Robert, are still fighting. When Ellen visits her mother at the senior residence she tells her mother of the awful things Robert does. Ellen's mother gleefully listens and encourages Ellen's sibling report. Linda's smile begs Ellen to continue beating up on her brother. This mother/daughter lunch often lasts two and a half hours, and when Ellen leaves, her mother's moderate depression has lifted. She also can hardly wait for the next brotherly beating.

Sixty-nine-year-old Robert has learned to visit his mother on the days that he knows his sister Ellen will not be there. Seated comfortably in his mother's small living room, Robert begins his report of the awful things his sister Ellen does. Once again his mother gleefully listens and encourages Robert's bad-sister report. His mother's depression lifts, and once again loyal Ellen and Robert take care of their mother by sacrificing their own relationship. This family drama has existed for more than sixty years, and most likely, even after their mother's death, Linda will reach back from the grave when each of her children recount how wrong the other is.

Unfortunately, sister and brother conflict is never resolved if they do not discover the source of their unresolved conflict. In Ellen and Robert's family the source was a mother who would not solve her own depression in a healthy manner.

> *Do you have unresolved conflict with your sibling?*
> *Now, in your retirement, do you know the source of this unresolved conflict?*

## Parents Who *Divide and Conquer*

Forty-three-year-old Carl is the youngest, forty-nine-year-old Brian the oldest, and right in the middle is forty-six-year-old Karen. From the time of their childhood, their father said, "The boys can take care of themselves." The boys were taught to be independent; Karen was taught to be dependent. The boys pleased Daddy by being independent, and Karen pleased Daddy by being dependent. These brothers view their wives as dependent beings, and their wives have given up and turned over most decision making to their husbands. The brother/husbands choose when to, when not to, how to, how not to, where to, where not to, and on and on. Karen turns over the decisions to her husband—a husband whom Daddy approved.

Seventy-five-year-old Daddy has died, and these three adult children are sitting in Bernard Wellstone's office. Bernard is the attorney who is the executor of their father's estate. Each of the three kids is seated in a comfortable leather Victorian chair. The attorney holds forth behind his large mahogany desk with all the trappings of a successful law practice. Bernard knows what is about to happen in his ornate office. Daddy is dead and gone, and yet he will continue to dominate. Carl, Karen, and Brian sit attentively in their chairs as the attorney reads all the legalese. Now comes the section on the allocation of Daddy's estate. In a slow and deliberate monotone, Bernard reads, "'To my son Carl, I leave the amount of $500. To my son Brian, I leave the amount of $500. To my daughter, Karen, I leave the amount of $273,405.'"

The atmosphere moves from quiet, calm anticipation, to confusion, to anger, and then to tension. These two brothers and their sister are surprised, and yet Daddy's voice resonates around the room: "The boys can take care of themselves." Bernard, the attorney, knows that he has witnessed and participated in a process of dividing these two brothers from their sister. Karen is moderately surprised and quietly gleeful. Carl and Brian are hurt, angry, bitter, resentful, and contemplating ways to overcome their father's legal wishes. In their state, if children are given at least $500, the will cannot be challenged. Daddy carried out his divide-and-conquer all the way to the graveyard and beyond.

Karen accepted her inheritance, and the relationship with her brothers never recovered from their Daddy's hurtful allocations.

When parents divide and conquer, their adult children's retirement years are often spent apart in both distance and emotion. This sibling noninvolvement with each other undermines the joy that no one other person can satisfy. Your sister and brother relationships are unique.

The opposite of parents who divide and conquer are parents who unite and nurture these same relationships.

## Parents Who Unite and Nurture

In my sixth-grade class, we held monthly elections for class officers—president, vice president, secretary, treasurer, and sergeant at arms. The first month I was elected president; the second month I was reelected president; and each succeeding month my classmates reelected me president. I was popular! I really did not know why. My mother was concerned, after my third presidential reelection, that the other kids in the class were not getting a chance. She was proud of me and concerned about the other kids in my class and the other kids in my family. But in all honesty, I never refused the nomination.

My mother nurtured me and wanted to unite me with my fellow students and my one sister and four brothers. I was able to convince her that I did not elect myself; the other kids elected me. That logic worked, as she was able to see how I was supporting the sixth-grade democratic process. At home she insisted that each of us receive our own bowl of ice cream. No one was left out. At her recent memorial service my three brothers and our sister were present. My only absent sibling was Harold, who has been missing for over five years.

Recently I attended a reunion at the very small high school that I graduated from in 1961. My class of twenty students—thirteen girls and seven boys—was the second graduating class from this small school. I sat in the same gymnasium where for three years I had played basketball, roller-skated, and jumped on the trampoline. In June 1961, to the rendition of "Pomp and Circumstance," I marched with my nineteen fellow classmates. What a joyous occasion with my family and friends. Fast forward to April 1999, thirty-nine years later.

In my gymnasium with three hundred–plus people—students, former students, spouses, and current and former teachers—the class rolls were called. For the 1959 forty-year honor class, five graduates stood and were applauded. For the 1960 class, there were no graduates. For the class of 1961, one graduate—me— stood and was applauded. I was disappointed that none of my fellow graduates came. All of the classes from 1962 to 1999 were called, and many people stood.

As I took a break in the foyer of the gymnasium, I saw Mr. Potynen, one of my teachers. He and I reminisced about many of my fellow high school graduates. I had to remind myself that Mr. Potynen is only eight years my senior. I experienced being both a high school student with him and, in the here and now, an adult with him.

As with the energy required to maintain sibling relationships in the retirement years, energy is required to maintain relationships with fellow graduates. The memories are not enough. Any of my classmates could have shared both then-and-there memories and have given an update on what has happened in their lives since 1961. Maybe in the year 2001, when we are the forty-year honor class, all of us fifty-eight-year-olds will be able to bring back the magic time.

These retirement years offer an opportunity for the expression of your energy to enhance all your relationships. When you sit on your energy and wait, all that may happen is that rigor mortis will get to you before you get to anyone else.

## The "Empty Nest"

The kids are gone! The kids are gone!

I became a first-time stepdad at age forty-two to five-year-old David when I married. Ten months and twenty-two days later I became a first-time biological dad with the birth of our daughter, Molly. At my reunion, many of my fellow students were parents and grandparents. I am the new kid on the block to parenting.

Two of my brothers and my sister are grandparents. When my daughter was eight, she informed me that I was old enough to be her grandfather. She quickly added that she wanted me to be her father, not her grandfather. I smiled.

Forty-three-year-old Lyla is a single parent who has reared her two sons by herself. Lee is now twenty-seven years old and Donald is twenty-five. After Donald left home four years ago, Lyla married her boyfriend of six years. Since her new husband works out of the country on three-month assignments, Lyla is left to herself much of the time. She enjoys this and notices a pull within herself to reconnect with her sister, Louise. Both of these sisters have grown children, are in the twilight of their working years, and want to fill in some sister time. Lyla and Louise meet once a week for an extended lunch, which often lasts for three or more hours.

Twenty years ago, seventy-two-year-old Peter and sixty-eight-year-old Ursula came to my office for marriage counseling. They had been married for forty-two years and had one son and three grandchildren. They had a traditional marriage in which Peter worked outside the home and handled all of the finances. Ursula managed the home and raised their son. Peter is an only child, and Ursula is the fourth-born of the children in her family. She has one deceased older brother and three living sisters. Ursula had devoted herself to her marriage with Peter and had little contact over the years with her sisters. They sent Christmas and Easter cards with short letters each year. Peter retired seven years ago from his work for the railroads. Peter and Ursula have a suitable financial retirement and enjoy each other's company.

I am seated opposite this couple, me in my chair and they close to one another on the couch. They appear to have a happy and contented marriage. After an exchange of routine pleasantries, I asked the question, "What brings you two to my office?" Ursula blurted out that Peter had stayed out all night and played billiards. I asked when that happened, and Ursula just as quickly blurted out, "Forty years ago." This was a red flag.

Within the hour the truth came out that Peter was dying of a kidney disease and wanted to protect Ursula from knowing about it. But she had learned about this illness from his doctor. She did not want him to know that she knew. They were each overprotecting the other. Within two additional marriage counseling sessions, the truth came out. They could now begin the preparations for Peter's death, and Peter could inform Ursula of how she would be taken care of financially after he is gone.

Peter encouraged Ursula to invite her three sisters to visit. He knew that they would be a bond for her. Ursula quickly accepted Peter's permission to reconnect with her three sisters, who live in Oregon. After the third session they terminated their marriage counseling. I never saw them again. Peter died six months later, and six months after his death I received a letter from Ursula describing how she was spending time with her grandchildren and her three sisters. Ursula's sisters have visited her four times during the past year and she has gone to them twice. Weekly sister telephone calls have become a ritual.

When children are gone and work is gone, retirement can be empty.

*How would you feel if you called your sibling(s)?*
*How would you feel if they called you?*

## Twenty-four Hours a Day and Seven Days a Week Retirement Changes the Twenty-four/Seven

Frequently, prisons use isolation to correct an inmate's behavior. We are social animals and most of us want contact with some of our fellow human beings. Contact can come in the form of physical touch, emotional touch, or touch by word. With the onset of retirement, the contact opportunities change. When my wife was eight months pregnant, she opted to take a leave from the hospital where she worked and remain at home. She moved from a setting where she had contact by word and physical presence with approximately a hundred people per day, to just talking to me, her best friend, and some neighbors.

She went from a high-stroking to a low-stroking environment, and I noticed how my extroverted and outgoing wife missed her daily contacts.

*How has your retirement changed your contact with other people?*

Each day when I go into my office, Judy Novak, my receptionist, says, "Good morning, Marvin." She recognizes me. When I retire I won't go into my office. Where will I get my recognition? Forty years ago, my grandfather retired at age sixty-five. My grandmother had never worked outside of their home, and she had her daily rituals that structured her time. Grandfather became a grump. He slept too much, and became restless, irritable, and not much fun.

Grandfather's solution to his lack of recognition and Grandmother's peace of mind came when my grandfather began going to auction sales, garage sales, and anywhere else he could obtain used and broken bicycles. His garage became his new shop, and between his sixty-seventh and his eighty-second years he received much of his needed psychological recognition through his bicycle business. He also made some extra money. He said it was for the money, and yet he knew it was also for his peace of mind.

> *In your retirement, how much recognition are you giving your sister(s), your brother(s)?*
> *How much recognition are they giving to you?*
> *Are you getting the recognition from them that you want?*
> *Are you giving them the recognition that you or they want?*

Retirement years can become ordinary to the point that life lacks luster. In this part of northern California where I live, around the first of the month when the Social Security checks come, the buses to Reno, Lake Tahoe, and the Indian casinos hit the road. It may be only once a month, but it *is* once a month. You are never too old for some form of excitement, unless you have drawn your last breath or you are a dyed-in-the-wool cynic.

Seventy-eight-year-old Luigi and his seventy-year-old brother, Carmine, play boccie ball at East Portal Park every day when there is no rain and the temperature is above sixty degrees. These brothers are both retired from the Southern Pacific Railroad. They have a combined work history of fifty-seven years. They both switch from English to Italian during their one and a half hours at the game. They share a bottle of red wine, bread, cheese, and Italian pastry. At the end of the one and a half hours, they grunt their good-byes and return home to their wives, Sophie and Helena.

Their boccie ball time satisfies their hunger for something out of the ordinary.

Imagine your life without, sights, smells, tastes, touch, or sounds. Nothing stimulates your existence. The sight, smell, taste, touch, and sound of your children are gone. The sight, smell, taste, touch, and sound of your work are gone. Where are your sisters and brothers? They have a past, a present, and a future with you. Their stories are stimulating, even if repetitive. They know your sibling language, and even though they are familiar, our brothers and sisters cannot be replaced by anyone else.

The familiarity of your parents is gone because they have passed away. The familiarity of your children is gone because through your good efforts they are out of and away from your home. And now the familiarity of your work is gone because of your retirement. What is left? Your lifetime peer group, those sisters and brothers, begin to take on a newfound importance.

## Living Longer and Golden Sibling Years

Dr. Calvin Somerston scheduled retirement six months after his sixty-fourth birthday. He died at age sixty-three. His retirement years with his physician brothers, seventy-year-old Larry and sixty-eight-year-old Eric, will never be. These brothers had planned on golfing vacations, cruises with their wives, and the companionship of each other.

Calvin's brothers decided to continue their plans for their retirement as a way to honor Calvin.

Our culture, with the many advances in medical science, affords us the possibility of many years of retirement.

*Where and with whom would you prefer to spend these years*

*Whether you have full retirement years or partial retirement years, where do your sisters and brothers fit into your plans?*

Most of us will live beyond the point of retirement. My father was retired during the last eleven years of his life. He had weekly telephone calls from his two sisters, periodic visits by his one still-living brother, and monthly visits from his two living sisters. He enjoyed his life with his female companion of twenty-three years and continued to keep a place for his sisters and brother in his life. They loved him and he loved them. When I watched them interact, I could witness what they were exchanging, and yet I was the observer and not the participant. During the last eleven years of my father's life, he received joy from sharing time with these special people. His two sisters, LaVerne and Peggy, and his brother, J.T., were my aunts and uncles, and they were his peers. Their conversations had a code that only they understood. Their words contained a sibling past, a sibling present, and a sibling future. Their shared stories showed sorrow over their losses and laughter over their happiness. And most of all, they had a joy of sharing time together.

My father and they enjoyed their partners, their children, their grandchildren, and their great-grandchildren, and they also continued to reserve that special place in each of their hearts for their brothers and sisters.

Life is made up of choices. Some choices are made externally by someone else, by the weather, by an accident, or anything else out of our control. The choices made internally will determine how we spend our twenty-four/seven time.

*How much sister/brother time do you want to spend in your retirement?*

*How little time do you want to spend?*

## That Special Support

The wrinkles and lines on the ruddy face of sixty-five-year-old Ernie reflect his forty-nine years as a hardworking and hard-drinking longshoreman. Ernie, the fifth-born of nine children, never married. He has five sisters and three brothers; one of his brothers died at the age of four and a half from cystic fibrosis. Ernie was born in San Francisco and has never lived away from the city except for his military service during World War II. Ernie returned to San Francisco upon his honorable discharge from the United States Navy and then resumed his work as a longshoreman.

Six months after his return, Ernie moved out of his parents' home and bought a small one-bedroom, one-bath house in North Beach. Ernie has lived alone in this home during the past fifty years. He frequently visits his parents and brothers and sisters. But only once have his parents visited his home. This was during the first week he lived there. Ernie loves his family and Ernie loves his time alone. Every Friday night Ernie meets his fellow longshoremen at the pier bar and enjoys his three Irish coffees that take him three hours to drink. Ernie bids his fellow longshoremen good-bye, and then he walks the half a mile to his house alone. This Friday-night ritual has been played out for over fifty years. Ernie loves his time alone and also his time with his fellow longshoremen. On Saturday Ernie reads. This fourth-grade school dropout has a subscription to *Time* magazine, and reads novels by Hemingway, Mickey Spillane, Tom Clancy, and most recently, John Grisham. Ernie's most prized set of books is his *World Book Encyclopedia* that he purchased in 1955. Each year he receives an updated volume. For breakfast on Saturday morning, Ernie cooks himself three scrambled eggs with sardines, three pieces of San Francisco sourdough toast with raspberry jam, a glass of orange juice, and one cup of decaffeinated coffee. During his one-and-a half-hour breakfast he reads *Time* magazine. Ernie is a self-educated man who has voted in every local, state, and national election since his twenty-first birthday. His only newspaper is the Sunday San Francisco *Chronicle*.

Saturday afternoons, after cleaning house, Ernie takes a one-hour nap. At the conclusion of his nap, Ernie reads about a city or a biography of a famous person in his encyclopedia. He then spends the rest of his day by reading one of his current novels.

Saturday-night dinners are spent in a rotation ritual at one of his brothers' or sisters' homes. These dinners are fun for Ernie, and he tells his nephews, nieces, and anyone else who will listen about the latest book he has read or about the latest ship that he helped unload. Ernie always leaves at nine-thirty and rides the cable car home. It is a given which sister or brother has the next Saturday-night dinner.

Up until the passing of his mother and father twenty and seventeen years ago, respectively, Ernie attended every Sunday-morning Mass with his mother and father. Four of his sisters and two surviving brothers live in San Francisco. His sister, Carmen, lives in Houston.

Two and a half years ago, Ernie contacted a doctor, complaining of a persistent and painful feeling in his midsection. The medical examination determined that Ernie had a kidney disease that would require removing one diseased kidney. In addition, in six months he would have to begin kidney dialysis.

Ernie asked for a meeting with all of his brothers and sisters, and after dinner he told then about his kidney disease. After a few tears and a few hugs, Ernie's sisters and brothers offered to do whatever was necessary to help him.

The following week the doctor performed the surgery. Ernie was now no longer able to work as a longshoreman. His long-shoreman buddies threw a retirement party at the pub, and each of them, with sincerity, promised to visit him and give whatever help he needed. Ernie knew they meant well, and he also knew that most of them would not follow through. His disease was too threatening to the longshoreman's creed of being tough. He loved them.

Within six months Ernie had to undergo kidney dialysis three times per week. He was referred to the Kidney Foundation and they rented him the equipment. The day that the kidney dialysis equipment arrived, his seven brothers and sisters were with him. The technicians set up the equipment in Ernie's small living room. The renal nurses then spent three hours educating Ernie and his brothers and sisters about the three-times-a-week ritual that would become the lifesaver for their beloved brother. The nurse then instructed each how to hook Ernie up to the equipment for the dialysis and also how to monitor how Ernie was feeling.

After the nurse completed Ernie's first dialysis, he was left alone with his siblings. His sister, Connie, spoke for all of them. They had devised a plan whereby each one in birth order sequence would spend the week with Ernie to tend to his needs and wants. Ernie began to cry tears of intimacy, the tears that come when love fills the room. There were also tears in everyone else's eyes, except Gino's. Gino looked up in order to hold back the tears—something he had learned to do as a kid in order to be strong.

For the next three years, the brothers and sisters whose turn it was, and their wives and husbands, brought in dinner, according to Ernie's special diet.

During their weekly stays, Ernie shared many of his memories. He recounted for his sister Evelyn how she made special cookies for him when he was a child. He recounted for sister Carmen the fight they had had over a tricycle; he recounted for sister Louisa how he was angry at her when they were children because she broke his favorite glass; he recounted for sister Barbara how she was his favorite sister. He thanked his brother Robert for teaching him the manly art of throwing and catching a baseball, and with his brother John, Ernie recalled the time when they were in their early teens and they sneaked into a baseball game. With each of them, Ernie recalled the time when their youngest brother, David, died of cystic fibrosis, and how the family grieved the loss of David.

Ernie finally became so weak he was unable to speak and had to be moved to the hospital. He died peacefully in his sleep two weeks later. Prior to his death Ernie had revealed to his sister Connie that he wanted to be cremated and have his ashes placed at the foot of his mother's grave. They honored his wishes.

At Ernie's memorial service, four of his fellow longshoremen recounted Ernie's love for his work, his love of drinking on Friday night at the pub, and his love for his brothers and sisters and their families. Ernie's sister Louisa spoke for the family of their love for Ernie and the kind and gentle soul that embodied his being.

At the conclusion of the service Robert invited everyone to his house to eat, talk, and remember Ernie. His longshoreman buddies stopped by Robert's house to pay their respects and then they retired to the pub. They raised their glasses in unison and, withholding their tears, said, "Good-bye, good buddy."

After all the guests left Robert's house, each of Ernie's seven surviving loved ones reminisced about Ernie until ten-thirty in the evening. They were all relieved that Ernie was no longer in pain, and also quietly relieved that their weekly rotation had ended. None of them ever complained about the time they gave him during the last three years of his life.

Ernie's retirement years were more of pain than of pleasure; however, his siblings made his retirement a golden time in his life. He shared these years with the people closest to him.

Your retirement years can be what you want to make them. While you may not have Ernie's experience and memories of his retirement, what do you want of your retirement years of experience and memories?

# 11

~

# *Who Will Die Last?*

The philosopher Plato said, "Practice dying." I failed to understand the statement upon my first reading. My close friend John reminded me that it meant live life to the fullest. Some people *wait* to grow up. Some people *wait* for Princess or Prince Charming, or *wait* to have children, while others *wait* for the children to grow up. Waiting for retirement means you probably dislike your career. Ask yourself, Is your life one of waiting or is your life one of enjoying?

Cancer specialist Bernie Siegel in his book *Love, Medicine and Miracles,* identifies some patients who are relieved to discover that they have a terminal illness. Dr. Siegel initially thought that all people wanted to survive. However, the patients who were relieved with their diagnosis of terminal cancer most likely had been unhappy with their lives for quite some time.

Ten years ago I shared this story with my twenty-four-year-old client Connie. She is an attractive, dark-haired, dark-eyed, well-dressed, articulate college graduate who works in the financial market. She is successful and enjoys being with people. Her ladylike posture was apparent as she sat down. I instantly liked her, and intuitively knew I would enjoy working with her.

Connie told me her story. "At nineteen, I was diagnosed with a life-threatening disease." The words from her physician's mouth came with reluctance and concern over Connie's diagnosis. At that moment, Connie said she experienced moments of both relief and pleasure. She disliked her life, but she was both shocked and surprised at her internal reaction.

When her disease went into remission, she continued to live an unsatisfying life until her mother's death. Connie was twenty-two years old, single, dated little, and lived alone. She enjoyed her work, but she wasn't moving ahead fast enough and she began to consider changing careers.

Connie originally came to my office for help with her feelings about her mother's death. According to Connie, she, her two brothers, and her one sister were not close. She recounted a childhood of severe verbal and emotional fighting between her parents. Her two brothers and sister lived their lives separately by having many friends outside of the home. When they were home, each stayed mostly in their bedrooms and seldom talked to one another. This created a depressed family. When her mother died Connie was devastated. Her mother's death also triggered Connie's unhappiness, then relief at the possibility the disease might take her life.

Connie grieved in our sessions over the loss of her mother. She cried. She expressed her anger about her parents' fighting and she talked of her fears of letting herself get close to other people. She shed tears. She also expressed anger and fear over her own loss of the childhood she wanted. She had not realized how much she had been *waiting* for happiness. Death to Connie appeared to be a welcome relief. Connie then made the decision to be happy and started acting that way. She began to talk with her two brothers and her sister, began dating, and within two years took a new career position in a city three thousand miles away. Her therapy was completed by the time she moved. I occasionally receive letters from her about her new career and her new boyfriend.

The extent to which we are willing to allow ourselves to be close to others is the extent to which we are willing to risk the loss of those others. This is a variation on "no pain, no gain." Sisters and brothers are part of this risk.

## For Better or for Worse

Familiar words spoken at the wedding ceremony. "Till death do us part." These same words could describe brothers' and sisters' relationships. The relationship of marriage has highs and lows—hopefully not too high and not too low. Sibling relationships are different in that they start in childhood, not in adulthood. Brother-and-sister relationships are like an arranged marriage. This same-generation brothers-and-sisters relationship lives on the surface of an ocean's waves. The waves are a sign of movement, and the siblings' waves create a life of action, memories, love, hate, resentments, and forgiveness.

Artimus and Jonathon are a sister and brother raised in San Francisco in an upper-middle-class neighborhood. Each went to the same elementary and high school, and later both went to the University of California at Berkeley. Upon graduation, twenty-two-year-old Artimus volunteered for the Peace Corps and was assigned to Malawi, in southeast Africa.

Other than one-week stays at summer camp, this was the first time Artimus had been away from her parents and Jonathon. During their childhood, she and Jonathon fought over food, friends, toys, parents, chores, and anything they could dredge up. Their occasional wrestling ended with a bloody nose or slightly bruised skin. The count was Jonathon, five bloodied noses, Artimus, three. No broken bones, but many tears, many trips to their parents, and many trips to their bedroom for the time-out.

Their high school fights were more sophisticated—no wrestling, no bloodied noses, and no bruised skin. They made fun of each other's boy- and girlfriends and they also continued to defend each other from outside criticism. They now fought with words and emotion. As with their childhood, an apology and forgiveness trailed these sister-and-brother fights.

At the university, they enjoyed an occasional lunch together, and continued to fight over politics, Artimus the liberal and Jonathon the conservative. They sprinkled their discussions and fights with university words, and their verbal sparing was a contest of one-upmarship. Both won and both lost.

Now came the time for Artimus to leave. Africa! What was Jonathon to do? They both knew that Artimus would be gone for a year before she could visit home. With Jonathon and their parents, Artimus felt her trip to the airport was filled with excitement and an occasional tear. Jonathon was surprised at his affectionate feelings toward his sister. Jonathon also had a disturbing intuition about Artimus's safety. He quickly dismissed it, however. At the airport Artimus hugged first her father and then her mother. She saved the last hug for Jonathon and, in their embrace, she whispered, "Thank you for our memories. I'll take them with me to comfort me in my moments of loneliness, and Jonathon, I love you." Jonathon repeated the words "I love you." Artimus walked away.

Artimus wrote Jonathon weekly, with separate letters to her parents. Both Jonathon and Artimus's parents also wrote weekly. Seven months later, a Peace Corps official and a chaplain came to the family home on that fateful Saturday to bring the news that Artimus had died in a bus crash near the small village where she lived.

Her body arrived two days later and they scheduled the services for the following Saturday. Parents, extended family members, friends, neighbors, and fellow students came. Jonathon requested that he be allowed the privilege of delivering Artimus's eulogy.

"Artimus was my friend and companion throughout our childhood. We knew we were special to each other. She had friends and I had friends. Our friends would come and go and Artimus and I stayed. Artimus is with me today, as she is also with our mother and father, family and friends. As children we fought, disagreed, sometimes hit, and always forgave, forgot, and made our sister-and-brother relationship stronger.

"As I stand here with my mother and father and each of you who knew and loved Artimus and knew of her dedication to make her world a better place, find comfort in that her presence will remain with me, our parents, and each of you.

"I have contacted the Peace Corps and informed them that in two years, when I finish at the university, I want to enter the Peace Corps and to be assigned to the village in Malawi to continue Artimus's work."

With tears in his eyes and tears around the sanctuary, Jonathon sat down.

Four years later, Jonathon completed his two-year Peace Corps duty in that small village in Malawi.

Twenty-seven years after the death of Artimus, Jonathon, an

architect, is married and is the father of three children: Johnny, age twenty-three, Paige, age twenty-one, and Jan Artimus, age seventeen. Jonathon's children never met their aunt Artimus; however, she lives through their dad's stories and his picture of his beloved sister. With Artimus and Jonathan, he will be the last to die.

Their strong relationship carried them through the better and the worse.

## Final Parting

As with all deaths, healthy grieving is the pathway to find happiness again. As noted earlier, Elisabeth Kubler-Ross, in *On Death and Dying,* identified five stages to assist in the grieving process.

### Denial

When I was eleven years old my favorite uncle died unexpectedly of a heart attack at thirty-nine. I attended his funeral, observed him lying in his casket, and, in my eleven-year-old mind, I told myself, "He is not dead;" he is working underground for the FBI and when his assignment is completed he will return." I never told anyone what I told myself.

The denial stage may be passed through immediately, it may take some time, or in some extreme cases this stage is never completed. Not speaking of the person who has died is a form of denial. Not being able to speak of the death of a brother or sister in order to protect parents may be an outcome.

When the stage of denial is completed a flood of feelings normally bursts forth.

### Feelings: Anger, Sadness, and Fear

Thirteen-year-old Darnelle was furious that a drunk driver who drove on the sidewalk killed her brother Tyrone. Darnelle understood her anger toward the drunken driver, but she was confused about her anger toward Tyrone. Why didn't he see the car coming and get out of the way? Why was he on the sidewalk at that particular time?

At Tyrone's funeral, Darnelle's anger subsided, and then the rush of tears came. When her anger toward Tyrone was completed then her sadness came in waves. She cried throughout the funeral and throughout the evening until sleep overtook her. With the death of a child, parents' are the best people to assist in bereavement. Unfortunately, the parent has also lost a child. Darnelle and Tyrone's mother, Tracey, and their father, William, were able to help Darnelle and their three younger children, Demond, Russell, and Terril, with the loss of their brother.

Next for Darnelle came her fear. What will her life be without Tyrone? Could death happen to another family member? Her mother? Her father? Or one of her other brothers? When Darnelle told her father of her fears, he gave her love and compassion. He had similar fears, and yet he knew that Darnelle needed reassurance from him. He stepped outside of his parental grieving to tell Darnelle that Tyrone died accidentally, and that he and Darnelle's mother would be with her and her brothers and that they would take good care of the family.

## Bargaining—"If only I . . ."

In the morning before she left for school, twelve-year-old Denise asked her seventeen-year-old brother, Carlyle, to pick her up from her middle school when he finished class. He agreed and left for school. At the end of class he struck up a conversation with his girlfriend, Stacy, and got lost in their conversation. Two hours later, Carlyle remembered his sister's request and rushed with Stacy to Denise's school. After a thorough search, they couldn't find Denise on the school grounds. Carlyle raced home—no Denise! Shortly afterward his mother arrived. Their search failed to find her. A search of the neighborhood yielded no Denise. Telephone calls to Denise's friends gave no reports of Denise.

Joe, Carlyle's father, was called at work and quickly came home. With chagrin Carlyle explained how he had forgotten to pick his sister up. Once alerted, police immediately canvassed the neighborhood and the school. As night fell, there was still no sign of Denise. The greatest nightmare for parents, the loss of a child, was beginning to unfold. By two A.M. the police called off the search until in the morning daylight hours. Carlyle, his parents, and some neighbors searched throughout the night.

At morning light, the grim-faced police came to the front door. The look on their faces told Carlyle and his parents of the tragic news. They had discovered Denise's body at a construction site near her school. The police said she apparently had stumbled and fallen into a drainage ditch and drowned. They found no evidence of foul play. At that moment Carlyle began a mind odyssey that he would play over and over, always with the same results.

The family was devastated, and later that day they sat together at the funeral home to plan services for their daughter and sister. With great sadness, Denise's parents honored her wish to donate her organs if anything happened to her. Her heart, lungs, liver, and corneas became gifts to other children. Four days later, when they held the service, Carlyle sat in his chair playing the odyssey over and over in his mind.

Carlyle held himself responsible for his sister's death because he failed to keep his agreement to meet her at school. No matter how much he tried to play a different tape, Denise was always dead. Carlyle was not able to move to the next stage of grieving. He remained stuck in this stage until his death at age twenty-seven in a car accident.

With professional assistance, most likely Carlyle could have continued his grieving in a healthy manner. Carlyle refused to talk to anyone about the loss of his sister. Understanding that his forgetfulness was an accident could have helped him through this stage of bargaining with himself.

### Depression and despair—"The Dark Pit"

Irvin D. Yalom, M.D., recounts the story of Penny in *Love's Executioner*. Her twelve-year-old daughter, Chrissie, had died of leukemia. Yalom, in describing Penny's grieving over the loss of her daughter, writes, "In many ways her sons were the real victims of this tragedy—as is often true of the siblings of children who die. Sometimes, as in Penny's family, the surviving children suffer because so much of the parents' energy is bound up with the dead child, who is both memorialized and idealized."

Candy Lightner, the founder of Mother's Against Drunk Driving (MADD), lost one of her twin thirteen-year-old daughters to a drunk driver. She has two other children, her surviving twin daughter and her son. Soon after her daughter's tragic death, Candy Lightner began the long campaign to change drunk-driving laws and develop MADD. She was extremely successful in lobbying for passage of legislation.

In retrospect, Candy Lightner acknowledged that she unintentionally neglected her surviving daughter and son in her pursuit. This can be a common occurrence in such tragedies. Rather than allow depression and despair to drag them down, some deflect this stage by overactivity in a cause. The cause then holds depression and despair in check.

Brothers and sisters of a deceased sibling almost always look to parents to assist in their grieving. Parents who have lost a child also have great difficulty in dealing with their own grief and the grief being experienced by their other children. The delay in this grieving stage will most likely prolong the stuck place.

The passage through each of these stages is not necessarily completed separately. Each stage is a unique passage for each person. There not a right way to handle this process. Throw away the clock and the calendar when you are on this grieving path. The grieving person may experience again the bargaining stage and return to a feeling stage or even back to denial. The transition through grieving takes a winding path with many cutbacks and reverse directions. Sometimes the bereaved person becomes lost on the path of grieving. As long as some movement occurs, the person grieving may reach the last stage, that of acceptance.

### Acceptance—"I Can Talk About My Loss"

Twenty-five years ago, thirty-eight year old engineer Benjamin, father of Colleen, Allen, and Regina, died unexpectedly from a heart attack. After the funeral the four of them did not talk about their loss. Then the next day their mother donated her husband's clothing and many of his mementos to the Salvation Army.

They limited any discussion of loss to comments about his paintings. The mother permitted nothing else. She refused to discuss the loss of her husband and told her children that he was gone and that was that. Colleen, Allen, and Regina followed their mother's wish and remained stuck between denial and feelings.

Twenty-five years later, thirty-nine-year-old Colleen, thirty-seven-year-old Allen, and thirty-five-year-old Regina, participated in an adult sibling session that focused on the death of their father. I sat in the room with these three and guided them through the experience. We placed three large pillows end-to-end on the floor; a blanket covered the pillows, and my sport coat lay on the blanket to represent their father. With their permission and my direction I said, "This represents your father and whatever words you want to say to him will be OK." Immediately all three broke into heart-wrenching sobbing and tears. My internal reaction was that it felt like their father's death had just occurred today, not twenty-five years ago.

For the next three hours, these sisters and brother moved through the stages of grieving by sharing their individual memories at the time of their father's death and their memories of the times since his death. They cried, talked of their fears about losing him, and shared their anger at his alcohol abuse and their happy memories of the times they had with him.

These three adult children moved to the stage of acceptance of their father's death during this session. They agreed that they would continue saying good-bye, in order to say hello.

Without the experience of a good-bye to a loss, a hello will not come. The hello is the beginning to that part of life where joy and happiness will reenter the bereaved's life.

## Childhood Brother or Sister Death

Childhood is the time of promise of things to come. At this time, children have the promise and don't have a clue. What they believe is that the present will be here forever, and so will their brothers and sisters. However, the truth is that some children lose a brother or sister during this precious time of childhood when the world is supposed to be a safe place.

Childhood sibling death can occur in three ways.

## Prior to the Birth of Younger Children

Donna was born forty-one years ago, the first child of May and Eugene. Because of a severe problem with Donna's heart she lived only three days. Her parents were devastated at going through the nightmare of losing a child. They together arranged the funeral services for their infant daughter. Family and friends shared in the parents' grief and were a comfort to them.

Two weeks later, May and Eugene made a pact that they would have other children and would keep the memory of Donna as a part of the family. During the next seven years, three sons and one daughter were born. On the fireplace mantel, May and Eugene arranged pictures of their wedding, as well as pictures of one-day-old Donna, six-year-old Michael, four-and-a-half-year-old Linda, three-year-old Brian, and one-year-old Louis. This is their family. The children talk about each other and their sister, Donna. May and Eugene share the excitement of all four of their pregnancies and also the three days they had with Donna. Donna to this day continues to be a part of this family.

## After the Birth of Some Children

David is the oldest in a family of four brothers. When David was five years old, his mother, Lydia, became pregnant with her second child. Her pregnancy ran full term, and yet in the later stage of the pregnancy she sensed something was wrong. The doctors reassured her that everything was all right. Unfortunately, her fears proved correct. Their son John was born dead. This family chose to go on, and three years later, Larry was born healthy. Three years later Jason entered the world.

None of the family members had memories of John. The parents had shared only that each of the children had a brother that they would never know. Very little was ever said about this second-born brother.

Unfortunately, with the death of John in his mother's womb, no memories would ever occur after his hoped-for live birth. This is a might-have-been and a very painful family experience, not only for the loss of their son and brother John, but also for what memories would have occurred.

## After the Birth of the Last Child

Six-year-old Sharon had an eight-year-old brother, Ronnie, and a four-year-old sister, Meagan. Sharon's grandfather Robert brought balloons for each of his grandchildren; then he sat on the floor while the children blew up the balloons. When they were finished Grandpa would tie them off. Sharon had a balloon in her mouth and was laughing at Grandpa's antics when she suddenly inhaled. Sharon's uninflated balloon stuck in her throat. Grandfather Robert frantically tried to remove the balloon, but before he could get it out Sharon died.

This family was devastated. Sharon's grandfather blamed himself for this tragic and accidental death. Both parents, Carl and Mary, were able to grieve over the death of their daughter and support their other children in their loss of their sister. Carl and Mary attempted to convince the grandfather that it wasn't his fault; however, seven years later at his death, he still hadn't forgiven himself.

A loss of any child is a parents' greatest nightmare. The loss of a brother or sister during childhood is especially poignant because it is not supposed to happen. Parents must help brothers and sisters through their childhood grieving and move them to the stage of a healthy acceptance of their loss. Children need reassurance that they will be safe and that they can say good-bye to their brother or sister.

*Did you lose a brother or sister to death in your childhood? How did you and your family grieve the loss of your sibling? If your grieving is incomplete, what could you do now to bring it to a conclusion?*

## Teenage Years—Sister or Brother Death

The family is set. Husband and wife—mother and father—and all children are established, and this is the family. The parents have been married for twenty years and their children are in their teens. This is a special time when children begin the early stages of emancipating from the family. The teens are not children and they are not yet adults. This is both an exciting and a difficult time. Teens are spreading their wings and parents are learning how to let go. This is a trial-and-error learning experience.

Think of your own teenage years as you exercised your wings and your parents anguished about your attempts to fly. You are no longer a kid—you are a teen, the time for dating, driver's license, boyfriends, girlfriends, staying away from home more than being at home, body changes, voice changes, attitude changes, rebellion, knowing everything and being scared of not really knowing much of anything. The time of your teens continues the promise of your long life to come.

You have had a lifetime relationship with your teenage brothers and sisters. They have always been with you and that is the way it is. You love them, hate them, make friends with them, hit them, hurt them, and forgive them as they forgive you. Brothers or sisters are not supposed to die in these years.

Seventeen-year-old Raoul and his nineteen-year-old sister, Carmen, live with their mother, Sheila. She has been divorced from their father for more than ten years. Carmen and Raoul have a special sister-and-brother relationship. Carmen admires and protects her young brother. Raoul knows how much Carmen loves him and he has respect for her. They have limited their fights and disagreements throughout their lives. They have always enjoyed each other's company, playing together as young children, and now in their teenage years they share information about boyfriends and girlfriends. Carmen advises Raoul about what girls want, and Raoul clues Carmen about the workings of teenage boys. Both love their mother; however, they both know in their hearts that their relationship is closer with each other than with their mother.

Without warning seventeen-year-old Raoul is killed in a single-car accident. He was returning from a high school football game, had dropped off his friend, Carlos, and continued on his way to his own home. He rounded the corner at a fast speed, skidded, and ran into a telephone pole, killing himself instantly.

The highway patrol informed Carmen and her mother of his death. Carmen continued working part-time and stayed in college. Her mother continued her work and the two continued to live together. Carmen did not share her sibling gap with her friends. She had been an older sister for seventeen years and now she was alone.

Carmen spent the next ten years in a marijuana fog. She finished three and a half years at her college, then dropped out and left her job for a full-time position with the electric company. When she was twenty-nine she entered therapy at her mother's request. Carmen had done some dating, had moved out of her mother's home, and had purchased her own home. She gave up marijuana when confronted by her mother.

Carmen's therapy soon identified her incomplete grieving over the loss of her brother ten years earlier. During the past ten years, she had visited her brother's grave only immediately after his funeral service. Within three months of therapy, in which her therapist gained her trust, Carmen agreed to complete the grief work that had been interrupted through her denial and her daily use of marijuana.

Carmen agreed to ask her friend Linda to ride to the cemetery with her to visit her brother's grave. Linda was asked to support her by remaining in the nearby car while Carmen walked slowly toward her brother's marker. The tears started and Carmen continued to walk. His grave marker read:

Raoul Luis Alvarado
January 23, 1962–October 2, 1979
Beloved son of Sheila and Henry
Beloved brother of Carmen

Carmen sat on the freshly mowed green lawn next to Raoul's marker. She sat in silence for what seemed a long time, her tears coming in a torrent. Then she spoke her brother's name out loud: "Raoul, I miss you." Between tears and words, Carmen began to tell Raoul about the last ten years of her life, and the gigantic gap that his death had caused in her life and the life of her mother. Carmen was surprised when she revealed her anger for his driving that caused his car accident and his untimely death. Her therapist told her that a variety of feelings—sadness, anger, fear, and happiness—may play a part in her grief work. Carmen continued talking with Raoul about her desire to have a happy life and asked him if that would be okay with him. In that moment, Carmen recalled their many earlier conversation about living their lives. Carmen told Raoul that she would be back to visit in the near future. She leaned over, kissed his marker, and slowly stood and walked back to the car. She had no sense of the time. Her friend Linda, still waiting patiently in the car, was reading a novel. Linda told her they arrived at the cemetery at one P.M. and it was now 2: 37. Carmen sat at her brother's grave for over one and a half hours. Carmen and Linda drove out of the cemetery without saying anything. They both understood the silence. Carmen drove Linda to her home, thanked her for her support, and said she would see her tomorrow at work.

In subsequent weeks and months, Carmen visited Raoul's grave several times. Carmen continued to tell Raoul about her life. Then the day arrived when Carmen told Raoul about Steven, her fiancé. Six months later, thirty-one-year-old Carmen married Steven. Carmen spent less time at the cemetery from then on, but continued to carry Raoul in her memory.

A beautiful spring day arrived, and Carmen drove to the cemetery with her husband, Steven, to introduce their two-day-old son Steven Raoul to her brother.

Carmen said her good-bye and hello to Raoul. The smile on Carmen's face said it all. She was happy.

Carmen delayed the grieving over the loss of her brother by ten years. She completed her grieving in the time and way she chose. The assistance from her therapist provided guidelines to complete her journey.

*Did you lose a brother or sister to death in your teenage years?*

*How did you and your family grieve over the loss of your brother or sister?*

*If your grieving is incomplete, what could you do to complete your grieving over the death of your brother or sister?*

## Adult Years—Brother or Sister Death

You and your sisters and brothers have made it through your childhood and your teenage years. You are all adults, have finished school, work, have a home of your own, have married, have become parents, have many memories of your brothers and sisters, and continue to see them at holidays, family gatherings, and births of children. When they moved away you kept in contact by telephone, letters, and most recently through the marvel of e-mail.

Thirty-nine-year-old Dan has two younger brothers, Eric and Landon, and a forty-one-year-old sister, Josephine. Among the four of them they have nine children. Dan lives within fifteen miles of the family home in San Antonio. Eric lives in a small town fifty miles from Dan. Josephine remains in the family home after the death of their parents in a car accident. Landon lives in El Paso, Texas, and visits his brothers and sister in San Antonio on a monthly basis.

On a cold and rainy day, Josephine surprised Dan with an early-morning telephone call. She asked to meet him for lunch at one P.M. Dan agreed, and on the drive to lunch he felt his gut become tense and fearful. Josephine's voice, while routinely nurturing to others, this time had an ominous sound. Dan sat opposite Josephine at a small table at the corner of the quiet restaurant. They ordered lunch, and the two of them began with small talk about each other's spouses and their children. Their food arrived, but neither sibling was really hungry and they each made small efforts to put food on their forks.

Dan asked Josephine first, "What is bothering you?" Josephine's answer came quickly and clearly: "I have terminal cervical cancer." The whole restaurant seemed to darken for Dan. His words did not come readily: "How do you know?" Josephine told him, "I came from my doctor's office after my eight o'clock appointment. Jim [Josephine's husband] was with me when my doctor gave us the test results. We went home, sat on the couch, talked, cried, held each other, and prayed. We had a strange reaction. Without words each of us got up from the couch and walked silently to the bedroom, where we made love.

"Afterward, we talked about how we would tell our children." In a loving gesture, Josephine's husband, who knew how close she was to her younger brothers, suggested that she meet with Dan for lunch. Neither could eat another morsel of food. Josephine asked Dan if he would arrange a time in three days when she could meet with him and Eric and Landon. She wanted to tell them herself and wanted Dan to support her. He readily agreed.

Three days later, Josephine, Dan, Eric, and Landon met at the beautiful green park near where they grew up. The sky was a clear blue, and the only other people in the park were a young family more than a hundred feet away. Josephine and Dan sat on one side of the picnic table with Eric and Landon on the other side. The other two knew something was wrong; they didn't know just what it was. Landon made a mildly humorous comment to reduce the tension.

Slowly, with tears in her eyes Josephine told her brothers of her disease and the outcome. Once again Dan had that awful feeling in his gut. Eric asked questions and Landon openly cried. Josephine had chosen to share this time with her brothers in the same way that as children, as teens, and as adults they all shared their lives together.

After two hours, all four knew that the time had come for them to return to their own homes to begin the pregrieving over their sister's death.

Josephine and Jim agreed to tell their children that evening. During the next four months and seventeen days, Josephine spent untold hours with her husband, with her children, and with her brothers and their families. These were precious moments, days and months that took Josephine and her family through to her death. She had asked for a memorial service with family pictures, a microphone for anyone's comments, plenty of food, and the release of forty-one balloons, each one representing a year of her life. As a last request she asked that the service be held at the park near their childhood home.

Dan, Eric, and Landon said good-bye to their sister and hello to continuing participation with her husband and her children.

Grieving before the death of a terminally ill loved one can be a deeply felt and satisfying way to say good-bye. With the permission of the ill person, each family member can cherish this time in a unique manner.

*Have you lost a brother or sister to death in your adulthood? How did you and your family grieve over this family loss? Is your grieving complete or incomplete?*

## Senior Years (Seventy and above)—Sister or Brother Death

The time has come, the children are grown, there are grandchildren in the family, careers have ended, retirement has come and stayed. You can still look at your sister and brother. Sure, the face is wrinkled, spotted, and has slightly drooping muscles, but you can still see that smooth facial skin on the face of the kid from your childhood. You can see your sister's smile and remember that same smile from childhood. You can see your brother's frown and remember that same frown when you took his baseball mitt.

Lyman's eighty-eight-year-old brother, Lucius, died while working in his beloved garden. Lyman had lived alone for the past nine years after the death of his wife, Irene. They had been married for fifty-seven years, and Lucius chose to remain in their house and continue gardening. Younger brother, eighty-two-year-old Lyman, made many attempts to get his brother to live with him and his wife. Lucius loved Lyman but knew that as much as he loved his brother, he could never stand to live with him. Lucius explained this to Lyman's wife, Ruth. Ruth chuckled, winked, and said with a smile, "I can barely live with him myself."

Lyman chose not to speak at the funeral, but his inside conversation brought tears to his eyes as he said good-bye to his big brother. Lyman was pleased when Lucius was laid to rest near his wife. Lyman was the last sibling left. They had lost their sister, Sarah, to diphtheria when she was seven. Now Lyman will be the last to die.

Later-age sibling death combines the long history of sharing and yet still seems to come too soon. With the exception of a painful disease, brothers and sisters generally prefer to keep each other alive and around. No one else, not spouses, children, or grandchildren occupies that special place.

*When you lost your sister or brother in these "golden years," how did you say good-bye?*

## My Sister and Brothers

I know five of us are alive. I don't know whether my youngest brother, Harold, is alive or dead. He has been gone more than five years. In checking with my attorney, I learned that when there is no contact and no one has seen him or knows of his whereabouts, my brother can be declared legally dead. This qualifies his three children for Social Security benefits. I asked Harold's wife if she wanted to do this. She did. I asked my sister and three brothers if they would agree to this declaration. They will.

I continue to enjoy my relationships with these special kids who have played a part in my life during the past fifty-six years. My hope is that we have many more years together, creating new memories, sharing old memories, laughing, talking, and hugging. I don't care who will be the last of us to die; I care how we will spend the gift of time that we have left. I love and enjoy them, not all the time and not every time, but most of the time. I hope it is the same for them.

## Your Sisters, Your Brothers

Many people look back over their lives and wonder what happened to get them to this point. Some people are old before their time, and others age but are never old. Twenty years ago my brother and I visited our ninety-four-year-old widowed grandfather at his senior residence apartment. It was apparent that many more women than men occupied the apartments. Grandpa had a good sense of humor, and when my brother asked, "Grandpa, do you ever get it on with any of these women around here?" Grandpa's face began to glow and the corners of his mouth broke into a wide grin. He said, "No, but I sure remember what it was like." Grandpa was still a kid. We all three laughed.

Our yearly family reunions were held near Grandpa's birthday, and when he spoke of my grandmother, his wife of sixty-four years, he would say, "I miss my wife." I was impressed that he referred to her as his first love.

In 1910, these two had arranged that then twenty-one-year-old Grandpa would come to the two-story farmhouse at midnight with his pickup and a ladder. My grandmother, sixteen-year-old Evie, had a bedroom on the second floor. He placed the ladder against the wall, climbed up to her room, and helped her down the ladder. They placed her packed suitcase and the ladder in the pickup. They eloped. They drove to a town fifty miles away, and when the justice of the peace office opened the next morning, they excitedly entered and within twenty-five minutes were husband and wife. Two days later they went back to the family farmhouse. Her sister had informed her parents where she was. Mr. and Mrs. Landress accepted their married daughter and her new husband.

Grandpa and Grandma were married sixty-four years, and he outlived her by more than ten years. Grandpa, the fourth-born of his six brothers and sisters, also outlived them.

Back to your sisters and brothers.

*Which ones are alive and which ones have passed away?*

*Have all resentments, hurts, slights, cheats, indiscretions, and any other "bad" things been forgiven?*

*We can be right or we can be close.*

*Which have you chosen with these special people?*

*When was the last time you talked with, visited, or wrote your brother or sister?*

## You Are the Last Sibling in Your Generation

Eighty-three-year-old Bertha rose from the pew and, with cane in hand, walked the twenty feet to the front of the sanctuary. The room was quiet, the smell of fresh-cut flowers wafting through it, and she heard the rustling of great-grandchildren. Bertha reached her seat unassisted and sat down near the casket of her eighty-seven-year-old brother, Arnold. It was apparent that she hadn't written anything to deliver. With a smirk, she started laughing and finally got out her words. With a finger pointed toward his casket, she said, "He could always make me laugh, and I want to laugh now to say good-bye to my brother." With her finger pointed toward family and friends, she said, "He wants you to laugh also." Slow giggles became belly laughs, belly laughs infected people, and as Bertha walked back to her pew, everyone, still laughing, stood and gave her an ovation.

The journey with yours brothers and sisters will be what you make of it. Have fun!